AN UNEXPECTED BLESSING

UNOMA NWANKWOR

KEVSTEL GROUP

KevStel Group LLC

Lawrenceville, GA 30046

An Unexpected Blessing © 2013 Unoma Nwankwor

ISBN 9780989073813

First printing August 2013

Printed in the United States of America

This is a work of fiction. Any references or similarities to actual events, real people, living or dead or to real locales are intended to give the novel a sense of reality. Any similarities to other names, characters, places, and incidents are entirely coincidental.

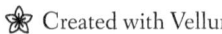 Created with Vellum

Praise for An Unexpected Blessing

"Unoma Nwankwor has penned a sweet romance with an important message about love and acceptance. She's definitely a writer to watch." ~ Rhonda McKnight, Black Expressions Best-selling Author of What Kind of Fool and An Inconvenient Friend.

"What woman hasn't felt the pangs of unfulfilled desire? In An Unexpected Blessing, Unoma Nwankwor weaves deception, cultures and the intrigue of love for a romantic journey that spans two continents and challenges the cornerstone of faith." ~Valerie J. Lewis Coleman, best-selling author of The Forbidden Secrets of the Goody Box. TheGoodyBoxBook.com

Revelation 4: 11

Thou art worthy, O Lord, to receive glory and honor and power: for thou hast created all things, and for thy pleasure they are and were created

To my husband, Kevin, and my kids—Fumnanya & Ugo.
Because of them, I am.

ACKNOWLEDGMENTS

This might be cliché, but I'll first like to thank the Lord God Almighty. Really, all the glory belongs to him. I am an avid reader but being able to put pen to paper is a gift given to me from God and I'm so thankful. My passion comes from providing hope and encouragement through Christ Jesus. By doing that for others, I'm also encouraged.

I had the desire and the passion but the push came from a man God placed in my life, my husband, Kevin. The day he saw the mountain of books overflowing from the shelves in my library, he said, "Babe you need to write your own". That was five years ago. Finally it's here and I couldn't be happier. He supported me, harassed me, pushed me, and scolded me, throughout the process. He knew I could do it, before I knew I could.

I am also thankful to my parents Professor and Mrs. P.I Osiegbu, their tireless support and prayers are invaluable. They gave me the foundation on which I stand and I'm so grateful to have them as mine. I would also like to thank my mother in law, Mrs. P. Efienokwu. Each time we speak, she never ended the call without asking "what about that book you are writing? O na ga kwa?" (Is it moving along?) Then she would proceed to pray for me. I'd be remised, if I didn't acknowledge my late father in law, Mr. Kingsley Efienokwu (RIP), he always pushed me to be the best I could be.

I would also like to thank, my brothers, siblings-in-laws,

especially Emefie, Novelyn and Uche, who always pushed my short stories out there. They gave me feedback and encouraged me along the way. Also to the man I fondly call Uncle Emma, Mr. Emmanuel Ojeah. He might not think anything of it but his support and encouragement of my family always eases my soul. Thank you sir! To my sistah girl Amoni Onuwaje, Adamma Okonkwo & Lolia Oruamabo. I appreciate you girls. Your "proud of you sis" texts are never taken for granted. Thank you!

To some special authors who without knowing it have inspired me beyond measure: Pat Simmons, Kendra Norman Bellamy, Brenda Jackson and Francis Ray (RIP).

Finally, to my two precious gifts from God; Fumnanya and Ugochukwu. You always understood that mummy needed to write and somehow also knew when I needed a break. I'm grateful to God for you both! May He always cover you with His precious blood. Through his grace, you will always be the head and not the tail. Love you with all of my heart.

PROLOGUE

LAGOS, Nigeria
June 2011

FERANMI LOVED HER CHILDHOOD HOME, but it was time to go. When she landed in Lagos two weeks ago for the summer break, she never thought she would miss Atlanta so much. She looked around her old bedroom one more time —her mother hadn't changed a thing. Feranmi often wondered whether her mother subconsciously thought her three kids would come back to stay one day.

She tossed her newly done micro braids over her shoulder and secured them with a pink beret. She then picked up her last piece of clothing, folded it, and placed it into her suitcase. Feranmi looked at her watch. It was 8:30 p.m. They needed to get going if they were going to make it to the airport in time. Her sister, brother-in-law, and parents all insisted on being her escorts. She pulled out her ticket to confirm her departure time.

Her flight would start boarding at 11:00 p.m. and she should be at Hartsfield Jackson airport by evening the next day.

Feranmi was about to change her blouse when she heard a knock at her door.

"Come in." Feranmi walked to the door to make sure it was unlocked. It was. On the other side of the door was her mother. She had a strange look on her face, Feranmi couldn't quite place it. She could detect melancholy and a little nervousness.

"Mummy, I was about coming to tell you that we needed to start heading out."

"*Ehen* I know. I wanted to talk to you before we got to the airport," her mother said. There was a brief silence then her mother continued.

"Olorunferanmi, my daughter."

Feranmi felt her heart skip a beat. Her parents only used her full name when they were angry or when the conversation was serious. She hadn't done anything to disappoint them so this had to be a serious conversation. "Ma?"

"Have you given anymore thought to what we discussed when you first arrived?" her mother asked.

"Mummy, I can't remember. What did we discuss?" Feranmi looked at her mom for some clue but there was a blank look on her face. The only thing Feranmi could remember them talking about with any seriousness was Bayo. This had better not be about him.

Bayo Ajibade was the only child of her parents' business partners, who also happened to be her godparents. Her parents, especially her mother, were hell bent on hooking her and Bayo up as husband and wife. And that was not happening if Feranmi had anything to do about it.

"Why are you avoiding the issue? I'm talking about Bayo," her mother said, with a hint of frustration in her voice.

"Mummy, please not this again. I've told you, I'm not

marrying Bayo. Stop trying to fix us up." Feranmi was so happy that Bayo was in South Africa with some friends. She had thought him not being in Lagos would lessen the pressure. She was wrong. Feranmi got up from the chair she had been sitting on and leaned against the dresser. Her mother still sat on the bed, and stared at her as if she had committed the worst crime on earth for not wanting to be forced into marriage with Bayo.

'Why, Mummy? I actually thought you and daddy would let me be on this issue. I'm not an old maid! I believe God will give me my own man. Even those who actually got to choose their husbands are not guaranteed happiness. So why would you want to decrease my own odds by fixing me up with someone?" Feranmi pleaded. Why couldn't her mother see it her way?

"Feranmi, listen to yourself. You'll be thirty soon. Do you want to be forty before you start having children? I don't see what you have against Bayo. He is a fine young man."

"Urgh... but he's not the fine young man for me. I've been trying to tell you and daddy that ever since you guys came up with the idea." Feranmi left the room. Her mother followed her.

"Young lady, I don't care how old you think you are, or that you live in America on your own. Don't ever walk out on me when I'm talking to you, again."

"I'm sorry. Mummy, but I'm just tired of this whole marriage thing."

Feranmi's father came out of the home office. "What's going on? I thought you women were packing. Leave you alone for a minute and you find something to bicker about."

Feranmi guessed he had probably been in there checking emails. *Oh Jeez, exactly what she needed; for her father to join the conversation.*

"Nothing, daddy. Mummy and I just have conflicting ideas

about an issue." Feranmi's eyes pleaded with her mom to let it go. The glare in her mother's eyes told her no.

"Dele, don't listen to her. All I did was mention Bayo and she got angry," Yewande Adewunmi made her way to the loveseat in the corner and sat down. "She has totally shut her mind on the possibility that he may not be as bad. Just one date and she never gave the guy another chance." Feranmi's fifty-five year-old mother, who stood at 5ft.2in, was a one-woman gang all by herself. Although she was petite—with curves in all the right places—she had the ability to wreak havoc when she had her mind set on something.

"Baby girl, you have to understand that your mother and I want what's best for you," her dad said, picking up the remote to bring down the volume of the TV.

This was beginning to sound like a Nollywood movie. Nollywood was the name coined for the Nigerian movie industry. If Feranmi heard that "what's best for you line" one more time, she would actually scream.

"Daddy, I'm grown and I know what's best for me. I appreciate you and mummy, but isn't it time to let me just do this myself?"

"You graduated from college four years ago in case you don't remember. Don't you see your sister is happily married with two kids? We are the ones that introduced her to Tunde, so why do you think we are not good judges of character? Just give this boy one more chance," her mother appealed.

Feranmi was almost sucked in by her mother's plea, but the memory of her one date with Bayo kept her grounded.

"Baby girl, you live in your apartment alone and we're worried. You need a man to protect you," her dad said.

"Daddy, I have an alarm system and God protects me."

Her father sat in silence, while her mother got up and adjusted her wrapper—she was ready to prove her point.

Feranmi couldn't take it any longer. She really didn't want to fight with them anymore. She couldn't leave home like this. They wouldn't be in the States for about another year or so and she had no idea when she would be back in Lagos. Her mother stopped pacing and stared at her. She opened her mouth to speak when Feranmi cut her off.

"I'm seeing someone and it's very serious," she blurted out. They stared at her. "I didn't tell you before because I wanted to surprise you."

"*Ehen*, you should have said so...who is he? Who are his parents? Where is he from and when do we meet him?" her mother asked enthusiastically.

"Slow down, Yewande. Let the girl answer one question at a time." Her dad turned his full attention to Feranmi. He was just as interested in all those questions as her mother. He just had a different tactic.

"So, baby girl, tell us about him." He gestured for her to sit on the couch next to him.

"He is Nigerian and a very nice man. I promise you'll meet him when you come to the States again."

Her parents smiled at what Feranmi knew was the magic word, "Nigerian." They never said it but Feranmi was sure her parents feared that she would marry an American – a fate worse than death in their eyes.

No such man existed, but if it made them happy, then it was all good. She was not about to be pressured into marrying anybody, just to be married. Besides they weren't coming to the States any time soon, so the lie was worth it.

CHAPTER ONE

ATLANTA, Georgia
October, 2011

FERANMI ADEWUNMI WAS ALMOST something she prided herself on never being. Late. Cell phone pressed between her shoulder and ear, attaché case under her arm, she pushed the "Up" button for the elevator. She was recovering from a horrendous morning of Atlanta traffic and now this...

"I'm getting married!"

Feranmi pulled the phone away from her ear and stared at it like an electrical current had shot through it. The commingled shrieks from Kayla Bell, the impending bride and her other bestie, Ini Ekanem, demanded that she return to the conversation. Feranmi was so completely caught off guard—so shocked—that she could hardly get a word out.

The elevator door opened.

"Feranmi?" Kayla's voice had dropped an octave. "You aren't saying anything."

"Are you getting in?" A husky voice floated down from above Feranmi's head. She turned to see who was behind her. He raised an arm to gesture toward the open door, but froze midway through the gesture. "Fera—"

Feranmi could feel her eyes bugging out of her head. Were they deceiving her? She dropped the phone to her hip. "Alex Montgomery."

His lips split, forming that trademark, perfect smile she remembered. Feranmi did a visual sweep of him from the fine, quality shoes to the edged haircut. She blinked, dismissed his perfection, regained her composure and stepped into the elevator. The space instantly became too small.

Alex opened his mouth to speak, but they could both hear Kayla's voice blaring from her cell phone. "Fera. Fera, are you there?"

Feranmi raised the phone to her ear. Her heart was thudding. She could barely catch her breath.

"Sorry, girl. I was stepping into the elevator."

Alex held a finger near the panel in the customary way people did when they were volunteering to push your floor number. Feranmi smirked and made the selection herself. He was staring at her. Memories of his heated gaze came back to her in a flood. The elevator continued to shrink. Feranmi turned her back to him slightly.

"So, you're getting married," she parroted Kayla's announcement.

"Isn't it great? Are you excited for me?"

"Of course, Kay. You know I am. I'm just surprised. This came out of nowhere."

"Fera, you've been working too many hours. The girl's been talking about the man forever and posting all those pictures on Facebook," Iniobong, affectionately known as Ini added. "I'm not surprised at all. Anyway, we always said she'd be the first to the altar."

That was true. Ever since the women's days at Clark Atlanta University, where they'd met as freshmen, they'd joked that Kayla would be the first to get married. Their taste in men was the key difference between the three. While Ini went for the bad boy type, Kayla was more flexible, while not compromising on her values. Feranmi, on the other hand, had a list and her future husband had to meet every criteria. He also had to be Nigerian. This bought her full circle back to the other occupant in the elevator. She couldn't keep her back to him. It was rude. She was raised better.

"I've got to call you back, Kay," she said. "Give me time to get to my desk and get settled." Feranmi ended the call without waiting for her reply. She knew her friend would understand why as soon as she called her back and told her she was sharing an elevator with Alex.

"Feranmi Adewunmi. It's a small world."

Feranmi stuck her phone in her purse. "It might be a bit too small." The elevator dinged, the doors opened and she stepped out. So did he.

"So, this is where you're working these days. Great for you," Alex said. He reached into his pocket and pulled out a business card case and handed one to her. "I'd love to have dinner and catch up."

Feranmi shook her head. Her mouth felt like it was full of cotton. "I'm not sure," she stuttered. "I'm kind of busy these days."

"You can make time for an old friend. I'm back in Atlanta now. Permanently." She noticed he placed emphasis on the word *permanently*.

"I think it'll be good to catch up." He stuck the card in the pocket of her attaché. She looked down at it, willing it to sprout wings and fly off.

"By the way." Alex shook his head a bit. "You look amazing."

Feranmi couldn't help but blush. She didn't have anybody in her life saying those words to her. Still, she wasn't having dinner with him. With Kayla's announcement and her parent's pressure she was vulnerable right now and being too close to Alex would be too risky.

Alex pushed the elevator button and the doors opened. "We should have that dinner. You know we may be seeing more of each other anyway, now that Kofi and Kayla are getting married." He smiled slyly, like a cat that had eaten the canary. Then he turned and stepped back into the elevator.

"I've got a meeting with a firm upstairs. Call me," he said. "Please, Fera."

The elevator doors closed. She stood there long after absorbing the shock of three words that had come out of his mouth. The first two were Kofi and Kayla. How did he know about them? The third was *please*. Feranmi made quick strides to her office and put her things down.

"Please, Fera." Alex's voice was not going to leave her thoughts until she let the memory of the last time they were together play out. She closed the door, took a seat and let herself remember the biggest mistake she had ever made.

Some people would argue that a man and a woman couldn't be best friends, but she and Alex were a case study of what that could look like. Although they went to the same school, they didn't run in the same circles. That changed when their paths collided in their final year. By some coincidence, they both signed up —with a couple of others— to attend a twelve-week mission's outreach class. Representatives from various churches around Atlanta participated in the program.

Almost immediately, Alex and Feranmi were drawn to each other. The same passion to spread the Word of God and help others burned in their souls. As time went by, they spent a lot of time together in and out of class. After the class ended, they volunteered to go on a one-week outreach to Burma. It was the practical phase of all they had learned in class.

It was on that journey that Feranmi realized she had fallen in love with him. The night before they were about to head back to the U. S., they had ministered all day and went out to eat. Dinner was filled with idle chatter at the end of which they strolled with the others back to the hotel. He walked her to her room and by some push of gravity, they shared a kiss. She panicked. He was perfect no doubt, the kind of man she wouldn't mind dating and eventually marrying, but there was a tiny problem. He wasn't Nigerian.

On their arrival back to Atlanta, Feranmi made it her mission to put some distance between them. It wasn't hard to do since final exams were around the corner. After their exams, his mother became ill and he decided to relocate to Chicago. Feranmi remembered their last conversation like it was yesterday.

After weeks of avoiding him, he finally caught up with her in one of the empty classroom on campus.

"Why have you been avoiding me?" Alex's brow was knit in an angry line.

Feranmi placed her pen slowly in her book and closed it. "I haven't, I've just been busy."

"Come on, Fera. Ever since we got back from Burma things haven't been the same. I know you aren't trying to ignore what we shared. We need to talk about it." Alex pulled out a chair opposite her and sat down.

"Alex, let's not complicate things," she said, not daring to make eye contact. "I don't want anything to happen to our

friendship. It means so much to me." She loved him but wasn't going to invest time and energy into a relationship that held no future. She needed her parents to accept anybody she married. With Alex being American, that was not going to happen. Why would she deliberately want to fight a battle she had no chance of winning? His impending relocation worked in her favor. She had to stay focused.

"You're leaving Atlanta anyway, so what difference does it make?" she asked. "It's not like I'm going to follow you to Chicago."

"That's not what we're talking about right now and you know it. People date long distance all the time. The separation doesn't have to be permanent."

"I like Atlanta."

Alex shook his head, stood, and walked to the door. "If you won't reconsider giving us a chance to be more than just friends, then whether or not you like Atlanta or hate Chicago is the not the issue."

Feranmi swallowed. She had no idea how much time had passed with him standing at the door and her sitting on the chair, their eyes locked in a battle of wills. She wanted to ask him not to leave, but she couldn't. *Fight for me,* she thought and then she dismissed it. There was no point. Her mind was made up. Wasn't it?

"Please, Fera," he said.

There it was. The fight. Men fought by begging, but she was resolute. She wasn't going to disappoint her parents. They probably had a point. It was better to stick to what she knew—a Nigerian. It worked better that way. Falling in love with an African-American man was all wrong for her.

"I guess I have my answer." Alex Montgomery pulled the door open and walked out of her life.

Feranmi pushed the memory aside. Four years later, she was no closer to finding the right Nigerian man than she was the day Alex stood in that classroom. She didn't mind that God worked in His time. Besides she had succeeded so far in keeping her 'marriage obsessed' parents off her back. Her friends, especially Kayla, always thought she was kidding when she told them about the pressure to marry Bayo. The reality was that some did find their true love through this arranged marriage thing and for some it was a complete disaster. Her older sister, Bimbo, was one of those whose husband, Tunde, turned out to be a godsend, but she was not her sister. Good or bad, Feranmi was determined to find her own husband. Her parents weren't going to have a second go round on this match-making stuff.

"WHY DIDN'T YOU TELL ME?" Feranmi weaved in and out of traffic as she headed up 400 North to Alpharetta.

"Before we get to that, can we resume the discussion where you tell me how happy you are that I'm getting married?" Kayla quipped on the other end of the phone.

Feranmi wanted to kick herself for not being more excited for Kayla. Kayla was her girl. Feranmi was genuinely happy that she'd found love with a good man and was getting married. But try as she might to be over the moon about it, her own pathetic situation was throwing shade.

"Forgive me. I'm thrilled. Tell me about the proposal."

Kayla didn't wait a second to do so. The details were painfully romantic and so representative of the Kofi that Kayla had been describing over the past few months. Fancy dinner, horse drawn carriage ride around the city, roses in the park, down on one knee...it was all divine. The joy Feranmi should have been feeling, finally made its way to her heart. "That sounds like something out of a fairytale."

"It was and the ring is to die for. I'm going to take a pic and send it to you."

"You do that. Right after you explain how Alex Montgomery knew you were engaged before I did." Feranmi's tone wagged the finger she couldn't make Kayla see. "Make sure you start at the part of the story where you explain how you and Kofi are even involved with Alex."

"Okay," Kayla said the word with a lilt of caution. "I told you Kofi and I ran into Alex at this networking thing."

"Yes, I remember."

"Kofi and Alex hit it off. They did some business together. They played basketball and golf. Girl, I don't know. I think they're like best friends or something."

"Kayla!"

"I tried to bring Alex up to you a few times and what? What did you do?"

Feranmi was steaming. Sure, she'd banned the name Alex Montgomery from their conversations, but if he and Kofi were friends...

"Fera, don't get angry. I didn't really know how cool they were at first. I also didn't know at the time that Kofi and I would be getting married, so... I tried to spare your feelings. I know how you feel about Alex."

"I don't feel anything about Alex." Even her best friends didn't know the extent of her true feelings for him. They suspected, but she would never admit it. Her love for Alex was a secret she guarded close to her heart.

"Yeah, that's why we're having this conversation about him, right?"

"I just didn't like being taken by surprise like that. I didn't expect it. You know I don't like surprises."

"Yeah, well let me get it out now so you won't be surprised. He's in the wedding."

"Kayla!"

"You'll survive," Kayla said. "You should try to holler. He's getting finer with age."

"Holler? See that's what I'm talking about. Women pursuing men who should be pursuing them."

"Don't start that American-Nigerian stuff. You know I'm not trying to hear that. No culture is perfect, and while you're at it, stop being pious about American men."

"I know it's not all of them."

"It's not most of them. Besides Nigerian men aren't all perfect. If they were you'd marry Bayo. Ouch." Kayla teased.

Feranmi wanted to wring Kayla's neck for bringing up Bayo.

"I've got to go. We're calling Kofi's parents before it gets too late in Ghana. Wish us grace."

Feranmi's heat cooled. "Grace, Sis. I love you. Tell Kofi I said congratulations."

They ended the call just as Feranmi pulled into her driveway. She stepped out of the car. From afar she saw a long Federal Express box on the front stoop. She had no idea what it could be as she hadn't ordered anything online lately that required shipping. She opened the door, put her things inside the foyer, and scooped up the long, rectangular box.

She made her way into the kitchen and pulled out scissors to slice it open. She was shocked at what her eyes were looking at. Red roses. A dozen of them. Feranmi searched inside the box for the card. She had no idea who on earth could or would have sent her flowers. They weren't from Deji, her brother, because he only sent them for her birthday.

She smiled, making a mental note to call him later. She

knew he was busy in school and their schedules were so crazy that they only talked once every two weeks.

She removed the card and read:

Feranmi – It was wonderful running into you today. I hope you'll bend your rules and call me for that dinner. – Enjoy, Alex

CHAPTER TWO

ALEX COLLAPSED on his sofa and took a long, satisfied chug from his glass. He looked around his condo. The house he now called home had really grown on him, but was a far cry from the four-bedroom house he had sold in Chicago. He'd been living in Atlanta since he relocated from Chicago about a year ago. He'd managed to settle down nicely after leaving behind a life that had turned into a nightmare. He shook his head against the thought of his past. He didn't want to revisit the bad memories tonight. Alex flipped between channels on his 52" LCD, not finding anything that was worth paying full attention to. He pondered on the events of the week and more importantly, the events of the last couple of days.

Feranmi. He'd finally seen her. And to think, the meeting was an accident. His plan was to make contact with her after he'd had more success with his business. He knew it was a little risky to wait so long. After all, she could meet someone and slip through his fingers, again. Kofi and Kayla subtly let him know that Feranmi was dating, but hadn't met anyone she thought much of, so he stuck with his plan. Truth be told, he was ready to make contact a few months ago, but he'd been unsure of how to approach her. They hadn't talked in a long time. It seemed there was so much between them...years and space, and of course his scabbed over heart, because there had been Tracie. He shook the memory of Tracie off, pushed his body deeper into the cushion and finished his drink.

Feranmi looked as good as he remembered. Her 5ft.6in frame was still as curvy as it had always been. Her mocha colored skin glowed like she had some kind of ethereal aura around her. She'd been wearing a form-fitting, pinstriped suit and had her jet black hair in loose curls pinned on top of her head. He liked it when she wore her hair off her face, because he saw more of her eyes. Although she'd been a bit bothered to see him, he still managed to get lost in her voice.

They once shared a closeness he couldn't explain. Alex shook his head and tried to clear her from his mind. The memories were still fresh. Her laughter, her smile, and the way she looked at him when she thought he wasn't looking. He couldn't have imagined the attraction between them. Then there was the kiss— pure heaven. But all that changed when they got back from Burma. It was as though she was a different person. She said she didn't want to ruin their friendship but to him, something didn't seem right. She was bent on not pursuing a relationship which he knew for sure was inevitable. And he thought she knew it, too.

Alex guessed he was wrong. He had learned a while ago not to assume anything when it came to women. His mother had tried to teach him that from the first time she noticed he was aware of the opposite sex, but he was hard headed.

As if on cue, his phone started to ring to Bishop Paul S. Morton's "I'm Still Standing." Alex smiled and picked up his phone. "Hi, Ma. It's like you're telepathic."

"Oh?" Amanda Montgomery asked.

He could detect her smile through the phone.

Alex stood and walked to the kitchen to discard his empty bottle. "I was just thinking about you. I miss you. I want to see you."

"Then you should get on a plane and visit."

Alex rested his body against the doorframe between the kitchen and living room. "I don't know. I'm not sure I'm ready to do that yet."

"You're being too hard on yourself and too self-conscious." His mother's concern reached through the phone and soothed him like only she could.

"It's not just that," he paused, trying to convince himself that there was more. "I'm busy trying to get work."

A beat of silence passed and then his mother said, "I'm not worried. When its time, you'll find your way home. 'Til then, I can keep coming to Atlanta."

He swallowed and released a long plume of air. "Thanks, Ma. That's why you're my number one girl. You understand me and you stood by me through everything, never doubting me or giving up hope."

"Alex, you are all I have and I know who I raised. I love you dearly, but you have to learn to forgive yourself for whatever mistake you think you might have made." He could hear his mother sigh heavily. It made him feel bad that he was upsetting her.

"I know." He choked the words out in a whisper. Sometimes speaking to his mother made him feel like a little boy, but it was in a good way. She didn't smother him or make him feel small, ever.

His mother continued. "God can give you that joy you desperately seek, but you have to let go first."

After a long pause, Alex said, "Thanks Ma, I'm going to arrange for you to fly down here to visit soon."

"I bet. You probably just miss my cooking," she joked.

"Yeah, that too." Alex rubbed his hand over his head and chuckled.

"Ma, if I don't say it enough, I love you."

"I love you, too, baby. Good night and please don't work too hard," his mother said.

He promised her he wouldn't and they ended the call.

Alex looked at the time on the microwave. It was getting late. Did he channel surf some more or just go to bed early? Neither was appealing. Being a non-dating bachelor was getting old as the Flintstones. This brought him back to his thoughts of Feranmi. He wondered what she was doing tonight. He'd hoped he'd hear from her, especially after she received the flowers but even he knew that hope was a stretch. That stubborn woman was not going to call him and give him the satisfaction of a conversation. No, she'd wait until her good manners and social etiquette forced her to pull out his business card and then she'd call and acknowledge the gift.

Right now, she was probably wondering how he'd gotten her address. She'd assume it was Kayla, but little did she know, Kayla and Kofi had not given him that information. He'd gotten that on his own. His plan had been to get his business on track first, and then see about Feranmi. At least that's what he told himself he was doing. Maybe he was doing what Kofi said—punking out.

Alex shook his head, turned off the downstairs lights and took the stairs two at a time to the upstairs bedrooms. He showered, said his prayers, and settled into bed. He had a big week ahead of him. His meetings with potential clients could give Montgomery Construction the desperate boost it needed. His company had suffered a great deal while he was fighting to clear his name. The negative press of a murder investigation cost him a lot of clients, which was another reason why he thought relocating to Atlanta was the right decision. The last big contract he had was to build a mini shopping complex in the Danville area, a city about one hundred and twenty miles from Chicago. He was fortunate enough to have a team that could carry on without him for the conclusion of the project, but since that job, business had dwindled to a state of nonexistence. He was hoping that would all change when he got the contract next week. He kept his thoughts positive about it, but just in case, he sent up another prayer, closed his eyes, and went to sleep.

IT WAS EARLY the next morning when Alex entered his office. He slept well, but couldn't sleep long. The advantage of getting to the office early was that he beat all the traffic. That was a headache worth rising early for.

He pulled out the proposal for the Anderson Group project. It was a job that was not only profitable, but important in terms of putting him on the map in the southern commercial construction business. Competition for projects was unbelievably fierce, especially since so many companies had put a halt to building due to the recession. It had gotten so bad that he'd even considered giving up and going into a different kind of business. In the end, he decided he couldn't do that. Building things was in his blood. It had been ever since his mother had bought him his first set of Lincoln Logs and Legos.

Alex heard the door open and knew it was his right hand man and foreman, Phillip Saunders. Phillip's willingness to relocate had been essential in the decision to move his business out of Chicago, because with Phillip on board he didn't have to build the key members of his team from scratch. When Alex advised him of his plans to move Montgomery Construction,

Phillip was more than happy to return to his home state of Georgia so he could be closer to his family. He was also glad to still have a job in this economy. Phillip started his career in Georgia. His connections and insight made the process of recruiting a formidable team stress-free for Alex, so he could spend his time and energy on rebuilding and rebranding, courting clients and crunching numbers.

"Morning, boss."

Alex raised his head from the work and returned the greeting. Coffee and newspaper in hand, Phillip entered his office. The 6ft.4in man who was built like a linebacker looked every bit the part of a site foreman.

"Your presentation is done. It looks like you're studying that proposal as though staring at it is going to make them call and tell us we have the job," Phillip said, raising his cup to his lips. He took a sip. "I thought you said you were going to move on to the next proposal and not look back and make yourself crazy about this one."

Alex nodded. "Yeah, I did say that, but I'm also touching and agreeing with this paper that that phone is going to ring."

Phillip took another sip of coffee. "Well, I done already said my prayers. I'm going to check on the supply order for the school renovation. It starts in a few weeks."

Alex twirled the pen in his hand. He was glad to have the renovation project, but it was a small job. They'd be in and out of there in less than a month. The temptation to open the Anderson Group file tugged at him, but he remembered what Phillip had said—prayers were already done. He had to have faith that God was going to give him what he needed. That was how it was going to have to be.

He was going to turn the pain of the last two years into gain. When Stacy, his assistant, informed him that the Anderson Group had called to set up a follow-up meeting, he couldn't believe it. Apparently, they were down to the final two bidders for the contract to build a shopping complex that would contain ten stores for rent. They wanted him to come in to provide some additional information before making their choice. He had done a lot of preparation to ensure he would be able to handle such a huge contract, so he had subcontractors lined up for the various pieces he would not be able to handle. Besides, he had plenty of other work to do. Chief among them... phone calls to make. He picked up the handset on his desk and heard the repetitive beeping sound that alerted him there was a voice message. He'd been the last man out last night and had made sure there were no unreturned calls, so he was curious who had called him so late. He pushed the code to retrieve the message.

Feranmi's sexy voice filled the room.

"Alex, thank you for the flowers. It was so unnecessary, but I didn't want to not acknowledge them. Have a good day."

The line went dead. That sneaky woman, calling on his office line instead of his cell. The office number wasn't even on the card he'd given her, so she'd had to Google it or search phone information to get it. I guess she figured two could play the research game. She'd probably called before she'd gone to bed.

Curious, he pushed the button to hear the time-stamp. 5:30 a.m. Alex laughed out loud. He surmised that Feranmi was attempting to call the office before he'd be there, so she'd get voicemail. But what she'd really told him was that *he* was the first thing on her mind when she'd awoken. He pumped his fist, turned on his iPad, and placed an order for another floral delivery.

CHAPTER THREE

WHO ON EARTH *can be calling at this time?* Feranmi answered the phone.

"Feranmi, are you still sleeping? Ah, ah, you are not awake by now?" Her mom's voice blared through the phone.

Feranmi's eyes jolted open. This had to be a joke. She looked at the alarm clock beside her. It was just 3:00 a.m. Her mother knew that this time of the year, Lagos was six hours ahead of Atlanta. *Why was she calling me at this time?*

"Mummy, *e ku aaro ma.*" Feranmi said "good morning" in her native Yoruba language. "Is everything ok?"

"Morning, my dear. Everything is fine. Are you still sleeping?"

"Mummy, are you serious? *Shebi*, you know what time it is. Of course I was sleeping."

"Ha! Sorry oh, sorry. I totally forgot. It was your father rushing me."

"Why. What's going on?"

"We are trying to fill out this Visa information and he

wanted to verify your address since you moved. The one we knew well was the address of the apartment."

"Hold on...are you guys coming to America?" A sudden chill washed over Feranmi's body. She pulled the comforter closer to her neck and longed for spring.

"Ah, ah... your father didn't call you?" her mother asked.

Feranmi sat up. "No he didn't call me. What's he supposed to be calling for? What's going on?"

"At the last minute, the professor that the University chose to attend the Martin Luther King festivities and conference in Atlanta decided to opt out because of family obligations. So your daddy was selected as his replacement." Her mother didn't seem to notice that Feranmi had mentally checked out of the conversation. She continued, "It still works out fine because we will be back here in time for Tunji's wedding."

Feranmi was wide awake now. Sleep had said its goodbye. Uncle Tunji was her dad's younger and only brother. When her grandparents died, her dad took over the role as a father figure, paying for his brother's education until he graduated from the University. This would be Uncle Tunji's second journey down the altar. His first marriage didn't produce any children and of course, he blamed his wife. She endured years of ridicule and just couldn't take it anymore so she returned to her home —Sierra Leone.

"Okay, quickly is it 8523 Polar Rd, or 8253 Polar Rd?" her mother asked.

"Umm...its 8253," Feranmi said. Her mind was racing. Her parents would be in Atlanta in less than three months. Although her mother didn't say it, Feranmi knew she would tag along to see the mystery man that somehow was never around when Feranmi talked to her parents on the phone. She rattled out the rest of the address. They talked a bit more and Feranmi got the details about her Uncle's new bride to be.

It wouldn't be a conversation with her mom if she didn't manage to weave in some kind of talk about the Ajibade's, her godparents. And she did. Feranmi stood up to go to the restroom. She was about to lay back down when she had the sudden urge to pray. She really needed guidance right now. She couldn't go back to bed anyway, or she would oversleep and be late for work.

She walked to the kitchen to put on the electric kettle for some instant coffee. Bible and devotional in hand, she sat at the kitchen table. She thought back to the conversation she had with her mom. They would be here sooner than she thought. Was that on purpose? If they hadn't forgotten the address, one day they would have called and told her to pick them up at the airport the next day.

The whistle of the kettle brought her out of her trance. She quickly made her coffee and sat back down. The aroma was as soothing as the beverage itself. Feranmi opened the devotional to the day's date. Staring right at her was Psalm 32:8: *I will instruct you and teach you in the way you should go; I will counsel you with my loving eye on you.*

Feranmi opened her Bible and read the whole chapter. She did believe and trust in God, so she was waiting for her man. But she didn't have the willpower or courage to fight her parents. She needed to come up with a plan. Her only option was to get a man that would pretend to be in a committed relationship when her parents got here. Not just any man, but a Nigerian. She hadn't intended to see them so soon and she felt bad about lying but after this everything would be over. She wasn't choosing a husband, just someone to stand in as a potential. There was a difference. Wasn't there?

"Lead me, Lord," Feranmi whispered. She rinsed her mug and headed up stairs. Where would she find a man on such short notice? Ini. Good thing they had planned to meet up tomorrow. It was time to get the ball rolling on her scheme.

FERANMI SLID into her car and cruised down Interstate 285 headed to Ini's place. She had spent the earlier part of the morning lazing about and performing little chores around the house while solidifying her plan. She had been so busy during the week at work that she barely had time to think about her issues. It was a productive week though. She made her sales numbers and had a lot more leads that she had to follow up on next week. Sales meant commissions so she was not complaining, not complaining at all. She had to feed her shopping and book buying habit somehow. She was having a great year at work and was thankful.

Feranmi chastised herself having not called Ini an hour ago. Ini was always late. She practiced "African time" effectively, which was funny for someone who, although Nigerian had not stepped out of the United States a day in her life. Ini's parents', who never married, met while they were in school at the University of Houston in the sixties. When she was two, her dad accepted a job in Nigeria and relocated, leaving Ini and her mother in the U.S.

Feranmi dialed Ini's number and waited for her to answer. "Hey, girl, I'm pulling into your subdivision now. I hope you're ready," Feranmi said.

"I'm ready. Don't get your panties in a bunch," Ini replied.

Five minutes after Feranmi pulled into her driveway, Ini's door opened.

"You better grab a sweater. I don't want to hear you complaining about the cold!" Feranmi yelled to her. Although the prediction was for a cool and breezy day, it was mid fall in

Atlanta and the weather was usually unpredictable. It was safer to dress in layers, just in case. Ini did not go back into the house. She slid into the car and tossed her monster-sized Hobo bag on the back seat.

"So diva, how was your week?" she asked, pulling her seatbelt around her. "I didn't get to talk to you. Each time I called the bank, you were busy."

Feranmi glanced to her side and smiled "Yeah, we talked. We just didn't spend time discussing your numerous potential men."

"Ha, ha, very funny. I see you got jokes," Ini said.

"For real though, work was really crazy and you know this was a busy week with the girls," Feranmi said. She mentored a group of girls at a local center. The "We Matter" program was aimed at making a difference in the lives of young girls', ages fourteen to seventeen. It was a program very dear to Feranmi's heart. She was blessed and counted herself as privileged growing up in Nigeria with educated parents. But there were still parts of the country and people who still viewed daughters as second-class citizens. Young girls were sometimes denied education since they were regarded as having no value to society except to be married and bear children.

"Those girls! You seem to be doing something for them every week," Ini said.

"Not every week, but those are my girls and helping them gives me fulfillment." Feranmi checked out her side mirror before taking the ramp to get on Interstate 20 towards Stone Crest Mall in Lithonia. It was a nice, urban mall that was closer to Ini's part of town, so they decided to start the day with lunch in one of the trendy new restaurants there and get some shopping done afterwards.

"So how was your week?"

"Apparently not as busy as yours," Ini said, with a bit of sarcasm.

Feranmi loved her girl, but she was a bit insecure. Feranmi had long sensed growing up without a father or father figure had been extremely hard, and although Ini would never admit it, her self-esteem had suffered as a result. She was intelligent and beautiful, but couldn't seem to attract the right kind of men. Although Ini denied it vehemently, Feranmi and Kayla actually suspected that some of her men had hit her a time or two.

Feranmi started to reply to Ini's sarcastic comment, but let it slide as she had more important things to talk about. Ini would be vital to the success of her plan. With the sounds of Pastor Marvin Sapp's new CD, *I Win* playing in the background, the two friends discussed their week and the upcoming plans for Kayla's engagement weekend.

Kayla, originally from Atlanta, had moved to Chicago when she got a lucrative offer from a multinational pharmaceutical firm. Feranmi was certain the three-day weekend was Kofi's idea. In Africa, it wasn't unusual to make big deals out of engagements and weddings. Feranmi knew that Kofi's country, Ghana, wouldn't be any different. They loved the idea when Kayla told them about it. It would give her and Ini a chance to check Kofi out. They needed to make sure he was right for their friend. Although at this point, it might not matter since the wedding date had been set. Date or no date, she and Ini still planned on grilling him. He was marrying their girl.

HOURS LATER, the ladies were relaxed on the patio of Ini's apartment going through their shopping bags. They were all smiles—another satisfying day of shopping. Quality without breaking the bank. Both of them had very different styles. Ini's style was more eccentric, going for bolder colors —a style that complimented her dreadlocks she had been growing for about five years. Feranmi was more conservative and chic.

Ini stood. "You want something to drink?"

"Yes. A cola please?" Feranmi slid her foot into a new pair of shoes. "And I need you to help me out with something. I need advice."

"Me, give you advice?" Ini plopped back down. "Well, that's a first. You don't let anybody tell you anything, so don't keep me in suspense."

"I'm going to ignore that comment." Feranmi took a deep breath and gave voice to what had been bothering her all day. "My folks are coming for a visit."

"Oh really? Why? What's the occasion? Didn't you just go home?" Ini asked.

"Girl, really long story, the short version is that my dad was chosen to participate in the MLK festivities and conference here in Atlanta," Feranmi said. "And of course, my mother is tagging along."

"That's a good thing, right? You seem worried."

"Depends on how you look at it. Remember I told you and Kay about the lie I told them when I was leaving home six months ago?" Feranmi's voice was laced with anxiety. "Well, they will be fully prepared to meet my imaginary man."

"You mean you haven't told them the truth since then?" Ini's eyes were bugged out.

"No, but that's beside the point. I'm not trying to hear all of that this time around, so I need a man quick or a makeshift one that will act as my man until they're gone." Feranmi covered her eyes with her hand and waited for Ini's scathing comments. She was positive Ini would have something to say. Feranmi never really understood why her friend would use her degree in

Business to open up a matching making business—Africans Dating in Diaspora. And now here she was asking for a favor.

Ini stood. "I'm going to get those drinks." She disappeared into the house and returned minutes later with their colas in tall glasses. They both took sips.

Feranmi waited while she watched the look on Ini's face grow more disconcerting by the second. This was not an Ini that was going to lash out at her for her crazy, trivial idea. This was the Ini who loved her and was concerned for her. Finally, her friend spoke.

"Fera, why can't you just tell them to back off? Tell them no."

"You don't understand how it is at home," Feranmi began. "It's almost a crime for a woman my age not to be married. My parents fixed my sister up and she's happy. They want to help me have the same 'happiness' with that Bayo guy I told you about. Their logic is, if I can't find a man, they'll find one for me since I'm ripe for marriage." Feranmi looked for some kind of reaction from Ini, but got none so she continued.

"I'm just tired of fighting them. I've been waiting on God to give me the type of man I want. I believe He will, but for now I've got to do something so that I won't have to argue with them when they visit."

"Fera, you've told me this a million times. I get that the whole arranged thing is still pertinent in some cultures. I hear you. But the thing is, you're here in the U.S. and you're grown. Why can't you stand up to them and just say, 'No. I'm not marrying Bayo'?"

"Because, I wasn't raised to say 'no' and just because I'm here doesn't mean I've abandoned my manners. I prefer to do things this way."

"This is not about abandoning your manners. It's about a culture that doesn't make sense. Don't you think they should be abandoned?" Ini asked. "I mean seriously, do you believe in Ethiopian women having their clitoris cut off?"

"That's different."

"No, it's not, girl. It's a culture. You can't tell the people who believe it's right that it's wrong, so what's the difference?"

Feranmi picked up her glass and took a long sip and returned it to the coaster. She couldn't seem to find the right words to describe what the difference was, but somewhere in her, she knew there was one.

Ini threw her hands up. "Okay, girl. I don't get it, but here's what we're gonna do... I'll set you up on some dates and hopefully you and one of them will click or one will be willing to put up the act for your parents."

Feranmi popped out of her seat and clapped her hands together like a child at a birthday party. Then she reached over and gave her reluctant friend a tight hug.

"Thanks. You're the best." Then she paused. "Please, don't make me fill out a profile. This is humiliating enough."

Ini laughed. "No, I won't. I'll handle this one personally. You won't believe how the service has grown in the past two years. There are a lot of y'all looking for love."

Feranmi knew she had that one coming, after all, she'd had a lot to say when Ini started her business.

"Seriously though, the only reason I'm doing this is because if you're willing to put yourself through a series of blind dates, I know you're desperate. You've always had too much pride for that."

"Desperate times call for desperate measures, so let's get this thing started," Feranmi said.

"Speaking of men, Kayla gets married in about four months. Why so soon? You don't think she has a bun in the oven do you?" Ini's tone was mischievous.

"Only you would think of such." Feranmi laughed. "No I

don't think so. She's celibate. Besides you know her, once she's made up her mind, she doesn't believe in procrastination."

"The wedding is in February. Exactly when are your parents coming again?" Ini asked, as they walked into the house to prepare dinner. It had gotten a little chilly, and the patio was becoming uncomfortable.

"January, sometime around MLK day. They can't wait to see you and Kayla again. They ask about you girls each time we talk. They consider both of you their adopted American daughters," Feranmi smiled.

"Aww... I love Dr. & Mrs. A. too. My mom admires and respects them," Ini said, visibly gushing at the memories.

Feranmi was happy with her plan. She never would have thought having a friend with a dating service would come in handy. The thought of dating brought Alex to the forefront of her mind. She willed her mind to focus on the issue at hand. Alex was a non-issue and she had to remember that. Although she would be lying if she didn't acknowledge that he did look better than she remembered. But all they had were memories and that was how it was going to remain.

CHAPTER FOUR

FERANMI'S gray Maxima moved through the streets of downtown Atlanta. Her destination-The Cheesecake Factory in Buckhead. This was the first blind date she was going on since she came up with her plan. The profile Ini sent her piqued her interest so she decided to give it a shot—not like she had a choice anyway. Time was not on her side. When Michael, her date, told her that he had made reservations here, it was too late to change the restaurant.

She and Alex had lunch there once with a couple of other people from the missions program. Although they were in the midst of many, it was as though they had the place to themselves. They had a wonderful time, laughing and getting to know each other. She remembered him teasing her about isolating her green peas on the plate. She shook her head to clear the memory. Today was a new day.

Feranmi entered the restaurant and spotted Michael immediately. He was seated at the bar. He told her that he would be wearing a checkered, purple, shirt and black dress pants. She nervously walked up to him. As though sensing her approach, he turned around. His eyes roamed her body.

Did he just size me up with his eyes? Ok Fera, calm down. She was going to keep an open mind. He stood. "You must be Feranmi." He extended his hand.

She placed her hand in his. The handshake was firm. "Yes, I am and you're Michael, right?" she asked.

"Yes, Michael Adoyo, III. Our table is ready." He turned around, got his drink, and moved towards the hostess. Feranmi followed, but she thought that was rude. He didn't even wait for her to go ahead of him. Strike one.

By the time she got to the table, he was already seated. He didn't bother to pull out her chair or at least wait until she was sitting down like a gentleman should. Peeking over her menu, Feranmi's eyes took in his features. Michael was average height with a brown complexion that matched his dark eyes. He wasn't what she would consider handsome, but he wasn't ugly either.

"So, tell me about yourself. What do you enjoy?" he asked, once the waiter took their orders and left.

Feranmi looked around the restaurant briefly; it was rowdy and noisy. It was a good thing Michael got a table by the window.

"I'm just a simple kind of girl. I work in a bank downtown and —"

"Oh, which one?" Michael cut her off. "My family sits on the board of most of the major local banks in the area." He dusted off a piece of lint from his shirt. Before she could speak he continued.

"Those banks were spared from the recent crisis in the financial sector because we had the best experts at the helm of things."

"Interesting, so I'm assuming you're a numbers guy?"

"Oh, no I'm not. My brothers and I fly planes. Have you ever travelled by private jet?" he asked.

Feranmi hadn't even answered the first question and he was down to the third. So he liked to talk about himself. He seemed rich, so should have his choice in women. Why was he finding love through a dating service? She decided to ask the question.

"You seem like a guy that has everything together, so why are you going on blind dates?"

He let out a loud laugh. "I just want to explore other territory. I was getting tired of the women in my circle," he said. "How about you? You're an attractive lady; I would think one man would've already snatched you up to take care of him."

"Take care of him?" Feranmi needed clarification on that one.

"Yeah, you know the whole wife and mother thing. That's what all the ladies want, isn't it?" His brow rose.

No, it's not!! She wanted to scream, but instead settled for, "Not all women. Some are fine just the way they are."

"Hmm, I'm yet to meet one," he said, using his thumb to wipe off the surface of his Rolex. She wondered if the watch was really dirty or he just wanted her to see it.

Feranmi opened her mouth to reply, but stopped as the waiter approached with their food. She didn't consider herself an extremist when it came to women's liberation, but her mother had taught her to be a strong, independent woman. Her mother also instilled in her that equal does not mean same. God created men and women for different reasons and with different visions. The world functioned better when everyone played their part. But this man was off the chain. He was as chauvinistic as they came. Strike two.

She bowed her head to pray when she noticed he was

already cutting up his steak. She finished and picked up her fork.

"So, you are one of those types?" he asked.

Feranmi's eyebrow rose. She folded her arms across her chest and asked, "And what type would that be?" She noticed his shoulders straightened at the brashness of her tone.

"Don't take it the wrong way. I just noticed you're among those who pray to something they cannot see or have never seen," he said.

"You don't believe in God?" she asked. She put her fork back down.

"Not necessarily. I do believe in a higher power that oversees all. I believe in the power of the universe, but I won't label it as God." He took another bite of his steak.

She saw the perfect opportunity to evangelize, but knew he would argue and she wasn't going to argue him into believing what she believed. Strike three. They ate the rest of the meal in semi-silence. She made up an excuse to cut the night short and headed straight home.

FERANMI LOOKED at her reflection in the mirror. She squeezed out some moisturizer from the tube and applied it on her hands and face. Satisfied that she had covered all areas of her face, she picked up a long-tooth comb and wrapped her hair. She was still furious, but there was no one to blame for this but herself. Had she been able to stand up to her parents about getting married, she wouldn't be in this mess right now. They'd be here soon and although this was the first blind date, there was nothing to say that it wouldn't go downhill from here.

Be anxious for nothing. The Philippians 4:6 verse popped

into her head. She looked up to the ceiling, Ok Lord, but I need help here...

Her phone rang. It was probably Ini calling to find out how the date went. She secured the satin scarf on her head and went in search of her phone. She was right, it was Ini. Feranmi answered the phone, placed it between her shoulder and ear, picked up the empty glass on her nightstand and made her way to the kitchen.

"Hey, girl, how did it go? Ini asked.

"It was terrible. The guy was rude, pompous, and he believed in a higher power. Can you believe it ...a higher power?" Feranmi paused to let Ini's laughter subside. She was glad someone was having a nice time. "It's not funny."

"Calm down, Fera. Your folks aren't here yet. You still have time, besides..."

"Besides, what?" Feranmi asked when she sensed Ini's hesitation.

"At the risk of you biting my head off, I was gonna say besides your buddy, Alex, is back in town. He could always help out."

"That's out of the question. Please find me another date," Feranmi snapped. She couldn't imagine asking Alex to stand in as her man. There was unfinished business between them that she had no intention of finishing. It wouldn't be fair to him or her. They both knew the way they left things. She had spent the last four years trying to get over him. But apparently that didn't happen, because ever since they ran into each other, he had constantly invaded her thoughts.

"Aren't we touchy? Have you at least thanked the man for the flowers?" Ini asked.

"Yeah, I left him one message the first time and sent a post-card to his office the next." Feranmi said, getting a cup of water from the dispenser.

"Coward, pick up the phone and call the man," Ini said. "And I will find you that second date. I gotta go." They said their good-byes and Ini hung up. Feranmi went back to her bed room. Ini was right. She would rectify that right now. Feranmi located the card Alex had handed her and dialed his number.

"This is a welcome surprise. I was beginning to think you were hiding behind voicemail," Alex said, his soothing baritone an octave lower. He must be in bed already. She smiled. He knew how to have his share of fun, but was a natural homebody.

"No, it's convenient that's all," she said.

"Yeah, right. You and I know better, but I'm glad you finally decided to call."

"I wanted to say thank you for the flowers. They were beautiful." Feranmi knew she needed to stay on track. Say thanks and good-bye. She missed his friendship, but she had to do what she needed to do to save herself the torture over someone she couldn't have.

"Beautiful flowers for a beautiful woman." Alex said, "We should do lunch or dinner sometime."

"Yeah, we should. It's close to the holidays and quite busy for me. We'll get to see each other during Kayla and Kofi's weekend. You'll be there, right?" Feranmi immediately hoped she didn't send the wrong message. Or would it be the right message?

"Yes, I'll be there," Alex replied.

Feranmi actually felt his smile through the phone.

"Okay, see you then." Feranmi said, and disconnected the call. She said her prayers and slipped in between the covers. Despite the tangled web her life had become, she slept with a smile on her face. There was only one reason for that—Alex.

CHAPTER FIVE

ALEX PUSHED the sliding door aside and stepped onto his deck. The evening was a little chilly, not uncommon for early November. He hadn't spoken to Kofi in a while and it was time to fill him in. He took his phone out of his pocket and hit speed dial. Kofi answered after the third ring.

"Man, you won't believe what's been happening to me in the last couple of weeks. Even I can't believe it," Alex said, as he leaned back into the patio chair.

"So, tell me what's been happening," Kofi said. "I haven't heard from you in about two weeks. Somehow we keep missing each other. Text messages keep me in the loop, but not enough."

"Sorry about that, man. It's just been crazy. I didn't have any jobs coming in. My business needed a serious overhaul, and I had lots of extra time for the devil to be playing tricks with my head." Alex explained.

"I hear you man, so fill me in. What's going on?"

Alex could sense the excitement in his friend's voice. Kofi was more like the brother he never had. When Kayla introduced them in Chicago some years ago, they discovered that they had a lot of things in common. They both had absentee fathers, but in Kofi's case, his mother had re-married a man who stepped in and filled that role to make sure he got what he needed from a male role model. Their similar circumstances were the foundation of the brotherhood that made them virtually inseparable. Kofi and his mother were the only ones that stood by his side when he was arrested and thrown in jail two years ago. That night was one he didn't want to remember. Alex felt separated from everyone and everything, even his God.

"How long you gonna keep me waiting? Fill me in." Kofi's voice jarred Alex back to the present.

"My bad! Anyway as I was saying, by some stroke of luck, or as my mama would say, through God's blessing, I was awarded the contract I bid for. It's turned my whole life around." The adrenaline that fueled Alex's excitement pushed him to his feet. With one hand in his pocket, leaning against the table, he went on to tell Kofi about the Anderson Group Project. It took a lot of preparation to make sure the proposal was just right. The follow-up meeting was a piece of cake. As soon as the job was his, he hired employees who were on the job six days a week.

"Man, I'm happy for you, but you need to also take the time to enjoy life. It's been two years since Tracie. You need to get out there. You don't want to become rusty do you?" Kofi chuckled.

"Just because you've gone off and proposed to the lovely Kayla doesn't mean that a relationship or marriage is on everyone's agenda right now."

"Alex, you have to learn to let go. Forgive and let go, not for her but for you. Only then will your heart be open again."

"Look at you going all soft on me. Kayla got you watching

Oprah already?" Alex joked, but Kofi didn't laugh so he continued, "Seriously though, I hear you but it's just taking time."

"Alex, get over it. You've had time. It's been two whole years. Remember God doesn't let any hurt we've gone through be in vain. There is always a greater purpose, but you have to let go to get it. Remember that text I sent you the other day; you know the one with the passage..."

"Oh yeah, I still have it here." Alex had memorized it. When he started mulling over his past, he pulled it out... *Ephesians 4:31 Let all bitterness and wrath and anger and clamor and slander be put away from you, along with all malice.*

"Kayla and I were praying that day and that happened to be the verse in our prayer aid. We thought about you immediately."

"It's easy for you to say because you weren't the one locked up behind bars while fighting to clear your name." Alex could feel his blood pressure rising. But his mom had said the same thing time and time again.

"Like I said, I hear you." Alex said in a calmer tone. "Speaking of getting out there, guess who I ran into?" Not waiting for a response, Alex continued. "Fera— that lady is still as fine as she wanna be, but still as stubborn as a bull."

"I can't wait to meet this lady I've heard so much about," Kofi said. "So how did it go?"

"It didn't at first. I sent her flowers, twice, but instead of giving me a call she sends me polite voicemails and a post card."

"Hmmm, that sounds like one determined lady. Determined to stay away from you," Kofi said.

Alex pondered for a moment "Stubborn is what she is...but that changed two nights ago. Out of the blue I get a call..."

"And...?"

"That's what I'm wondering. She said she called to thank me for the flowers. When I ask her about lunch, she makes up some excuse about being busy." Alex let out a sigh. "There she goes again sending these mixed messages, but this time around I'm going to enjoy playing her little game."

"And I'll be there to watch," Kofi said.

"Is that right?" Alex asked. "So, when you coming to Atlanta? Haven't seen you since I left Chi town."

"As a matter of fact, later this month, we're having this three-day shindig in Atlanta Thanksgiving weekend. That way, Kayla's family who won't be able to come to Chicago for the wedding will get in on some of the festivities."

"Interesting, you haven't met Kayla's girls right? Are you ready for their test?" Alex asked, chuckling. He was so sure the ladies wanted to check Kofi out before the wedding.

"Nope, haven't met 'em but we talk on the phone from time to time. Oh you think that's funny, being under the scrutinizing eyes of those ladies?" Kofi asked.

"It won't be that bad. The most outspoken of them all is Ini, and believe me her bark is louder than her bite." Alex smiled when he remembered how she had given him a hard time with Feranmi. She was convinced they were dating and wanted to know his "intentions." Ini was also the most protective one of them all and also inadvertently gave him the first real hint that what Feranmi felt for him might be more than friendship.

"Yeah, you should have heard her when I talked to her on the phone for the first time." Kofi said. The men laughed.

"I don't know about you, but this get-together works out perfectly for me. I'd like to see how Fera would avoid me then." Alex stood and began walking the length of the patio, plotting his strategy.

"Hey, I got an incoming call. Be on the lookout for your invite in the mail," Kofi said.

"Okay. Be easy."

"Later, man."

ALEX STOMPED his muddy boots on the pavement. His walk through the uncompleted structure made him happy. Things were coming along nicely and they were on schedule. If everything continued this way, the project would be completed on time. His car wasn't hard to find since the parking lot was virtually deserted. There was an unusual snowfall two days ago and in Atlanta, that meant everything stood still. It was a huge contrast from Chicago where this kind of snowfall would be considered insignificant. He shifted the gear into reverse and swung the car around.

The holidays were approaching fast. As the years flew by, the holidays became more bearable. In the years that he and Tracie were an item, they alternated between spending Thanksgiving with her family in Virginia and Christmas with his mom in Chicago. Since the demise of their romance, it was really difficult finding meaning in the season, but he had a sneaking suspicion that this year would be different. Thanks to Kofi's Thanksgiving engagement weekend. If things went according to plan, he would be spending Christmas with Feranmi.

Alex looked around at the residual traces of snow on the highway. It reminded him of that day, two years ago. It was late September; a little early for snow even in Chicago. Tracie has insisted on having dinner out, which was uncharacteristic for her. She hated precipitation of any kind. She'd normally want to stay indoors even if the snow was light. That struck him as odd and should have been his first warning that this might not be the romantic dinner he thought she wanted. She'd been acting strange for a few weeks. She was easily irritated, and everything he did was wrong. He couldn't please her. Tracie had beaten him to the restaurant and she was seated when he arrived. The fact that she'd barely let him kiss her before he sat down should have been his second clue that something was off.

"Rough day?" he asked as he slid into his chair.

"Something like that," she said, raising her water goblet to her lips.

The waiter came to the table and offered them the wine list. Tracie shook her head. She wasn't going to drink. McCormick and Schmicks were known all over Chi-town for not only their food, but their exclusive wine list. Tracie never passed on an opportunity to sample some exclusive, overpriced wine; another oddity. Now he was sure he was in trouble.

"I know I've been working a lot, sweetheart," he began. "I hope you understand. It's not about me. It's about us. I want to make sure we have everything we need and want, because the day you agreed to marry me —"

"Alex, I know." She met his eyes for the first time that evening. "I have something I've wanted to tell you...for, well, awhile." She dropped her eyes and raised them again. He could see that tears misted over them. Her energy was anxious. She was twisting one of her fingers back. That was only something she did when she was nervous.

He swallowed. "Don't keep me in suspense."

"The time never seemed to be right. You've been busy with work and not home until late, so this has gone on longer than I meant. I want you to know, it doesn't have anything to do with you."

"Wait a minute," he said. "Am I about to get the 'Dear John' speech?"

"Alex, it's me. Please understand."

Alex was befuddled. If anyone had told him that this morning was going to be the worst day of his life he would have called them a liar. "Look," he said placing both palms on the *table.* "*Whatever you're going through, whatever you think we're going through, we can work it out.*"

"*Let me say what I need to say before I lose my nerve,*" *she pleaded and the first tear of the night spilled down her cheek.*

"*We've been together two years. I don't want to hear nothing that will end in you thinking you can just set me to the side.*" *Alex scowled.*

Tracie raised her hands and covered her ears like a child. "I'm pregnant and it's not yours."

The blaring of an automobile horn pulled Alex from his memory. Setting his car in motion, he continued to drive. He'd left the site a while ago and what would have normally taken him just about forty-five minutes was taking him almost two hours. When the weather was bad, people just didn't know how to drive.

ALEX COULDN'T BELIEVE this was happening. He was just at the site two days ago and everything looked ok, now this. He glanced at the papers in front of him and up to his foreman. He studied the papers as though his hard stare would change the information on them. The raw materials that had been ordered late were now going to be late in arriving, despite the fact that they paid for their expedited delivery. This was going to leave him with men that couldn't work for another three weeks. This caused two major headaches.

Alex stood from his seat and walked around to lean against his desk. One, he couldn't afford this kind of delay in the schedule, and two, he had a scheduled tour with one of the representatives from the Anderson Group in two weeks. He thought the building would be farther along than it was. He had given his word that they were on track, now he was running the risk of being a whole month and a half behind.

"Alex, I take full responsibility and will make sure the men are available and ready to go once the items arrive." Phillip had already apologized five times, but it wasn't going to fix the problem.

This was the first major mistake that Phillip had made in all the years he had worked for Alex, so he couldn't really come down hard on the guy. And from the looks of things, he was already coming down hard on himself.

"That's okay, Phillip." Alex sighed. "What's done is done. We just have to come up with a strategy to ensure we stay as close to keeping this thing on track as we can." Walking back around his desk and taking a seat, Alex continued, "You know this is the first major project we've had in a while and glowing recommendations after we're done are critical to our continued success in Georgia."

Phillip walked to the door and put his hat back on. He cracked open the door, turned around and looked at Alex. "I won't let you down, boss." He exited the office, closing the door behind him.

Fear of the unknown gripped him. Alex never wanted to be at that place he found himself two years ago—busted and broke. If anything happened to this project, that's exactly where he'd be. He was going to work his tail off to make sure that didn't happen.

Alex rubbed his head when he thought about the call he was going to make to Kofi. He dreaded it. He had been all set to attend the engagement weekend events coming up, but now it seemed impossible as the raw materials were now set to arrive at the same time. He was not going to take any chances. Kofi was his boy so would be undeniably disappointed, but unless some miracle happened and he could get everything on track or as close to it as possible; he wouldn't be able to attend.

Alex picked up the newspaper his secretary left on his desk. Work would be busy in a few weeks, so he might as well enjoy the last free weekend he would have in a while. He browsed the events section. The State Fair caught his eye. He hadn't been to one in a while. In fact, the last one he went to was with Feranmi. This delay wasn't just about Kofi; it also set his plans with Feranmi back a bit. Now he wished he hadn't run into her. She had been on his mind lately and he was finding it hard to focus, but he wasn't going to let any woman distract him. Getting his business back to where it used to be was his primary aim. Everything else would have to take a back seat.

CHAPTER SIX

FERANMI PUSHED herself off of the leather seat behind her desk and walked towards the door. The growling sound that came from her stomach reminded her it was lunch time. It was one of those cold and rainy days. She had lived in Atlanta for eight years now, but had yet to adjust to the cold, winter weather. She didn't feel like going out, so decided to try the cafeteria downstairs.

Tomorrow, she had another date and was not quite sure what to expect. This experience had been awkward for her. By nature, she was an introvert—quiet and reserved. Being the middle child of three, she often didn't know where she belonged, which was one of the reasons why living on her own in the States was so appealing. During this journey, she had a chance to discover who she was, her strengths and her weakness. She had grown into her own woman who knew what she wanted; and being fixed up was not one of them. Despite her independence, she couldn't escape the idea that women aren't considered accomplished until they became somebody's wife.

She hoped that this date would be better, although somewhere deep down she had a sneaking suspicion that it wouldn't.

The cafeteria had the usual lunch crowd. The aroma coming from the kitchen made her stomach growl even more. The line at the sandwich station was the shortest, so her decision on what to get was made easy; a sandwich. While she waited in line, Feranmi decided to call Kayla. They hadn't had a chance to catch up. She took out her Blackberry from the waist holder and dialed Kayla's number.

When Kayla answered, Feranmi could hear pots clanging in the background. Kayla must be cooking. "Hey, what are you doing at home? I thought you'd be at lunch by now."

"I got so much to do before we head to Atlanta and I can't do it if I'm hemmed up in the office all day, so I took the day off. Do you approve?" Kayla asked jokingly.

"Umm ...Let me think about it?"

"So, what's up? We keep missing each other ever since your dinner disaster," Kayla giggled.

"Yeah, you are one busy woman...Mrs. Adoo to be. I'm so happy for you, girl," Feranmi said. Another loud sound came from the other end of her phone.

"Girl, what are you doing in there that pots and pans are being banged together like cymbals? Are you ok?"

"Fera, I'm about to hang up on you. I'm trying to prepare a Ghanaian dish for my man and I need full concentration," Kayla replied.

The chef motioned Feranmi forward. It was her turn. Covering the mouthpiece with her palm, she placed her order for a grilled cheese sandwich and sweet potato fries. After paying the cashier, she found a secluded table.

"Hey. You still there? Sorry about that, I'm seated now so we can talk. Don't want all these people in my business,"

Feranmi said. After getting the go ahead from Kayla, Feranmi spoke.

"Kay, how do I get out of this one? I just don't have the energy for another bad date. This would be the third one."

"You don't. When you started this hunt, I told you not to go through with it. God's timing is the best and your parents will just have to be patient. You should've told them that a long time ago but no, you decided to lie so why are you complaining?" Kayla asked.

"What about Alex anyway...and I know you don't like talking about him, but too bad, because we are."

"What does he have to do with this? There is nothing between Alex and me."

"Yeah, right. Then why do you get so hot and bothered at the mention of his name? Okay suit yourself. I still think the two of you look cute together."

"This isn't why I called, Kay..." Feranmi said, her thoughts trailed back to a couple of nights ago. After the conversation with Alex, she made up her mind that she had to stay as far away from him as possible. Or she would be right where she was four years ago—broken hearted over someone she couldn't have.

"Go on the date. What's the worst that can happen? You never know. He might be your African knight in shining armor."

"Oh, so now you're a jester."

"Where are you guys going?" Kayla asked.

"The State fair is this weekend, so we decided to meet there. I'm tired of the restaurant thing. At least there, I can have a good time if the date goes south."

"Remember to keep an open mind. I gotta go. Love you, sis. Call me. I want to hear everything."

"Will do. Love you back. Let me get back to the office so I can leave early."

Feranmi would try to keep an open mind. She and Richard had talked on the telephone a couple of times and he sounded nice. No red flags at least over the phone. She hoped the same held true in person.

———

IT WAS A BEAUTIFUL SATURDAY. Nothing could compare to the strength of the bare trees that surrounded the parking lot of the fair grounds. God was simply awesome. Just to think that a few short months ago the leaves were green and the grass was lush. The dried up leaves that littered the parking lot crushed under her feet as she walked.

Feranmi willed herself to believe that it was going to be a good day. She and Richard decided to meet at the first refreshment concession stand at the South entrance. From the picture Ini showed her, he was a looker. The smell of candied apples and pumpkin pie greeted her as she entered the park. That was one snack she never understood how people could eat. A fruit and candy at the same time didn't make sense to her.

It was noon and the fair was in full swing. Families walking together having fun, couples hand in hand as if they had no care in the world. Feranmi admired that life, but it had eluded her so far. There was one person that did make her feel that way; Alex. Why did he have to be African-American?

She pulled her woolen cap a little further down her head. The briskness of the wind was messing up her hair. She saw Richard approach. His picture didn't do him justice. She sent up a silent prayer. *Please, Lord, let this be it.*

He must have recognized her too, because when their eyes met, his lips formed a smile. "Feranmi, right?"

"Yeah. Richard?"

"Nice to meet you," he said, extending his hand. Feranmi put hers in his. It was damp. *Ewww...was he nervous?*

"Likewise. Have you been waiting long?" Feranmi asked.

"No, I haven't." Feranmi began to move forward and Richard fell in step.

"Do you want anything to eat or drink?" His voice was deep.

"No, thanks. I'm fine. Let's explore the grounds. Maybe later," Feranmi said. Richard stood at about 6ft. tall, brown complexion with a shiny bald head reminiscent of Boris Kodjoe. The only hair on his face was the pencil thin moustache that shaped his lips perfectly. His Sean Combs jeans and multi-colored sweater told Feranmi that he took his appearance very seriously. This looked promising.

They went around from stand to stand taking in the sights and sounds. Richard was a medical doctor. He worked in one of the area hospitals. He was very polite— sometimes too polite for Feranmi. But at this point, she was willing to give it an honest shot. *This is me keeping an open mind.*

"Do you want to get on the rollercoaster?" he asked.

"Sure, I love the adrenaline rush." Feranmi was excited and actually having a good time. As they strolled along, she saw this beautiful piece of art. It was the same piece she saw in Alex's apartment years ago. She wondered whether he still loved art. He used to go on and on when they found what he called bargain pieces.

"Richard, let's go in here. I want to look around," Feranmi said. She knew she should be making new memories instead of surrounding herself with old ones. But she couldn't help it.

They entered the store and began looking around. There were many beautiful paintings and sculptures. She coughed. The store-owner must love incense as its scent overtook the store. A well-molded mother and child sculpture caught her eyes. She had a sudden urge to call home and speak to her mom. She would send her a Blackberry message instead when she got out of the store.

"I see you like this one? It reminds you of home, right?" Richard asked.

Feranmi was about to respond when the store door chimed. She glanced around just in time to see Alex. Her heart leapt in betrayal at the sight of him. This couldn't be. Of all the stores, he had to come into this one? Their eyes met and his lips feigned a smile. He began to walk towards them and she could tell that he wasn't too happy. Was he jealous? As much as she tried, she was not prepared when he came to a halt right in front of her.

"Good afternoon, Fera," Alex said, his eyes fixed on her.

"Hi." Feranmi couldn't recognize her own voice. Why was she allowing him to have such an effect on her? She had to stay focused on the reason they were not together. He was wrong for her.

"Surprised to see you here—"

"I bet you are," he said. "Aren't you going to introduce me to your friend?"

She recognized his emphasis on the word friend. He was trying to goad her. She knew him so well. Her eyes narrowed at him. He smiled slyly.

"Richard, this is Alex. He's an old a friend of mine." At the mention of the word "friend", Feranmi felt Richard's arm snake around her waist. Typical man, he was trying to mark territory. Richard extended his hand. The two men exchanged cordial greetings.

"Glad to see you were able to take time out of your busy schedule and enjoy yourself," Alex said, not taking his eyes off her. She knew he was referring to her excuse not to have lunch with him.

"Um...yeah." Her voice was laced with guilt. She missed her friend, but her heart was on the line. At that moment, she decided that the least she owed him was the truth. This had gone on long enough. It was okay keeping it from him, when she knew he was in Chicago, but now he was back in town she needed to level with him.

"I'll see you later, then. Call me," Alex said. He gave her a lazy smile and nodded at Richard before he walked away.

"Feranmi, are you ready to go?" Richard asked. She eased out of his arm and exited the store. They spent another hour walking around the fair grounds and got on a couple of rides but Feranmi was distracted the whole time. Her excitement had faded. She couldn't take her mind off Alex.

"I'M glad both of you think this is funny, because I don't." Feranmi snapped at her friends. She stretched her legs out on the ottoman in her living room and crossed them at the ankles.

The three of them had been on a lot of calls recently. The weekend they had been waiting for was a week away and the excitement level was high. Feranmi and Ini handled most of the arrangements and filled Kayla in along the way just in case she wanted to change something. Presently, the guest count was about twenty-five of the couple's closest friends and family. The plan was to make sure everyone had a marvelous time. The weekend would kick off with a casual dinner at a new, trendy restaurant in the heart of the elite community of Buckhead on Friday night.

"Why wouldn't we laugh? Umm... Miss 'I got a list and he

must be Nigerian'." Ini giggled on the other end of the line. "It's that mentality that's messing you up now."

"Ini, stop being so insensitive," Kayla said. "Fera, the fact that you've got a list is admirable but you have to bend a little and be open. You're too close minded."

"So has Alex called you since then?"

"No. He hasn't and it makes me wonder what he's up to," Feranmi said.

"Why should you care? He's not right for you, remember?" Ini teased.

"Cut it out Ini, Fera, why are you worried about Alex? You said Richard was pretty decent."

"He is, but he's not...," Feranmi muttered under her voice.

"He's not who? Alex?" Kayla asked. Why do you torture yourself so? Just tell your parents to get over it. We're in 2011 for goodness sake."

"There you go again. You can't eat your cake and have it. It's either you put your tail between your legs and go beg that man for being foolish four years ago or make do with your Richard," Ini said.

"Fera, what about the Kenneth guy? The one before Richard. We didn't hear anything else about him. What happened?" Kayla asked.

"That one wasn't even worth it. After the first few minutes of conversation, I could tell that he was a recent divorcee who was just looking for a mother for his kids. Dinner conversation was more like an interview for a nanny position." Feranmi sighed heavily.

"Why can't a man like my sister's husband come and sweep me off my feet? The way Tunde treats my sister is to die for," Feranmi said.

"You have such a man—Alex. He's just not in the package you want," Kayla said.

Feranmi knew Kayla was trying to be encouraging, but she needed solutions right now. He wasn't an option.

"Enough about me. I'm going to try and make this Richard thing work and stop whining," Feranmi said. "At least I have a good prospect and he just might be a keeper." Feranmi wasn't sure whether she was trying to convince her friends or herself.

"That a girl! You can't be in control all the time. Live your life and wait and see what God brings your way, but also be open to receive it," Ini said. Although she liked to act as if she didn't really care about anything, Feranmi knew deep down Ini cared about her.

"Thanks, divas, you're always there when I need to whine. Kay, you know we can't wait to grill Kofi," Feranmi said.

"Yeah, girl we can't wait. This is going to be good."

"Y'all better not harass my man."

"Whatever...," Feranmi and Ini said in unison.

The friends chatted a bit more, going over details for the engagement weekend before hanging up.

The sharp pain Feranmi had tried so hard to ignore for the past four years pierced her heart. She remembered the time she and Alex spent together. Although short, it was the most memorable time of her life. His kind spirit and caring nature were probably what drew her to him at first. But his strong, always in control nature was what made him exciting.

Feranmi turned off the television and made her way upstairs. It was time to put those memories behind her and concentrate on the future and hopefully that was Richard.

CHAPTER SEVEN

ALEX BOLTED UPRIGHT in the bed when he heard the phone ring. The sun shone through the window of his bedroom indicating it was probably mid-morning. As he predicted, his raw materials arrived about the same time his boy, Kofi, got into town. He hadn't been able to attend dinner last night. His daily routine now included a visit to the Anderson Group building site. He and Phillip stayed late at the site making sure that every man had their assignments and the materials needed to get the project back on track.

When the phone rang again, he wiped the sleep from his eyes and reached over to get it. "Yeah?"

"Hey man, don't tell me you're still sleeping." Alex winced as Kofi's voice came through the other end of the phone. Alex felt it was too early for his friend to have this much energy. He glanced at the clock on his dresser. 10:00 a.m. He had overslept. He had to get ready; he and Phillip had made plans to meet at the site in an hour.

"Got back late last night. How was dinner? Sorry, I couldn't make it, but you know what's at stake. I'll stop by to see you and

Kay later," Alex said. "I've got to move this project along so come February, I'll be able to enjoy Chi town without any worries."

"I get it, man. No worries about me. But you should be worried about your girl."

"Who?" Alex got out of the bed, left the bedroom, and headed towards the kitchen. He needed his caffeine fix.

"Is there another? Even when you were with Tracie, the only one I kept hearing about was Fera," Kofi said.

Alex hadn't heard from Feranmi since he ran into her at the Fair. Quite frankly, he hadn't let his mind think about anything else but getting his business back together. That was the original plan. Unknown to her, when Alex saw her with Richard, her reaction told him everything he needed to know. Richard wasn't a threat. He would do what he needed, to do then see about Feranmi.

"What about her? Is she okay?" Alex asked.

"From what I saw she is. She had some dude with her at dinner last night," Kofi said. "I forgot his name...umm—"

"Richard." Alex snapped. He was beginning to see red. He couldn't believe what he was hearing. For Feranmi to bring Richard around their friends, it meant that the guy was more of a threat than Alex originally thought.

"You know about him?"

"Yeah, I ran into them the other day." Alex put on the coffee pot.

"And you didn't tell me?" Kofi asked. "I don't understand, so you ok with it? I thought the plan was to get her back."

"I'm not worried about him. I know her and he's not even her type, so I decided to face what I had in front of me and see about her later."

"Based on what I saw yesterday, you need to be worried. I understand this whole wanting to get your business together, but you have to find some balance," Kofi paused. "Not to bring Tracie up, but you were so busy trying to build your business that she slipped through your fingers right into another man's arms."

Alex felt his anger rising even more. Kofi knew better than to bring up Tracie. That whole affair made him cringe. Kofi went on to tell Alex about dinner last night and how Kayla had to check him a few times because of his hostility towards Richard. Alex was glad Kofi had his back, but it was time to make an appearance.

"Alright, I hear you, man. I gotta make a stop at the site. Hopefully, I'll be at the bowling alley in time," Alex said.

They said their good byes and hung up. He had walked away once, giving Feranmi the easy way out. He wasn't going to do it again. Feranmi had avoided him long enough. That was about to change. First, he had to get rid of the competition.

ALEX LOOKED around one last time and nodded with a satisfied grin on his face. With the project being in its critical stage, he wasn't leaving anything to chance. Everyone worked sun up to sun down, seven days a week and now everything was looking good. Even if they were behind schedule, it probably would only be by a couple of weeks.

He barely had an hour to head back home, change, and make his way to the bowling alley. Things hadn't gone according to plan. He stayed at the site longer than he intended. He was more than an hour late, but when he visualized "what's his name" being chummy with Feranmi and their friends, his determination to make it to the bowling alley grew stronger.

Turning into the parking lot of the 300 Bowling Alley, Alex

found a good parking spot. He walked into the alley and headed straight for the shoe section. He got a pair of size eleven bowling shoes and proceeded to the area where he was informed the Bell/Addo party was camped. He spotted Kofi, who had his back to him talking to a group of people. Kayla had her arm around his waist and her head on his shoulder.

"Um, aren't you supposed to be bowling, man?" Alex asked, sneaking up from behind. He cleared his throat in a feigned cough.

Kofi whipped around suddenly and stared at his friend. The two embraced in a man hug, giving each other pats on the back. Their reunion was interrupted by Kayla.

She tapped Alex on his back, "Don't I get some love, too?"

"Come here, girl." Alex pulled her into an embrace.

"You might wanna ease up off my woman," Kofi joked.

"Whatever, man. Kay, you look good as always."

"Thanks, dear. I hope you have everything under control at work now? I was going to wring your neck if you had missed another day. I was kinda disappointed I didn't see you yesterday."

"I knew you'd kill me. Thank God it all worked out," Alex's eyes were roaming the room looking for Feranmi and her Richard. Things weren't completely under control but that was his and Kofi's little secret. He had to be here.

"Oh, so you weren't scared of what I'd do?" Kofi asked.

"Nah...you I can take." Alex continued to scan the room. *Where was she? Was she with him somewhere?*

"She went to the ladies room," Kayla nudged him.

"Am I that obvious?"

"Yes man...very," Kofi said. "Babe, excuse us. Come on, let me introduce you to everyone." Kofi kissed Kayla on the check and led Alex away.

"I'm happy for you, man. Glad you decided to grow some

sense and ask that woman to marry you," Alex said when they were out of earshot.

"Yeah, I'm blessed." Kofi turned around to glance at his wife to be. "You deserve this too, man. I'd like to see you happy as well. You've been through a lot."

"Don't want to talk about that here. Let's have some fun," Alex said, dismissively. "Where are they?" Alex recognized the impatience in his voice when the words came out.

"Relax—he stepped out to take a call, while she went to the restroom, I think." Kofi let out a chuckle.

"What's so funny?

"I thought you weren't worried,"

"Whatever, man," Alex gave Kofi a stern look.

"Why are you looking at me like that? You must have me confused. I ain't scared of you." Kofi was still trying to suppress his laughter when they got closer to the crowd.

"Hey, everybody, I want to introduce Alex Montgomery. He is my brother from another mama. He lives here in Atlanta," Kofi shouted over the loud noise. After making his rounds giving handshakes, Alex settled down to join in on the fun.

They had a competition going. It was between the ladies and the men and right now it looked like the men were being schooled or they were letting themselves be schooled, he couldn't tell which. From the scores, he would presume the latter.

ALEX COULD RECOGNIZE that laughter anywhere. He turned around and saw Feranmi approaching with Kayla and Ini by her side. He was really amazed at how close the three of them stayed after all these years despite Kayla's relocation.

"Are you having fun yet?" Kayla asked, as the ladies advanced towards him.

Alex got up and walked towards them. "Yes, I'm mingling. But not playing yet. Waiting 'til this round is over." He was talking to Kayla but his eyes were fixed on Feranmi, who was trying as much as possible not to make eye contact.

"Hey, stranger so you finally decided to show your face," Ini said.

"Hi, Ini. It's been ages."

"I know, come here. How've you been?" Ini walked forward and gave him a hug. He always admired her for her straight talk.

"I've been good. Hi, Fera," Alex said, his eyes searching for hers. She looked stunning in her hot pink Polo-T shirt and blue jeans. She had on that fragrance that played with his senses.

"Alex, glad you could make it today." Feranmi looked up and crossed her arms across her chest.

Alex knew she was nervous. "You missed me?" They had an audience, but he didn't mind. He liked teasing her.

"There you go, delusional again."

"If you say so. We both know better."

"We'll give you guys some room while we check on the other guests," Kayla said, and nudged Ini to move.

"I've got to go and check on the lunch table and make sure everything is ready. Lunch is supposed to be served in an hour," Feranmi said. Alex recognized her game. His eyes darted to Kayla.

"Don't worry about it, girl. We got it," Kayla said as she and Ini hurried away.

Alex smiled slyly at the killer look Feranmi gave her friends. "So how've you been?"

"Good. What about you? I heard about your setback at the

site. I've been meaning to call you. Is everything ok now?" Feranmi asked.

She cared. Alex also noticed she was uneasy. She was probably looking around for Richard.

"Yeah, everything is great now. We're back on schedule." Alex gestured for her to sit down about two rows from where the rest of the crowd was. "So, where is Richard? Is he your man now?" His voice hardened. He figured there was no use stalling. He needed to know what his strategy would be.

"He's outside, taking a call. He'll be back soon. And no, he's not. We're just hanging out," Feranmi answered. Her mouth formed to say something, but no words came out. She stared behind him. Alex looked back and saw Richard approaching. Alex stood to his full height and sized up the competition as he closed the gap between them. Richard came to a stop right in front of Alex. His smile was cool and phony just like the first time they'd met. He extended his hand which Alex took, returning the fake smile.

"Alex..."

"Richard..."

The handshake was firm and brief with each man nodding. Alex noticed Feranmi didn't stand by either of their sides, but remained seated.

"I didn't know you would be here. Feranmi mentioned you had a slight problem at your workplace." Richard moved closer to Feranmi. She stood and he placed his arm around her waist.

"Oh, did she now?" Alex asked, smiling. Underneath he was fighting to control the bout of jealousy rising within him. One would think he was in love, the way he was feeling right now. He missed his friend and some part of his ego wanted answers for four years ago. He even wanted a chance, but love? No.

Alex watched as Feranmi shifted uneasily, scratching her

neck. She always did that when she was uncomfortable. Alex concluded that either she wasn't feeling Richard or she was fighting what she felt for him. Alex decided that either way, there was no cause for alarm as Kofi thought. Everything was under control.

"Let me see what the others are up to. You guys have fun," Alex said. He nodded in Richard's direction and winked at Feranmi then turned around and rejoined the crowd.

ABOUT AN HOUR LATER, the eight couples that had come to celebrate with Kofi and Kayla sat down to lunch.

"I didn't know you girls had skills like that," Kofi said.

"I know! When I got here and saw the score I thought you guys were letting them win, but now I know better." Alex wiped his brow with a small towel.

"Oh, you did huh? You men are something else," Kayla said. Alex could tell he was about to have the ladies gang up on him.

"I'm playing, y'all. Just playing." He started to laugh.

Alex noticed Feranmi was unusually quiet. She had been fixing her hotdog forever. He wondered what was running through that head of hers. With her, one never knew. When it was time for the second game to begin, Alex paired up with one of Kayla's friends that just happened to have stopped by. The men had lost that round, too. God bless Ini, because out of nowhere, she announced that they'd be trying something new— switching partners. And just his luck, he was paired with Feranmi. The hard stares that Richard sent his way didn't go unnoticed, but Alex wasn't bothered. He and Feranmi had a good time on the lanes despite the insane number of gutter balls she threw. At a point, he was tired of losing so tried teaching her how to play.

The laughter he remembered returned. The tension that had been between them since he ran into her had disappeared. It was short lived when Richard called her to the side to talk to her. His pager had gone off a few minutes earlier and he stepped outside. Alex assumed it was the hospital where he worked. Kofi had filled him in on the guy and told him he was a doctor. Shortly after, Richard said his goodbyes and left. Since then, Feranmi's demeanor changed. Alex's body tensed when he remembered the current that passed through them when he tried to teach her how to throw the ball. He felt something. He knew she did, too.

After they finished lunch, everyone gathered in the parking lot, talking in small groups.

"I'm really glad you came out this weekend," Kayla said, giving Alex a hug. Feranmi avoided him the rest of the day. After lunch, she left quickly saying she had a headache. Alex and Kofi made plans to meet up later that night but he wouldn't get to see Kayla 'til tomorrow—Sunday—for brunch. And since they planned to leave for the airport right after, Alex decided to have a little chat.

"Yeah, glad I did, too. It was worth getting a break from work to hang out with my boy and his lady," Alex replied. "So what's up with your girl?" He thought he had made some progress, but apparently not.

"Alex, I'm staying out of you and Fera's business. If she knew I was talking to you about her, she would kill me. Literally," Kayla said.

"Okay, I respect that. Guess I'm going to have to do this by myself."

"You know I love you like a brother, but Fera is my girl. Can't get into it unless I really need to. Besides, if you feeling her like you say you do, you don't need any help." She gave him a parting kiss on the check and started to walk off, then paused.

"Alex, a little hint of caution, before you start anything, you need to come clean about Tracie and all that mess in Chicago two years ago." She smiled, turned and left.

Alex was taken aback that Kayla would bring that up. It wasn't a time he was proud of, but what did that have to do with Feranmi? He pushed the thought aside. From what he remembered about Feranmi's headaches, they were terrible. He pulled out his phone and began composing a text

I hope you feel better. See you tomorrow – Alex

THE RESTAURANT WAS NOISY; the banging of pans and yelling of orders were the sound bites that greeted Alex when he approached the booth where Kofi, Kayla and the rest of their friends and family were seated. It was near the kitchen, so he guessed it was the largest space they could get. There must be some truth to what he heard about the chicken and waffles at Gladys's Knight & Ron's Chicken and Waffles restaurant. It was barely mid-morning on Sunday and the place was packed.

He arrived just in time. He thought he would be late since he decided to attend church first. From experience, he knew one missed Sunday would turn into two then three until he found every excuse not to go.

He and Kofi had hung out at his place 'til late last night. They were able to catch up on a lot; things that texting and short phone conversations didn't allow them to. Alex was grateful for the brother he had in Kofi and was really happy that Kofi had found his soul mate in Kayla. Kofi expressed his concerned about Feranmi's obvious mixed messages. He didn't want to see Alex hurt again.

"You made it." Kayla was the first one to speak.

"Yes, I did. Hey wassup, everyone," Alex said. He scanned the room—no Richard. He slid into the seat next to Feranmi. She turned to him. He nudged her slightly with his shoulder. She looked flawless. Strands of her shiny black hair fell on her shoulders shaping her lightly made up face. A stubborn strand of hair played across her face. It took everything within him to resist the urge to tuck the stray strand behind her ears.

"Hey, you. Thanks for checking on me yesterday. I had it bad and needed to leave," Feranmi said.

"No worries. That's what nice guys do. I'm glad you're better."

Feranmi blushed. Alex leaned in closer and whispered into her ear, "You look very beautiful this morning."

"Thanks. You clean up good, too." She beamed at him and he slightly bowed his head.

"Where's your boy?" Alex asked. He smiled when she saw her hazel brown eyes, narrow. She always did that when she was displeased with something.

"What? Isn't he your boy?"

"You just like teasing me, don't you?"

"I love it is more like it..." He took a sip of water. "So where is he?"

"He had to work," Feranmi said. Alex was about to reply when they were interrupted by the waiter, who took their orders, reclaimed the menus, and headed back to the kitchen. Most of them decided to go with the lunch menu instead of breakfast, but Alex had a taste for waffles. There was light conversation flowing through the group. Alex noticed Kayla constantly checking her watch. She has always been a stickler for time. Kofi was the exact opposite.

It didn't take long for their food to arrive, and the chatter immediately died down. Alex watched Feranmi shove her green beans to the side of her plate.

"I see you still don't like green beans."

"Never said I don't like them. It's never spiced enough and the hot sauce isn't making it any better." She glanced at him then concentrated on her mission of separating the beans from the rest of her food.

"Then why did you order them?" he teased.

"I thought they would be different. Any other questions or are you going to allow me to eat my food?" she joked. He enjoyed it when she wasn't too serious.

"Besides, you don't see me bothering you about eating breakfast in the afternoon."

After a brief moment, with their meals almost a quarter gone, Alex turned to Feranmi and said, "So tell me, apart from work, what else have you been up to?"

He saw a sparkle in her eye. "Umm, nothing much, work and the girls occupy most of my time." She must have seen the puzzled look on his face because she smiled and continued. "Oh no, not my girls as in Kay and Ini, but I mentor a group of girls at the center."

"Are you kidding me? For real? That's great." He paused to drink some water. "Tell me about them."

For the next couple of minutes Feranmi explained the program. He was so proud of her. This was this kind of outreach that drew both of them together in the first place.

"Oh, wow. That's great Fera. In Chicago, I volunteered most Saturdays at the Boys and Girls club."

Feranmi let out a sigh. "The feeling you get when you give back is so—"

"Satisfying."

"You took the words right out of my mouth." A brief silence

passed between them and she said, "You're welcome to visit the center anytime."

"Cool. I just might take you up on that offer. It'll just be like old times." He winked.

They laughed and teased each other for the rest of the meal. It felt nice. But Alex reminded himself not to assume anything when it came to Feranmi. He learned that from experience, but he was comfortable that he was breaking down the brick walls she had built around her.

The party broke up with an hour for Kayla and Kofi to get to the airport. The couple expressed their gratitude to everyone for coming out. They said their goodbyes and left. Alex, Feranmi and Ini were left in the parking lot. They escorted Ini to her car.

"Okay Alex, don't be a stranger now. Anyway, something tells me you won't." Ini winked at Feranmi, then got in her car and slammed the door.

"So, what are you doing later?" Alex asked.

"Oh, nothing. I'm just going to relax and call my parents," Feranmi said.

Alex watched her frantically searched her handbag.

"What are you looking for? Your keys are in your other hand."

"I know. I'm looking for my phone. I want to make sure my folks haven't called." She rested the bag on the hood of the car. After a couple of seconds, she said, "I think I forgot it inside. I'll be right back." Feranmi walked towards the restaurant before Alex could respond. He remembered he hadn't checked emails today so pulled out his Android and began scrolling while he waited.

Feranmi walked up to the hostess' stand. "Excuse me, I think I forgot my phone at the table."

"Yes, the waiter found it. Here you go." The hostess handed Feranmi the phone she had stored in the podium.

"Thanks," Feranmi said. She checked quickly—no missed call. Without looking, she turned around and bumped into a couple with a small child. She raised her eyes

"Oh, I'm so sorry I wasn't looking...Richard?"

CHAPTER EIGHT

"I'M LAUGHING because you've got the craziest stories lately," Ini said. Kayla was silent.

"Kay, you there?" Feranmi asked.

"Yes, dear, I'm here. Just shell shocked, that's all. So when you called his name, what did he say?"

"Nothing, he just stared at me. I didn't want any drama. The chick he was with was ready to take me down with one wrong move." Feranmi parked her car outside the Tropical Food store. She was on her way home and needed to pick up the key ingredient to cook the Nigerian dish she craved—coconut rice.

This was the first time she could get both of her friends together since Sunday. They needed to hear her latest twist at the same time.

"But what beats me is, why would he be registered in a dating service when he's married?" Ini asked.

"Ini, haven't you been listening? He isn't married. He said she just had a child for him," Feranmi explained, her voice a notch higher.

"And you know this how?" Kayla asked.

"Because he has sent me five texts saying so—"

Ini interjected, "Says the same guy that lied in the first place. Fera, come on now."

"What am I coming on for? Did you hear me say I believe him? I'm just saying what he said."

"Honestly, I'm not even bothered by him. I'm just mad that I invested all that time going out with him. Three whole dates. I really kept an open mind here. He was a good prospect—at least I thought so. Now this just takes me back to square one in my search for a make-believe man." Feranmi sighed.

"You're joking, right? After the drama of the last months, you're still seriously thinking about going through with this ridiculous plan?" Kayla asked.

Feranmi knew she was concerned.

"Ha! I'm serious, oh. I talked to my big sister yesterday. She hinted that my parents were talking about this Bayo guy."

"So, that doesn't mean they're still planning to hook you guys up," Ini said.

"Yes, it does when my name was mentioned in the same sentence. My sis took her kids over to see the folks and that's when she heard them talking. Especially since they're yet to speak with my "man." My sister knows how I feel, so she called me this morning on my way to work." Feranmi found the coconut milk she was looking for, but decided to pick up a few more things. That way she wouldn't have to come here for another couple of weeks.

"Hmmm. I'm so glad that at least my parents have grand-children. If they didn't...they might have auctioned me off. I swear." Feranmi said. They all broke into a fit of laughter.

"So what did Alex say?"

There it was. She was wondering when Kayla would get to asking her that.

"Why do you girls always go to Alex when we're talking about me? Should I go back to banning his name from our conversations?"

After an awkward silence, she continued, "If you must know, he didn't do anything because he didn't know. I ran into Richard inside the restaurant. I would've died of humiliation if it happened in front of Alex."

"I think you should give this thing up. These are signs that it's bound to blow up in your face sooner or later," Kayla advised.

"I agree. I really think these are signs that you can't control every aspect of your life and that it's time to take a stand concerning your parents," Ini said.

Feranmi paid the cashier and left the store. Outside, she paused and took in her surroundings. The trees were bare and swayed from side to side due to the heavy winds. The holiday spirit was definitely in the air. Almost every store front was decorated with Christmas lights and had carols playing inside. She was suddenly reminded that she would be alone again this Christmas. Alone she could do. She had trained herself to be ok with it these past years, but she knew this year would be different. Alex was in the same city. This past weekend reminded her that she missed him like something crazy. After she let herself relax, the memories of their friendship came flooding back. Somewhere deep down she knew that the disappointment of Richard was probably a blessing. There was silence on the other end of the line. Her friends were waiting for her to say something.

"Okay. I hear you. I'll think about it. But don't hate me if I call you tomorrow asking for another guy." Feranmi teased.

"We'll never hate you. We don't understand it, but we support you anyway. Sisters for life, remember," Kayla said. She was always the one with the calmest head.

"Yeah, sisters for life," Ini and Feranmi said in unison

"Love you, Divas." Feranmi unlocked her car and got in

"Love you back." Feranmi and Ini replied. Feranmi disconnected the call. She pushed the gear into drive and headed home.

FERANMI RAN her fingers through her hair one more time before sliding her feet into her boots. She checked her reflection in the mirror. She was satisfied with the grey and red cashmere sweater and black jeans. It was a gorgeous, Saturday afternoon and she was headed to the center. There was a guest speaker coming today who was going to speak to the girls at the center about being proud of whom they were, regardless of their size, shape, skin color or texture of their hair.

Feranmi smiled when she remembered the conversation with Alex at the restaurant. It brought back memories of their time together. He was impressed. Talking about the center reminded them of their days in missions training and that life-changing trip to Burma. He was so excited, that she couldn't resist the urge to invite him over to the center, to see for himself. He had chosen to come out today. According to him things were better at work so he could ease off. They would meet at a local coffee shop and ride together.

Feranmi's heart raced with emotions she couldn't explain. She had enjoyed sharing those types of experiences with Alex. The only drawback was that it brought them too close to memory lane. Everything would have been perfect if her parents were not so against her marrying an American. Feranmi dismissed her issues. Today, she was going to have a good time doing what she loved. Keys in hand, she left her house.

Feranmi and Alex arrived at the center just in time. Everything was arranged in a classroom setting. The podium was in its place with potted plants on each side. The temperature in the room was comfortably warm. It was a welcome change from the chill outside. The five girls she mentored were all there with their parents or guardians. As usual, they ran to her the minute she entered the small room.

"Hi, Miss Fera, we were wondering when you were going to get here," Donetta said. She was the only fifteen year-old amongst the group.

There were three sixteen and one seventeen year-old— Ada. Since Ada was the oldest, she often doubled as Feranmi's assistant—a responsibility she took seriously. Their bond formed gradually over the year Feranmi had been involved with the group. It took time to build trust among the girls, but took longer with Ada. During their first encounter, Feranmi knew immediately that she had some self-esteem issues. She didn't stand up straight, nor did she make eye contact when speaking. She often wore heavy makeup for her age and used an obscene amount of hair gel to slick her hair down, but her natural tresses always found a way to break through. Ada was smart, but Feranmi noticed she dumbed down when she was around her peers, especially boys. She had made remarkable progress, even agreeing to go to college next year. Feranmi couldn't be happier.

"So, who do we have here?" Ada asked, sizing Alex up mischievously. She then turned to Feranmi and gave her a smile.

"Girls, this is an old friend of mine, Alex Montgomery."

"Hi girls—"

He barely got the words out when one of the girls burst into a song.

"Miss Fera got a boyfriend," Donetta sang.

"No, I don't. Now take your places let me check on the speaker. She should be here by now." Ada took Alex's arm and dragged him away to a seat beside her. Feranmi thought it was charming how he played along and followed.

She powered on her iPad to check her email. No word. It was almost the top of the hour. She should be here by now. Her thought wasn't even complete when her phone buzzed notifying her she had a text.

"I'm so sorry Feranmi. I have a family emergency I must attend to. I won't be able to speak tonight. I'm sorry for any inconveniences- Brenda Taylor

Feranmi frowned. Could things get any worse? From the scent of his cologne, she could tell Alex was behind her.

"What's wrong?" He asked. Feranmi could see he genuinely cared.

"My speaker just cancelled. The girls will be so disappointed. I'm going to have to cancel. I hate it." Feranmi knew she shouldn't show despair, but she couldn't help it.

"Calm down, it's going to work out. I thought I taught you how to relax—" he joked

"Alex, I have no time for games now." She shut down her iPad and placed it back in its case.

"I could speak if you want me to. I could talk about how I started my business."

She stared at him speechless. Just like old times, he was coming to her rescue.

"That would be great! I don't know how to thank you."

"We'll think of something." he winked and headed to the podium. "We'll think of something."

Feranmi knew him well enough to know he would indeed think of something.

CHAPTER NINE

FOR THE FIRST time in weeks, Feranmi was at peace. And she owed it all to Alex. Feranmi adjusted herself on the couch and flipped through the pages of a magazine. Yesterday was just like old times. In addition to teaching the girls about his business, he emphasized the importance of being proud in their skin. Feranmi noticed the girls were so attentive that they didn't recognize that he had spoken for an hour.

Feranmi beamed with pride when he spoke. That passion was still there. She admired that about him. Truth be told, he was part of the reason, the 'We Matter" program was so important to her. It was like living what they had learned and practiced years ago. They ended the evening on a high note with Alex asking her out to dinner. This time she accepted. Later today, they would meet at Maggianos. Right now she was having a lazy Sunday.

Service was refreshing. The pastor preached about giving thanks in all situations. It was as if he was talking to her. She had spent too many weeks whining about her problems. Her mother hadn't bothered her recently, work was good, and she had her health and good friends. Things couldn't be better.

A vibrating sound coming from between the cushions on the couch alerted Feranmi that her phone was ringing. She picked up the phone and looked at the caller ID— unknown number. It was from Nigeria; she grinned and answered the phone. Her mom. As she had done so many Sundays before, Feranmi's mother called to find out how her daughter was doing. After they exchanged pleasantries, Yewande began telling her daughter about the lunch guests they had.

"Hmmm...mummy de mummy, I trust you threw down. You're the best hostess I know. You go all out whether you are asked to or not," Feranmi said. Her mother hissed and she laughed. She remembered those days growing up. Her dad would call to say that he was bringing people from the office over.

"Just for drinks. They want to look over some papers I forgot to take to the office this morning," her dad would say. And before they knew it, the china would be flying out of the cabinet, yam would be boiling for pounded yam, and fruit would be cut for a fruit salad. She and Bimbo would be summoned immediately for duty they didn't sign up for. How did "just for drinks" translate into a three course meal and dessert? It never made any sense to her. Her mom was the quintessential homemaker and Bimbo had followed in that path, but Feranmi always believed there should be more. Nothing wrong with being a homemaker. She admired her mom, but she could have it all. She had to have a passion outside of her family.

"Oh, you are being funny, *abi?*" Her mom knew she was teasing. Feranmi missed home a lot and talking to them made her feel she was there.

"You can laugh all you want with the nice young man you will marry one day. You'll be forced to do the same. Modern or not, a man needs a homemaker. Your sister Bimbo hasn't brought me disgrace and neither will you!" her mother said, emphasizing the word disgrace.

Oh Lawd, here we go again with the marriage thing. Well today was not the day. Feranmi was going to side-step that comment.

"Is that your friend there? I don't understand why we haven't talked to him, yet." her mother said. "Are you people having problems? What is his name *sef?*"

It just occurred to Feranmi that she never gave her parents a name. They just referred to her imaginary man as her "friend".

"Mummy, he isn't here. *Shebi* you guys are coming...you'll see him then." Feranmi hoped that would be enough and she'd let it go. Because right now, she had no idea who they'd see when they got here.

She heard her mother being distracted in the background by gateman. From the one-sided conversation, Feranmi could tell he was informing her mother that one of her friends was here. *Good just what I need, a distraction.*

"*Ehen*, sorry my dear, I have to go now. What did you say his name was?" her mother asked when she returned to the phone some seconds later.

"Mummy, isn't someone waiting for you?"

"Ah ah Olorunferanmi, is there something you want to tell me? Why are you avoiding my question? What is his name?"

"Mummy, what will I be hiding? I just don't want you to keep your friend waiting. We'll discuss later—"

"She will wait. What is his name? If you don't give me a name—"

"Alex. His name is Alex." Feranmi said in a mere whisper.

"Okay, hmm...Alex. I'll talk to you soon. I love you. Tell

80

Deji I said he should call home sometime ah, ah." Her mother hung up.

Feranmi stared at the phone, dazed. She couldn't fathom what she had just done.

A COUPLE OF HOURS LATER, Alex pulled his car into the Maggiano's parking lot. He couldn't believe he was actually nervous, but it was understandable since he hadn't been out on a date in so long.

Alex was glad he accepted Feranmi's invitation to the center. Wow! He missed doing that kind of thing—talking to young people. Another added benefit of that decision was that he and Feranmi were rapidly getting to a good place—void of the initial tension. The way she was around those girls reminded him of what attracted him to her in the first place—her passion to help. She was invading his every awakening thought. She was the first person he thought about in the morning and the last person he thought about at night. Now he really wanted answers to four years ago and tonight, he intended to get them.

When he got to the restaurant, she hadn't arrived. The weekend crowd had started to gather because the restaurant was rowdier than he normally knew it to be. He ordered water for both of them, telling the waiter he would hold off on ordering anything else. Alex decided to check his emails on his phone while he waited. He was probably on the third email when, instinctively, he raised his head to see Feranmi approaching. She was stunning in her black and white striped sweater and red pants. Her scent played with his nostrils. He had to find out what it was. He loved it.

"Hey, sorry I'm late," Feranmi said when she got to the

table. Alex stood to pull her chair out. When his hand slightly brushed against hers, he felt a tingle.

"Hey, yourself. It's not a problem, I just got here." Settling himself back in his seat, he looked up and motioned to the waiter.

"Quite frankly, I did think I'd sit here for a while." He smiled at her. "So did you get what you wanted?" He teased as the waiter took their drink orders.

Feranmi had called him earlier and told him that she had to make a quick stop at the mall. He had remembered their last shopping experience—two days before they left for Burma. She had bribed him with lunch, and asked him to accompany her to the mall. He did, and swore he'd never do it again. She was dangerous around books and clothes.

Feranmi took a sip of water. "Yes, I did, but I promise I wasn't bad."

Alex raised his brow. She must have remembered that day as well. Almost immediately the waiter returned with their drinks and proceeded to take their orders. Alex was starving. He had been so nervous that he skipped lunch. He also didn't want to spoil his appetite for tonight. From what he remembered Feranmi was a hearty eater and he didn't want her to feel alone. She wasn't one of those ladies who tried to be cute by ordering a salad when out on a date. The only time she ordered a salad was when she actually wanted one.

Without looking at the menu, Feranmi ordered the Parmesan Crusted Tilapia. She handed the menu to the waiter and waited for Alex to place his order. After looking over the menu, he decided to try the Beef Tenderloin Medallions. As soon as the waiter was out of earshot, Alex turned his attention to his dinner date.

"Come here often?"

"Not anymore since I moved further north of the city. The

girls and I used to come here a lot before Kayla moved. Ini and I still come here once in a while."

"That explains why you knew exactly what you wanted."

"Did you check up on Phillip?" Before he could answer Feranmi shook her head and smiled. "I remember you always talking about owning your own construction business. I'm so glad that things worked out for you. Just the way you wanted," she said.

"Yes, I did. Everything is moving along. And thanks, that means a lot." He just realized that she remembered more about him than she let on.

"Alex, you don't know how much yesterday meant to me. I'm so glad you were there to step in."

"No problem. That's what friends are for right? Friends?" He asked the question as a challenge. She didn't take the bait, bowing her head and playing with her silverware. He decided to let it go for now. The night was young.

"Did you hear from the speaker?" he asked.

"Yes. Her child sprained his ankle playing soccer and since her husband was out of town, she had to attend to him," she said. A beat of silence passed between them.

"I was pleasantly surprised when you agreed to go have dinner with me," he said. "My charm finally wore you down, huh?"

"What charm? I decided to say thank you for helping me." She grinned at him, then chuckled.

"So, I had to earn a date with you. I'm hurt." He placed his hand on his heart, and winced in fake pain. She laughed. Her laughter always had a soothing effect on him. After the laughter died down, he straightened in his seat. She must have seen his demeanor change because she became serious. Alex couldn't hold it anymore, he needed to know.

"So what's the real reason?" he asked. "I've asked you to go to dinner with me once or twice and you refused. Why so difficult?"

"I don't know what you're talking about."

"You want me to spell it out? Getting time alone with you." His eyebrow rose.

"Don't you have any other ladies to have time alone with? If that's what you needed."

"She got jokes, y'all," Alex let out a hearty laugh. Feranmi joined in.

The waiter arrived with their meal. They ate in partial silence, talking about a range of topics in between bites. Alex caught her up on everything that had gone on the last four years, everything except Tracie and his murder case. That he couldn't tell her yet. He had such a relaxing time that he didn't want the evening to end. Judging from how freely Feranmi was talking to him, he had a feeling that neither did she.

Fifteen minutes after dinner, over their refills of coffee and water, they lingered, continuing to indulge in a relaxed discussion. She shared things that she hadn't shared with him before. He found her culture interesting, but not drastically different from some of the old traditions that his mother always talked about when he was growing up. After they had talked for a while, Feranmi got a nervous look on her face and said,

"Alex, I've got something to ask you." Her face was downcast and she avoided eye contact.

"Fera, look at me. What is it? You can't be shy." He teased, staring at her intently when she raised her head. She didn't utter a word.

"What is it?" He was anxious about what he was about to hear.

"Could you pretend to be my man when my parents get here?" She blurted out.

CHAPTER TEN

ALEX WAS SILENT. His body stiffened. All he heard were the words pretend and man. "You say what now?" She had to be kidding.

"My folks will be here in a couple of weeks. They are pressuring me to get married and I need to get them off my back," she explained with urgency.

"Why? How? I don't get it." He paused for some seconds waiting for her to explain.

"It's a long story—one which I'm too embarrassed to go into —but to get them off my back, I sorta have to show them I'm in a committed relationship that will eventually lead to the altar." She took a sip of water. She had her eyes fixed on him. Alex knew she was waiting for a reaction.

"So let me get this straight. You want me to help you lie to your parents, but don't want to tell me why?" Alex inquired with a puzzled look on his face

"But, I just told you why...umm it's to get them off my back." Feranmi began to fidget with her wristwatch.

This must be awkward for her, but he at least knew her

well enough to know that there had to be a very real reason why she just asked him to do this. But then she knew better to expect him to just play along so he needed more than she was giving. Granted he was still attracted to her after four years, but she had rejected him once. And he had worn his heart on his sleeve for Tracie. He was not about to be that kind of man again.

"But why are they on your back in the first place? Why can't you just tell them that you don't have a man?"

Her face changed immediately. He had hit a sore spot.

"It's not as simple as that. Are you going to help?" she asked, her frustration level rising.

"Up until now, you didn't want to have anything to do with me. Then, all of a sudden, you come up with this ridiculous idea and want to use me," Alex said, his brow knitted in disbelief.

She began gathering her things. "You know what, forget I asked. I shouldn't have." She stood.

"Whoa! Whoa! Where do you think you're going?" He reached for her hand, but missed by a couple of inches.

"I know you didn't expect me to just go along, no questions asked." He got up reached for his wallet and threw a fifty-dollar bill on the table. He turned back around and she was gone. His forehead crinkled in confusion. What just happened? He hurried to the parking lot and caught up with her. He grabbed her hand to get her to stop.

"Now, wait just a minute. You're acting irrational so this must be important but I ask again. Why can't you tell them you don't have a man?" Alex asked.

Feranmi didn't raise her eyes from her shoes. He placed his index finger under her chin to lift her head. She looked at him. He tried to stay focused. He had always had a thing for her hazel brown eyes, but now they were misted over with unshed tears. His heart ached, but he willed himself to keep it together.

"It's a long story—"

"We've got time. Spill it. Why do you need a pretend man for your parents and why me?" His voice was stern.

Feranmi looked up at him, then down at her shoes again. More seconds passed between them, but he was willing to wait.

"When I went home last year, I kinda led them to believe I had a man." Feranmi then told him what he knew to be the abbreviated version of her trip home and the pressure to get married.

"Hold on. So you mean you not only told them you had a man, but a Nigerian man?" Anger rose within him. It all came together perfectly. The reason she had fought him so long was that he wasn't Nigerian.

"Yes," she said, barely audible.

"I think I know the answer to this, but I'm going to ask it anyway." He paused. "Did the fact I'm not Nigerian play any part in you wanting us to remain friends?" Alex felt his anger continued to rise with each second of silence that passed. She continued to stare aimlessly. Not sure of his next reaction, he said, "I guess I have my answer. Good bye, Fera." He then turned and walked to his car.

ALEX TOSSED ASIDE THE FOLDER—IT was a new proposal he was putting together. The Anderson Group was so pleased with the job he was doing that they sent a referral his way. Franklin LLC was a company based out of Jacksonville, Florida and they wanted to build a small office complex.

Two days later and he was still infuriated with Feranmi. How could she be so jaded? He thought he knew her. And the agony she had put both of them through these past four years. Had her mind not been so warped, he wouldn't have met Tracie nor would he have been caught up in that murder mess two years ago.

His intercom buzzed. He reached across the desk and pressed the button to speak.

"Yes, Stacy?"

"There is a lady here to see you. She says her name is Fera," Stacy said. Alex had ignored all Feranmi's calls. He needed to make up his mind on how he would handle Feranmi Adewunmi.

"Send her in, and please hold all my calls."

Alex heard a soft knock on his office door. He stood and put one hand in his pocket.

"Come in."

Feranmi entered his office wearing a navy blue pant suit with a navy blue and white polka dot blouse. Her black pumps added about an inch to her height. She must have left work early because a quick glance at the clock on the wall indicated it was 2:00pm. He could tell she was nervous by the way she rubbed her hands together. She took him in with her eyes. He knew she was trying to read his expression. He saw remorse and misery written all over her face. But he wasn't willing to let her off so easily. He wanted answers and he was going to get them.

"Is there something you want?"

WHEN FERANMI OPENED the door to Alex's office, her heart leapt. He looked like he just stepped off the pages of *GQ* magazine. His pink dress shirt was tucked nicely into his pinstripe dress pants whose jacket hung behind the chair. His freshly shaven face and clean haircut completed his ultra-suave look. It took a special type of man to wear pink so confidently. His stance was intimidating and he had every reason to be angry, but she knew him. He would at least give her a chance to explain.

"Alex, before I give any explanation, I want to say I'm sorry," Feranmi said.

"Sorry, for what exactly?" He continued to stare at her with a blank expression. The fire in his dark brown eyes told her she had her work cut out for her.

"For everything—"

"That's not an answer."

"Alex, please..."

"I'm not letting you off that easy. I want to know exactly what you're sorry for." He walked from behind his desk to the small leather sofa in the corner. He gestured for her to sit down. She studied him for a minute and sat.

"I don't even know where to start." She sighed.

"As they say, the beginning is always best." Alex sat next to her and crossed his legs.

For the next half hour, Feranmi told Alex about the pressure her parents put on her and her sister. Not just about getting married, but to a good Nigerian man. She told him about their preference that he be at least African. They—especially her mother — was against another American in the family. Feranmi told Alex about Aunty Sade—her mother's younger sister—who came to the United States in the seventies to go to school but found love, or what she thought was love, instead. For the next couple of years, Aunty Sade stayed in an abusive marriage using the money the family sent her to feed Ronald's—her husband— drug habit. It wasn't until a distant family member who visited America on vacation ran into Aunty Sade and was able to tell what was going on. By then it was too late. She had no degree and had become a drug addict.

Feranmi couldn't tell what Alex was thinking, but the fire in his eyes was gone. There was an extended pause between them. His eyes never left hers. She felt like he could see into her soul. She caved under his gaze and let her eyes fall to the sofa.

"Where's your aunt now?" Alex asked, in a low tone.

"The family chipped in and brought her back to Nigeria, but she didn't survive the shame. She later passed away." Feranmi felt a tear escape and roll down her cheek. That had been a very sad time.

"I'm sorry to hear that."

"Alex, please understand that single event has shaped the way my sister and I were brought up to think about who we should end up with."

"I understand your mom, but come on, Fera. You've been in the U.S for a while. You can't possibly think Ronald was totally to blame for everything.

"I don't—"

He cut her off, "Then why didn't you give us a chance?"

"I couldn't disappoint them…"

"So you were willing to put our happiness on the line to please them?" He asked. Feranmi saw the look in his eye challenging her to deny the attraction between them.

"Before I met you, I'd avoided all relationships with African-American men. The time I spent with you tested everything I knew. So I pushed you away."

"And now?"

"You want the truth?"

"Nothing less would do," he said.

"I can't say I'm totally sure. My mind is too clouded right now to think of you and me. I just want to get through their visit." She waited for his reaction. This was the moment of reckoning. Alex stood and walked over to the window. He stared out of the window a while then turned.

"Since I'm not Nigerian, how will my being your man please them?" he asked with his hands in his pockets. She stood up and walked towards him.

"You'll pretend to be. Ini is Nigerian, and she hasn't been there before. I could give you a story so believable; they'll think it's real." She was getting excited but didn't want to show it.

"You've got this all figured out."

She remained silent. She was being selfish, but needed this.

After a few moments he said, "I'll do it."

"Thank you! Thank you! Thank you!" She threw her arms around his neck. She caught herself, and quickly removed her arms from around his neck and stepped back.

"Don't get too excited 'til you hear what my condition is." He snickered.

Her mood changed as quickly as it did before. Alex wasn't sure why–whether it was because of what he said or that she was suddenly aware of the heat that passed between them when she hugged him.

"When will your folks get here?"

"Mid-January. What's the condition?" she asked cautiously. He had a sly look on his face. "I'm almost afraid to hear it."

"Don't be. The condition is we do a practice run 'til they arrive."

Her jaw dropped. "Exactly what do you mean by that?"

"I mean, we practice dating. You know, we hang out get to know each other again. You remember that, don't you?" he said, with a hint of sarcasm.

This was blackmail, but it wasn't like she had a choice. With her eyes downcast, she agreed.

CHAPTER ELEVEN

"SO WHAT GIVES, man? You seem to be on top of the world each time I talk to you lately," Kofi said.

"And why does something have to give? Can't I just be happy?" Alex countered quietly laughing. Scanning through his closet, he finally picked out a blue, casual dress shirt.

His thoughts flooded back to Feranmi and their arrangement. Initially she was taken aback by his condition and protested to blackmail. He reminded her it was either that or face her parents alone. It didn't surprise him when she opted for the former.

They had talked on the phone every day since then. Today, they were going to see a movie. Normally, Alex wouldn't be caught dead watching the chick flick she chose, but tonight, the kind of movie was not as important to him as was the time he would get to spend with her.

"Stop playing, Alex. What's up?" Kofi asked again.

"I'm just happy, man. That's all. Things are going great, my project is moving along just fine. I just had another client call me to put a bid together. They were referred by the Anderson

Group." After a long pause he continued, "And I'm seeing someone."

"Someone? Who is she? Do I know her? That's great. It's about time. I've been telling you to live a little," Kofi said.

"Thanks, man, and yes you know her. Its Fera ...umm, but there's a catch. So I need you to keep it to yourself," Alex said, quickly putting on his shirt. For a moment he forgot that Kofi was not just his boy, but Kayla's fiancé. He didn't need any added pressure on Feranmi. Although this had been her idea, she was still a bit hesitant about them.

"About time you guys got it together. But what do you mean, a catch? Either you're dating her or you are not," Kofi said.

"The short version of the story is that she needs someone to pass as her man when her parents arrive in a couple of weeks. Has something to do with them pressuring her to get married." Alex looked at his reflection in the mirror before picking up his keys from the dresser and making his way to the car.

"And you went along? Are you crazy? You just got emotionally delivered from that whole Tracie drama... and the next thing you do is to re-enroll yourself in some Fera drama?" Kofi asked.

"I can't believe you went along with this. Do her girls know? Kayla didn't mention anything."

"Cool it, man, I know what I'm doing. I like this girl, so while she thinks its temporary, I'll be working on making it a permanent arrangement." Alex unlocked his car. If he didn't get a move on it, he would be late to the movie theater. "Besides, she's my friend, and in need." Those words didn't even sound right to him, but Alex had repeated them so much to himself that he was beginning to believe them.

"Okay, man. If you insist. Just looking out for you.

Remember this girl, cool as she may be, still insists on just being friends. I don't want you to put yourself out there again."

Alex heard Kofi's door chime. "Saved by the bell," Alex said.

"No, you're not because we'll continue later. That must be Kayla. We're headed to the church to talk to the Reverend Father Winston about some changes to the program."

"Hey, I'm not sure her girls know anything about this. It was hard enough for her to ask me. I don't wanna hear you go blabbing to Kay. I know you can't keep anything from her, but do this for me," Alex pleaded.

Alex heard his friend heave a heavy sigh. "Okay, man. Let me go get the door, we'll talk more later.

"Take it easy." Alex said before Kofi disconnected the call.

Alex let down the garage with the automatic opener, pressed on the accelerator and sped out of his subdivision. After Tracie, he hadn't wanted anything to do with any woman. Feranmi had always been at the back of his mind, but he couldn't let go of the hurt and pain of the last two years. Tracie's betrayal had cut deep. Despite his mother and Kofi's insistence on letting go, he was still not convinced he could give himself another chance. That all changed earlier in the year. Pastor Edwards taught a message titled, "A New Thing." Alex remembered the sermon as if it was yesterday. It really spoke to him.

Teaching from 2 Corinthians 5: 17 *"Therefore, if anyone is in Christ, he is a new creation; old things have passed away; behold, all things have become new."* It was a verse Alex had heard so many times before, but this time it was preached in a new way. He advised the congregation to become renewed in Christ and cast their burdens onto the Lord. Letting go of all hurt, pain and any resentment. He called for them to look upon any mountains they had to climb, or stuff they had to go through as changers of their destiny which shouldn't be carried like a chip but used as a learning opportunity in God's plan for their life. He gave the same call to action he made at the beginning of the year; which was to unpack the old baggage and embrace your new being.

INI AND KAYLA were totally in the dark over this one. Feranmi would have them laughing for days if she let them know what she was up to. Kayla would be nice about it, but Ini would be sure to play the, "I told you so" card. Feranmi was confused as it was and didn't need the added pressure. Her friends meant well, but she had to keep this thing to herself—at least for now. She parked her car as close to the theater entrance as she could. She let down the visor to check on the annoying pimple that had developed on her cheek— stress. Her phone rang. It was Ini.

"Hey, girl. Wassup?' she asked as soon as she picked up the phone.

"Hey, boo, what's going on?" Ini asked.

Feranmi heard loud noise in the background. Ini was probably at Tristan's, her on again off again boyfriend. Feranmi wondered what Ini saw in him. He was controlling, rude, and in her opinion, didn't treat Ini the way she deserved. She and Kayla pointed it out a couple of times, but Ini quickly defended him telling them she knew what she was doing. She then got used to saying, "He's not that bad." They became worried, but could only pray that she saw it for herself soon.

"Nothing much. Just work." Feranmi felt bad about lying, but it wasn't a complete lie. She was busy with work, too. "What about you? How's the match-making business? It's the holidays. You guys should be busy?" she laughed.

"Oh, I see you can now joke about my business?"

"Sorry," Feranmi said, trying hard to suppress her laughter

"Hey, I'm with Tristan—"

"Figured as much—"

"Don't start. Anyway, wanted to know if we're still on for next weekend because he and I wanted to make plans."

"Yeah, we're still on. Remember, we had to bully and beg to get that appointment." They were having the second fitting for their dresses. Feranmi was surprised that Ini would even ask that considering what they went through since the wedding was on such short notice.

"Ok, never mind then, I'll just make plans for the next day. Did I tell you we'll be going to the Georgia Mountains for Christmas? I hate to leave you alone," Ini said. Feranmi could tell she was concerned.

"No, you didn't, but I'm good. Really I am." That was all she was going to share and hoped it would be enough. The phone buzzed in her ear. She had an incoming call—Alex.

"I gotta hang up. I have an incoming call. I'll call you later tonight, okay? Say hello to Tristan. Muah!"

Although Feranmi didn't care much for the relationship, she still respected Tristan because her friend somehow saw something in him. She knew that Ini was about to start asking a host of questions which she wasn't ready to answer just yet. She quickly switched the phone over to answer Alex.

"Hi. You here yet? I'm in the theater lobby, but I can't find you," he said.

"Hi, there. I'm not in the lobby yet. I was talking to Ini. If you want, you can buy the tickets. I'll get the refreshments." Feranmi got out of the car. She turned the automatic locks on and did a quick glance at her appearance through her car window. Liking what she saw, she made her way to the theater.

A COUPLE OF HOURS LATER, after the movie, Alex and Feranmi decided to take a ride through downtown Atlanta. They left her car and took his since they would pass the theater on their way to her house later. Feranmi was glad he made an attempt to enjoy the movie with her as she would be the first to admit it was a real sappy one.

"I'm sorry for making you sit through that movie," she said with a grin.

"No, you're not. But don't worry about it. You having a good time was okay for me." He glanced at her quickly before returning his attention to the road.

"Look at you being all gentlemanly and accommodating."

"No, babe I am a gentle man, but you've been so busy running you haven't been able to find out," he said and winked.

"If you say so."

They drove in silence, each consumed in their own thoughts. When they arrived at Centennial Park, they found it had been turned into a winter wonderland. Christmas lights were everywhere. Carols were being blasted from hidden stereos. It was a beautiful sight. Couples cuddled up enjoying the view. Alex got a nice spot to park that had a beautiful view and handed her the Dunkin Donut coffee they had gotten from the drive-through on the way. After they'd had time to sip on their beverages, Alex turned serious and faced her.

"Fera, I've agreed to your plan, however, I'm still confused. Why are your parents so concerned about you being married? Does it have something to do with the culture?"

She remained silent for a couple of seconds, then said, "It's not so much the culture, but the perception about the single woman. Back home, societal pressure is placed on a woman who has gotten to a certain age and isn't yet married. Don't ask how it started or when or why it's that way. Right after college, my older sister found the man of her dreams—well not actually found since my parents had a hand in it. But the point is, she got married right on 'time'. I, on the other hand, decided to come to America to go to college. My parents, especially my mom, are obsessed with making sure I don't forget that to be 'complete,' I need a man's last name attached to mine." She gauged his reaction while she took a sip of her drink.

"Okay, so I get that. Do you have anything against marriage?" Alex asked.

"No, I don't. In fact, I'd like to be married to some amazing guy someday and have beautiful kids. But I want to be able to have a say in the matter." Her thoughts drifted to what a home with Alex would be like. She envisioned a son that would be a miniature version of Alex. She smiled.

"I like it," Alex said.

"What?" she knew exactly what he was talking about but wanted to be sure.

"Your smile." His gaze was intense, she shifted in her seat.

"Flattery..."

"Truth baby, truth." He smiled back at her. "So you wanna come over and fill me in on my fake story?"

Feranmi tried to picture what his house would look like. She'd bet he had an oversized leather seat in there somewhere. She felt the energy between them. At that moment, she knew she was treading on dangerous ground. But her heart had a mind of its own.

CHAPTER TWELVE

ALEX TOOK one last look around and nodded in satisfaction. Feranmi would arrive any minute for lunch. It had been a week since he had seen her. With the holidays approaching, their schedules became tighter. They did keep in touch through texts and brief phone calls. He smiled at the thought that today, he would be schooled on his Nigerian story. He also couldn't wait to hear what Feranmi had come up with.

He couldn't forget her surprise when she found out he could cook. Alex guessed that was another stereotype she had about African-American men or maybe it was all men. There was so much he had to correct and he was going to have fun doing it.

He went into the kitchen to check the indoor grill. They were having grilled fish with rice pilaf and a medley of veggies. He opted for a light lunch since they planned to later attend a jazz concert that was being held in Stone Mountain Park and might grab dinner while there.

When he heard the doorbell, Alex subconsciously straightened his shirt, and then went to answer the door. He opened it and gawked at her. She was casually dressed in jeans and a cashmere sweater, but she looked incredible. She had a way of taking his breath away. He had to get his emotions under control so he didn't scare her off.

"Aren't you going to let me in?" she asked. The sound of her sultry voice laced with traces of her Nigerian accent brought him back to the present.

"Pardon my manners. Come in." He stepped aside to let her through.

Feranmi entered and began looking around. He watched her take in the spacious condo that had a nice view of the city. He considered himself lucky that the seller was desperate to sell, so he got it for next to nothing. He decided to go with blue and chocolate brown colors when he moved in.

"Nice, it's so you. I see you haven't given up your love for art." Feranmi said.

"Thank you. I'm glad you approve."

"You do know that all these appliances hooked up like that are a fire hazard waiting to happen," she said, referring to the electronics attached to his huge LCD.

"Don't worry about it. There are all hooked up properly. It's only a DVD and stereo," he said, with a smile.

"If you say so," she said, raising her hands in surrender. Not shy at all, she walked around his living area, admiring the paintings and his DVD/CD collection. Feranmi stopped when she approached the mantle, and saw the small Asian statue she had given him. Some days before they left Burma, she bought him the piece as a souvenir. It and his memories were the only things he had to hold onto for four years.

Alex watched her fight tears. He couldn't find the right words to say, so remained silent. After a brief moment, she sniffed the air. He saw her smile at the aroma and proceeded to locate its source. He followed her to the kitchen.

"So what are we having?" she asked, walking around and nodding at what she saw. "I see you've been busy. Hope it tastes as good as it smells." He had the perfect comeback, but was stopped when she pointed to his appliances.

"Do you really use all this stuff?" He had a coffee maker, a waffle iron and a George Foreman breakfast grill.

"I'm a bachelor, so I like things easy. I use each and every one of them." Alex leaned against the fridge with his arms folded, watching her. He admired the way she walked around in his kitchen like it was hers.

"I never would've imagined you knew your way around a kitchen." She walked out of the kitchen.

"That's another thing you didn't wait around to find out."

"Where is the restroom? I'll like to freshen up before lunch. By the way, you never answered me on what we are having, so I'm waiting to be surprised." After a short pause she said, "It better be good because I'm starving." She took off her wrap and laid it on the couch.

He laughed. "It's right there on your right." He pointed in the direction of the restroom. "Everything is all set. When you get out you'll see what we're having." He was glad for the opportunity to be alone for a moment to get himself together. The woman was making him lose his mind and it was too early, too soon. *Maybe it wasn't such a good idea to invite her over after all.*

He walked across the room and pulled out the latest gospel CD by her favorite artist, Lexi. He slid it into the stereo and let the tune fill the room. It was a really good album. He had never heard of her before 'til he saw the CD lying in Feranmi's car.

SHE HAD UNDERESTIMATED AGAIN the effect he had on her. In the restroom, Feranmi breathed a sigh of relief. She breathed in an out several times trying to regain control. When he'd opened the door, her heart almost stopped. His hair was cut and shaped almost to perfection. He had on a pair of jeans and a black shirt that stretched tautly across his broad chest. And those shoulders— they made the room shrink.

The combination of his inward genuine kindness and his handsome features were exactly what made her run the last time and not look back. Her love for him grew more when she saw the statue she gave him all those years ago. Words failed her. She couldn't believe he kept it. This couldn't be happening. She had to keep on task. This was just an arrangement— she couldn't let her feelings ruin everything now. Her parents would soon be here. They'd put on a show, and her parents would leave. Only then could she afford to listen to anything her heart was saying. While washing her hands, she looked into the mirror and repeated to herself several times, *Stay strong*. Satisfied she had gained control, she opened the door to rejoin Alex.

Feranmi walked over to the table where Alex was pouring water into their glasses. He looked up when she approached. His dark brown eyes sucked her in. She looked away.

"There you are. Lunch is served." He pulled out the seat next to the head of the table. She sat down and her eyes roamed the spread he placed on the table. Alex sat down next to her and extended his hand. She couldn't be touching him. She needed to stay focused. Her facial expression must have given her way.

"I don't bite, Fera. Let me have your hand. Let's say grace."

"I didn't say that..."

"But your face did." She slid her hand into his, they bowed and he blessed the food.

"You see? All done. Nothing happened to your hand did it?"

"You love teasing me, don't you?"

"Only when you have it coming."

"Okaaay... let's eat."

They enjoyed light conversation over lunch. She told Alex about the road trip she was taking the girls on next spring. He told her about the new project he was bidding for in Florida. Feranmi swooned in his deep baritone voice. She shared stories about growing up in a family of three and being the middle child. He talked more about the struggles he had growing up as an only child with his mom. The love and admiration for his mom emanated through his voice. She respected and appreciated him so much more. Any man who loved and admired his mom like that, almost always treated his woman the same. *His woman? Where did that come from?* She was reading too many romantic novels.

"So, fill me in. What's my Nigerian story?" Alex asked rubbing his hands together, customary of someone in anticipation. There were done eating, but lingered at the table.

"Stop saying it like that." Feranmi said "You make it sound awful. I wouldn't have you do this if I had a choice."

"You do have a choice, which is to tell your folks the truth." He must have seen her demeanor change—she wasn't proud of herself. "But it is, what it is. So let's have the story."

"Okay, I talked to my folks yesterday, so I've already laid the ground work. You're a Nigerian that has never been to Nigeria before. By the way, from here on out, I'll refer to Nigeria in slang—*Naija*." Feranmi watched for a reaction. He nodded with a smirk on his face. Feranmi ignored it and continued,

"You're from Ibadan..."

"Huh? Say that again?" Alex asked. Feranmi laughed. She

was going to have to spell this out in phonetics. "It's pronounced 'E-ba-dunn'. It's the capital of Oyo State. You got it?"

"I got it, Fera. Keep going." Alex smiled.

"In my house, we speak the Yoruba language and pidgin English. Pidgin is another name for broken English—"

"I know you're not about to teach me two languages before January." Alex looked alarmed. Feranmi laughed so hard at the puzzled look on his face that her sides began to hurt. When she regained her composure, she saw he wasn't laughing. She realized that he was still waiting for an answer.

"No, I'm not. I'll just give you some phrases or words, so when my folks say them, you wouldn't be clueless." She saw his expression relax.

"Okay let's see what you got."

"My dad, you don't really have to worry about him. But my mom loves saying; *shebi* and *abi* a lot. Once in a while, she may slip in *kini*—they are Yoruba words."

"I don't have to say 'em, right?"

"Yeah, you don't have to say them. I just want to tell you what they mean." She paused. "You could surprise me and say 'em if you like." Feranmi winked at him.

"I'll pass."

"Whatever. *Shebi* is almost always used in a rhetorical sense. Loosely it's used like isn't." Feranmi saw his confused look. "As an example, *shebi* Michael Jordan is black?" Alex nodded.

"*Kini* simply means 'what'. *Abi* is a word used for confirmation. Another example, Mr. Obama is the president of America, *abi*?" Feranmi stopped. "Alex, you got it? You're not saying anything. You're just staring at me."

"'Cause you're beautiful, that's why—"

"Be serious—"

"I got it, babe. *Shebi, abi* and *kini.*" Alex said. Feranmi couldn't help but laugh at his pronunciations. "Are we done with today's lesson?"

"Yeah, I'm not going to overload you."

"Thank God for mercies—" Alex stood. He and Feranmi started gathering the dishes.

"Oh, one more thing, how far—"

Alex looked puzzled "To where?"

Feranmi giggled. "No. *How far* is pidgin for 'what's up?' My parents wouldn't say that, but my brother—Deji— would." She paused. "And your response will be *I dey.*"

Alex shook his head and walked into the kitchen. Feranmi followed him trying hard to suppress her laughter. He was doing all this for her. She loved him more.

CHAPTER THIRTEEN

ALEX WASHED, Feranmi dried, and within minutes the dishes were done. After returning the kitchen to its original state, they decided to watch some TV. Alex settled in on the black, oversized, leather couch while Feranmi opted for the matching arm-chair. Flipping through channels, Alex realized that there was a game on.

Feranmi thought it was considerate of him to ask if she minded if they watched. She didn't. Her dad and brother sold her on sports a long time ago. After all these years, she still hadn't grasped the concept of American Football or why they called it football instead of handball. The ball rarely touched their legs, unlike the soccer games she was used to. In between commercials, Alex tried to teach her the basics. She took as much in as she could. It wasn't much.

The game ended thirty-five minutes later.

"The team you were rooting for lost," Feranmi said.

"Yeah, too bad. Wasn't my team anyway. Let's see what else is on." Alex flipped through the channels and stopped once Feranmi saw a romantic comedy. They had seen it before so spent the time laughing and discussing the movie as it played. Feranmi noticed the exact moments when Alex stole side glances because she had stolen a couple of her own.

"I need some water," Feranmi said. Alex made an attempt to get up, but she stopped him.

"Don't bother getting up. I'll get it. I can find my way around a kitchen. Need anything?" She made her way around the side table in an attempt to get by. Alex grabbed her wrist and pulled her down by him. They gazed into each other's eyes. She felt the pull and slowly his parted lips captured hers. At first, he was slow as though afraid she would fight him off. Then he deepened the kiss and she began to respond. The sensations Feranmi felt four years ago consumed her as she lifted her arms and wrapped them around his neck, massaging the back of his head. He deepened the kiss even more. A part of her wanted to pull back, but she seemed to be tied to him like a magnet to iron. So she hung in there and allowed him to continue the attack with his mouth. The kiss was increasing in intensity when she pulled back.

Feranmi stood—a bit disheveled. She absently smoothed out her sweater.

"We shouldn't have done that," she said, not looking at him. Standing to his full height, Alex placed his hands gently on her shoulders and turned her around to face him. He cupped her face in both hands.

"Look at me." She raised her eyes to meet his. She saw something there she hadn't seen in while from anyone—desire.

"Apart from the fact that as Christians, we almost went too far, I don't apologize for any of it," he said. His gaze was soft.

"I should go." She got her wrap off the sofa and began putting it on. Then she picked up her purse and headed towards the door. Alex stopped her.

"You're a very attractive woman and I've been praying to

God to help me keep my hands off you for fear of running you away. Why are you so bent on denying us a chance because of something that happened to someone in the past?" She heard the frustration in his voice.

"Let's just stick to the—" her phone started to vibrate. She was about to complete the thought but it continued to vibrate. She pulled the phone out of her pocket –a text. She read it and panicked.

Miss Fera, could you come get me please...please...hurry. I'm in the JCP store at South Lake Mall. - Ada

What had Ada gotten into now? Feranmi knew Ada's mother was out of town. So, for Ada to send for her, it was not good.

"I've got to go..." she scrambled to the door.

"What's wrong? Who was it?" Alex asked. His eyebrows were scrunched up, and concern was written all over his face.

"It's Ada, one of the girls from the center. I gotta go."

"Do you want me to come with you?"

"No, thanks. I'll call you." She set her hand to turn the door knob when she heard his voice.

"Do that. We have unfinished business," he said. Feranmi opened the door and walked out.

FERANMI TRIED CALLING Ada during her drive but she was not answering the phone. She glanced at the dashboard: 5:00 p.m. The mall would close in an hour. Feranmi sped down the highway cautiously, not wanting to attract unnecessary attention from the police.

With just a few more minutes left to closing time, she raced into the store. It didn't take time to find Ada—she was in the Juniors' section of the store. She ran to Feranmi and gave her a tight hug. It was tighter than usual, since she normally didn't show emotion. Pulling back, Feranmi did a quick look at her. No marks, no scratches, although she could see the line that dried up tears had made on her face.

"What happened? Why are you here? I thought you were supposed to be at Tiffany's house this weekend since your mom went out of town." Since she could see no physical harm, Feranmi was angry and wanted answers.

"Umm... yes I was supposed to be there, but Brandon called and asked if I wanted to hang out at the mall. I didn't see any harm, so I followed. Miss Fera, he is the coolest boy in school and he asked me out," Ada explained, twisting her fingers.

Feranmi fought the urge to speak. She'd let her finish. She had learned that was the only way to hear everything.

"So we got here and we were ok 'til he started behaving funny—touching me and grabbing me. I just wanted to hang out. Then he got a phone call and there was some party he wanted me go to. I said no and wanted him to take me home, but he refused and said the only way I was getting back into his car was to go with him. When I refused, he drove off and left me here." At the end of her story, Feranmi could tell Ada was embarrassed just re-telling it. Feranmi calmed down and decided to change her tactic.

"Let's go," Feranmi said, firmly. The mall announcer just announced the mall was closing. They walked to Feranmi's car in silence. It was cold, so Feranmi turned on the car so the heat could run.

"Ada, I'm going to say this as calmly as possible because I care for you— all of you—and I'm so proud of your growth. You have to make wiser choices. When you were making the decision to sneak out of Tiffany's house to get in the car with a boy you barely knew, I know you really didn't think it was wise, but you did it anyway. And I bet more so to please him than your-self. Since your friend Tiffany isn't here with you, I'm assuming you were too scared to call her parents to come get you because you did what you weren't supposed to. So I had to come here all the way from Roswell. I don't mind doing it, but it would've been unnecessary if you stayed where you were supposed to be." Feranmi let that sink in.

Ada's mom was an African immigrant who worked very hard. Her husband died in an accident some years ago and her focus was on making sure Ada made something of herself. It hurt Feranmi to see Ada give the woman so much grief with her antics. Enrolling in the "We Matter" program was supposed to be a way to change all that.

Ada looked up for the first time, "I'm sorry, I wasn't thinking."

"Don't be sorry; learn from it. You were lucky. Suppose it didn't end this way. Listen to me, there is a time and place for everything. Concentrate on what you've got to do in this time and the rest will come in due course. Your sole focus should be on God and your books. Trust me, everything else will come in due time. There'll be boys better than Brandon, but you have to be worth something to attract the right kind. Remember a God fearing boy is better than a good looking one. But then, God will only give you the best. You can have both!" Her mind conjured up Alex's face. He was both, good looking and God fearing. They do exist.

"You got it?" Feranmi asked.

"Yeah, I got it...I'll do better. Please don't tell my mom."

"This is our secret. Send Tiffany a text, so she'll know to let you in. When does your mom get back?"

"Tomorrow," Ada said. Feranmi pulled out of the parking lot and headed west. She feared that at this rate, Ada would end up down the wrong road fast.

Feranmi's mind flashed back to Alex. It felt so good being in his arms, it took every ounce of will power she had to pull away. If she wasn't careful, she would be right where she was when Alex left four years ago. She had to take back control. Her parents would be here in three weeks; she would just avoid Alex until then. Their business would just have to stay that way for now—unfinished.

CHAPTER FOURTEEN

ALEX GLANCED across the conference room in a trance-like state. He hated to admit that he hadn't heard a word the inspectors said after the word "pass." It was the week before Christmas and he was just glad that the holidays would be worry free. The inspectors had just concluded their walk-through and were pleased. They requested this sit down meeting to go over the dates they would be visiting again and the key areas of concentration. He was of no use here. He excused himself, giving Phillip the look that told him to take over, and headed back to his office.

Alex was seated on the swivel chair behind his desk, his interlocked fingers held up the back of his head. He had to slow down. Feranmi was invading his every awakening thought, more so since they shared that kiss. He had to remember the main reason she didn't date him years ago—her parents. Alex knew family was important to her so this thing between them could go either way, especially since she was going through all this trouble to please them.

Alex remembered her laughter, smiles and the hope that he

could feel again, even weirder —she made him think about marriage. After that kiss, he knew for sure that his feelings were not one-sided. But she was on a mission to fool her parents and she couldn't even see it. With her, he was learning to let go of the past. Thoughts of Tracie still angered him, but they were few and far between. He wasn't fully there yet, so had to keep reminding himself about forgiveness and letting go.

Feranmi had called him later that night to fill him in on Ada. He wanted to reach out and hug her when he heard the despair in her voice. In his opinion, she was too attached emotionally to the girls. Since then, Feranmi had successfully avoided him for days and it was driving him to distraction—a situation he was going to remedy tonight. They talked every day, but she always found some reason to get off the phone. She was on the run again.

"Boss, are you okay?" Phillip asked when he entered Alex's office about half an hour later.

"Yeah, I'm ok. Are they gone?"

"Yeah. I came to check on you. Normally you'd sit through the meeting with the client. Not that I mind being left in charge."

"Appreciate you taking over. Just got a lot on my mind and I knew you could handle it." Alex got up from his seat and walked over to the window. The clouds had turned grey and the atmosphere was hazy. Mother Nature was about to unleash something heavy. It was December. He missed the snow.

"I was just relieved that we got a passing grade, with the go ahead to continue to the next and final phase," Alex said, absentmindedly.

"Yeah I'm glad, too. If there is anything I can do, let me know," Phillip said. "The men and I will be leaving early today because of the impending weather." Phillip turned around to leave and bumped into Stacy. Apologizing, he left.

"Come in, Stacy. Have a seat." Alex spent the next thirty minutes going over a list of things he wanted her to do before she left for the holidays next week. They were busier than ever these past few months; not just with this large project but a couple of other smaller ones. Things were looking up and he was so grateful to God—not taking a day of it for granted. His destiny might have been delayed by the time he spent caught up in mess that shouldn't have happened in the first place, but he was back on track—all thanks to God. The awesomeness of God continued to amaze him.

Alex picked up his phone and dialed the number he now knew from memory.

Feranmi's sultry voice came through the phone line. "Hello."

"Are you at home?" Alex asked. Her hesitation was his confirmation. "I'm coming over." He didn't wait for a response before he hung up, grabbed his keys and left the office.

Hours later Alex pressed the bell for the second time. Thunder rumbled, lightening flashed. He would make this a brief visit, but he had just to see her. He put his finger to the doorbell again about to press when the door opened.

"Alex, didn't you hear the forecast? You should be headed home." Feranmi said, looking at the greyed skies.

"Hello, to you, too." He decided to ignore her question. She was effortlessly sexy in her matching sweats.

"Hi, I'm surprised that's all." She stepped aside for him to enter. "Come in." He entered but deliberately didn't move, trapping her between the door and his body. He was so close that he could hear her breathe. Alex knew he wasn't playing fair, but neither was she. After some moments, she looked up to meet his eyes.

"Running from me again, Fera?" He stroked her face with the back of his palm. He felt her flinch at his touch. She didn't answer, but side stepped him and walked into the living room. He followed, admiring her gracious stride. Even in sweats, her sway left him breathless. Alex took of his jacket and placed it over the arm of the chair.

The room was warm and inviting. Somehow, this was exactly how he had envisioned her home. It had a grey and pale pink theme. The couches where adorned with pillows tossed all over. A miniature Christmas tree stood in the corner. The candles burning at both sides of her mantle filled the room with a scent of cinnamon and spice.

"Want something to drink?" She asked when he sat down. His tired body felt good against the cushion of the sofa.

"A bottle of water would be fine, thanks."

She escaped into the kitchen and returned some seconds later.

"Here you go," she said, handing him the bottle. She sat on the chair next to him, tucking her feet under her. He took a long gulp of water and then put the bottle on the side table.

"To answer your question, I'm here to see you." His eyes challenged her. She remained silent. "We had a deal remember? A trial run until they get here."

"Have I said otherwise?"

"Said? No. But I know you. You're trying to place me in your little box 'til you need me. That's not about to fly, sweetheart. You keep your end of the bargain, I keep mine."

"I'm just trying to make sure we stay focused."

"You're trying to control everything. You can't do that. Haven't you learned that by now?"

"Let it rest. How are things at the site?" she asked. Alex noticed her attempt to change the subject.

They weren't done yet, but he would let her slide. "All good."

FERANMI WAS tired of arguing with him. When she first asked, it seemed like the genius plan for Alex to help her out, but now she wasn't so sure. She should've known her avoidance strategy wouldn't last long. She studied him for a moment, her heart beating rapidly. Feranmi hated when her heart didn't listen to her head. For the past couple of days, Alex Montgomery had filled her thoughts more than ever before. She loved him and couldn't take being so close. And truth be told, her parents would never go for their relationship. So why put herself through the pain of starting a doomed relationship? She was trying to spare both of them the pain. So for this reason, she had avoided Alex like a plague. She wasn't ready to talk or acknowledge anything.

"Have you had dinner?" she asked. She was just about to eat when the doorbell rang.

"No, I haven't. Why?" he asked, startled by her question.

She got up and headed towards the kitchen. She leaned on the door frame, placed her hands on her hip and replied, "One, you don't look like you've been home, yet. Two, I was about to eat and it would be rude if I ate alone. Three, I was trained to always offer my guests a meal." Not waiting for a response, she entered the kitchen. She felt his presence the minute he entered the kitchen. He sat on the barstool and watched her.

"So what's it gonna be?" she asked turning the oven to 350 degrees. She would reheat some left over hen and serve over fried rice. Luckily, she had just enough for two. In the coming weeks, she was going to try cooking less. She didn't want any food wasted when her parents got here. As usual, she would hand over the kitchen to her mother. It was a tested and tried theory that both of them could not share a kitchen.

"I'd love something to eat. Thanks." She could feel his stare as she walked around the kitchen putting their dinner together.

"Need help with anything?"

She gave him a smile for the first time that evening.

"You can get us something to drink. Not sure what you'd want to drink but I have nonalcoholic wine and some colas."

"Cool. Where is the restroom so I can wash my hands?"

She pointed the direction. When he got back, his sleeves were turned back to about three quarters length and he busied himself getting the table ready.

Dinner was ready in twenty minutes. Hand in hand, they bowed their heads and said grace. Over dinner, the discussion revolved around work. He told her about the inspection and the passing grade. She was so happy for him and then gave the full details about the episode with Ada last week. They continued to eat in partial silence. Feranmi watched as Alex drank water with every two spoonful's of rice. She suppressed a chuckle. She forgot to tell him that it was spicy. She wondered what he'd do when he shared a meal with her parents and had to eat her mom's cooking.

"You seem to be avoiding me since the day you were in my house."

"Alex, we've talked every day since then," she said.

"You know that's not what I'm talking about. It's different. Even when we do talk, you're in such a hurry to get off the phone."

"I just don't want us to confuse things." She got up and took her plate to the kitchen praying he would just let it go. She really didn't want to talk about it. He followed her.

"Thanks for dinner. That was really good. It was the spiciest thing that I've ever had though," he said.

"When you said fried rice I was expecting what we eat at the Chinese restaurants. So I'm guessing this is the Nigerian version?"

"Well, you can say that. It's cooked differently for sure." She began to giggle. "Leave your plate there. I'll get it later." Feranmi pointed to the sink.

He looked at her funny. "Amanda Montgomery would have a fit if she found out someone was nice enough to cook for me and I dared leave the dishes for them to clean up," he said, with a mocked look of disgust on his face. He turned on the faucet.

He does dishes...sweet she thought sitting on the same stool he sat on earlier.

When he finished washing the dishes, they returned to the living room. The second they sat down, thunder rumbled and lightening flashed. The power went out and came back on almost immediately.

"I completely forgot about the weather. I better start heading home." Alex picked up his jacket.

Feranmi went to the door and peeked outside. "It's pouring out there. See what happens when you hang up on me? I was trying to remind you about the weather," she said with a smile, making her way back to the living area.

Alex looked up to the light fixture on the wall, "Do the lights go out often around here? I hate to leave you alone in case the lights go out again."

"This is the first time it's happened. I'll be fine." She walked him to the door. She spoke too soon as the lights went out again, but didn't come back on as quickly as before. They were left with the light from the candle flames. He reached into his pocket and got out his phone.

They waited for about ten minutes, but the lights still didn't come back on. The flame from the candles began to flicker. "Seems like this will last much longer. Do you have any tea lights or some more candles?" he asked.

"Yeah, this way." Feranmi led him to the coat closet under the stairwell. She handed Alex some of the lights and he lit them and began placing them in strategic places around the room.

"This has never happened before. I hope the power lines didn't go down completely and they'll restore power soon."

"Yeah, I hope so, too." He patted his pocket for his keys and headed for the door.

"Where are you going?" she asked, with a puzzled look on her face. "Alex, I'm not heartless. I can't let you drive in this storm."

He opened his mouth to protest.

"Don't even think about arguing with me." She walked to the stairs and placed her foot on the first one when he asked,

"Is that because you care, or you are just being nice?" His expression remained unreadable.

She wrapped her arms around herself and cocked her head to the side. "To be nice means I have to care. Let me go get a spare blanket and pillow and I'll show you where you can sleep."

"Fera, I really can't sleep under the same roof as you. I've tried to control myself all night, but I'm just a man who, at the very least wants to hold you in his arms," he confessed. "I've been doing well so far, but there's no reason for me to test God. I'm not super human."

"So, are you calling me a temptress now?" Feranmi joked. "Alex dear, you have two options. Either you control yourself, or you possibly meet your maker early. I trust you'll make a wise decision." She continued upstairs. She got to the landing and looked down at him.

"Relax, I have a pullout in the office downstairs. You'll sleep there if the storm doesn't let up early."

"Okay. Promise to behave now and stay upstairs," he said. She threw one of the pillows down on him. He dodged it and they laughed.

CHAPTER FIFTEEN

IN THE MORNING, Alex found his way around the kitchen and had coffee brewing by the time Feranmi waltzed downstairs. She had on flannel pajamas, her hair was slightly disheveled, but she had a glow on her face that he rarely saw. She looked breathtakingly sexy. She must have slept as peacefully as he did.

"Good morning, beautiful" he said.

Feranmi blushed, tightening the strap of her housecoat.

"Morning." She yawned.

"Still tired?"

"Not really. Hope you managed to sleep well?"

"Yeah, made some coffee, I remember you're no good without it." He took a final sip from his mug. "I gotta go. I need to run a few errands. What are you doing for Christmas?"

"Nothing much. It falls on a Wednesday so no service, but I would love to volunteer at the Food Bank in the morning then just relax at home. And you?"

"Didn't have any real plans but now that you mention it, volunteering would be nice. You want company?"

"Sure, why not?"

"Then it's a date," he said.

"What about breakfast? I can whip something up quickly."

"As tempting as that sounds, I'm going to have to pass. I'll grab something on the way. I want to have an early start." He walked towards her, closing the gap between them. He caressed her cheek with his hand "Why do you fight us when it's obvious you care?"

She didn't answer. He kissed her on the lips and made his way through the foyer. Alex opened the door and came face to face with Ini.

Alex and Ini exchanged pleasantries. He then got into his car and left, destination —carwash. He needed to get his baby clean. The storm had passed, making room for sunshine and freezing temperatures. The memories of yesterday came flooding back as he drove down the lonely street. He kicked himself again because yesterday was the perfect opportunity to share the last two years of his life with her and he completely 'chickened out.' He didn't want to scare her away. At least there wasn't any need to until he really knew where they stood.

LAST NIGHT WAS A GOOD NIGHT. Feranmi smiled. She had her favorite artist's CD on full blast as she did chores. It was a beautiful day. The last time she had so much fun was with Alex was four years ago. The storm didn't let up as they thought. By the time it was midnight, they decided that he would indeed sleep over. They talked and played a game of Scrabble. She taught him some more about the Nigerian culture. Feranmi chuckled when she remembered the look on his face when she described *amala* and *ewedu* soup. It had been one of her favorite meals growing up. He didn't understand how a white powder would turn black when stirred in hot water. Or the fact that people actually ate it.

Feranmi also taught him about greeting older people. That should have been the first lesson—she couldn't believe she almost forgot it. She had fun showing Alex how to bend over and drop his hand to his feet in the customary way that Yoruba males greeted older people.

"You mean almost like I wanna do a cart wheel?" he had asked.

"Yeah, something like that but one hand folded behind your back and the other to your feet." She had said. "You absolutely cannot walk up and say 'hi'."

The phone rang, bringing her back from memory lane. Feranmi turned off the stereo and went to answer it.

"Hey, girl. What's going on? Did you forget something?" Feranmi asked.

"No, hold on..." Ini said.

Feranmi heard a beeping sound which could only mean one thing—Ini was connecting Kayla. A few seconds later they came back on the line.

"Kay, are you there?" Ini asked.

"Yeah, I'm here. Girls, I hope this won't take long. I have a lot to do. So should I call you back later?" Kayla asked. Feranmi still had no idea what this was about.

"No, we're not going to be long. Hold on. It took me a little bit 'cause Fera refused to answer her phone."

"Hey, Kay."

"Hey, boo, you sound groggy. You ok? You didn't call me back last night," Kayla said.

"My bad. I was going to get to it much later today," Feranmi said. "Hope you're keeping calm and haven't started fretting yet. Remember delegate, delegate, and delegate 'til Ini and I get out there and take over."

"Hold up. I'm the one that got us on this call. Remember. I got something to say about our little Miss 'I can't date an African American' here," Ini said.

"Ini, are you serious? Is this what you got me on the phone for? I thought it was something important. Don't listen to her Kay. She's just making a mountain out of a molehill," Feranmi said, irritated.

"Is one of you going to tell me what's going on? Kayla asked, impatiently.

"Okay, the short version of the story. There was a serious storm in Atlanta last night, and on the news I heard that Fera's part of town was experiencing a black-out. I tried to call her several times and the call kept going to voicemail. Being the caring, loving friend that I am, I left my house early this morning and drove straight to her house. Guess who I bumped into?" Ini asked.

"Who?"

Feranmi hissed and Ini continued, "Alex Montgomery!"

"What? Alex slept over?" Kayla asked. "Fera, what's going on? Are you keeping secrets now?"

"Hey, slow down. To answer your question, yes, he slept over, but not the way you think. You should know Ini by now. She blows everything out of proportion. She just loves drama." Feranmi tried to calm Kayla down before she flew off the handle.

"He came over last night or evening I should say. I fed the man, and we were watching TV when it began to storm and then lights went out. I didn't feel good about putting him out in those conditions, so he slept on the pullout bed in the office and left early in the morning. Case closed," Feranmi explained. There was silence so she continued, "Then here comes Ini. She saw him and jumped to all kinds of conclusions. I gave her the same explanation I'm giving you now, but apparently she didn't believe me, because if she did, we wouldn't be on this call."

"Okay, come on Fera, Ini might not be totally wrong about this. There's more to it than you're letting on. We've known you for years. How did you go from avoiding Alex to letting him sleep over? Don't even get me started about feeding him. Your feeling must be stronger than you let us believe," Kayla said.

"That's exactly my point. For years, she'd sworn off African-American men as if she had taken an oath before coming to college that said she could only marry a Nigerian man. I'm totally confused." Ini said.

Feranmi had to admit that they were totally blindsided, so could understand their questions.

"Why are you talking about me like I'm not on the phone? This is why I didn't tell you anything. It's really not what it seems." Feranmi cradled the phone between her shoulder and her ear. She opened her refrigerator to pour herself some juice.

"So, how is it, Fera?" Kayla questioned

"Yeah, Fera, how is it?" Ini echoed.

Feranmi went on to tell her friends about the phone call with her mother.

"I was prepared to stand up to them, but my mom constantly works marriage into every conversation, then started pressing me for a name. So I blurted out his." She paused. Her friends were listening, not saying a word.

"Wow! Back up. You mean you've asked him to pose as your man?" Ini asked.

"Yes." Feranmi took a sip of her juice.

"And he agreed?" Kayla sounded surprised.

"Yes, he did."

"And what's the catch?" Ini asked.

"Why must there be a catch?"

"Come on, Fera. This is Alex we're talking about. The guy

you let walk out of your life the last time. There has to be a catch 'cause we know he's still got a thing for you," Kayla said, emphasis on the word "thing."

"He asked that we do a test run—"

Ini's laughter cut her off. "So you guys are test dating? Fera, either you're really scared of your parents or you totally dig him, but you're too scared to admit it."

"Fera, darling, I agree with Ini. What's going on? Do you like him? It's ok to change your mind. I told you that all those ideologies you have about African-American men were purely stereotypes. It's true that some of them are violent, lazy and irresponsible and seem to have given up their God given responsibility when it comes to accountability and fending for their kids, but you can't label all of them the same way. The media doesn't do a good job of highlighting the good, hard-working educated men who are doing right by themselves, their families and God. The same way I can't label all Nigerian men polygamists, scam artists, cheaters, and chauvinistic. There are exceptions and I've been telling you this for years." No one spoke. Feranmi knew she had this sermon coming.

"He is saved, right? That's the only requirement— that we shouldn't be unequally yoked with unbelievers. But if he's sold out to Christ, he'll be sold out to you," Kayla said.

"Kay, I hear you and truth be told, getting to really know Alex has changed my perspective. Shot down most of the things I grew up to believe." Feranmi sighed. "I'm not that naïve to think that all Nigerian men are perfect, but at least I'd be playing in familiar territory."

Feranmi waited for a response but got none. "I specifically asked God for what I wanted and Alex wasn't on my list. I don't want to step out of His will."

Ini faked a yawn. "Fera, we've heard you say that before. Don't you believe that sometimes what you ask for might not always be what God knows you need? I don't claim to be knee deep in the Bible, but sometimes we hide fear of change under the guise of waiting on His will."

"True. We're all guilty of it, but Fera something isn't clear. If your parents are against an African-American, why do you think Alex will pass?" Kayla asked.

"Don't scream...I'm having Alex pretend to be Nigerian." Feranmi said. She held the phone away from her ear until their screams subsided.

"Now, I truly believe you have lost your ever loving mind," Kayla said.

"I'm gonna need some popcorn to watch this drama play out when your parents get here," Ini said.

"It will be fine. I've got it under control."

Feranmi then told her friends about Alex's fake Nigerian story and the lessons she had given him on the culture. They talked a little bit more, sharing their plans for Christmas and New Year. Ini and Tristan would be leaving in two days. Kayla and Kofi were spending the Christmas with his family, but the New Year alone. Feranmi shared her own plans, but didn't feel the need to bring up Alex again. She had had enough for one sitting.

CHAPTER SIXTEEN

"MA, calm down. It's not that serious." It was Christmas morning and Alex was on his way to pick up Feranmi. They had solidified their plans to go to the Food Bank. On his way, he decided to call his mother.

"If some young lady has you going to do charity work on Christmas morning, then it is serious," his mother said. "I want to meet this girl, baby."

"Okay, Ma, you will, but don't go planning any weddings. It's not even like that now," Alex said. "I'll talk to you later or tomorrow. Please don't work too hard at the soup kitchen. Love you." Every holiday his mother and some of the other ladies from church volunteered at different causes.

"Love you, too, baby. And I won't.

Dressed in faded jeans and a hooded sweat-shirt. Alex turned his car into Feranmi's subdivision. The sun was in full blast and the air was cool and crisp. Car parked, he glanced at the mini shopping bag seated on the passenger seat. He hoped she liked it. It was a birth stone sterling silver necklace and bracelet set. He had it inscribed with the letter 'F'. Snatching up the gift, he zipped up his jacket and got out of the car. She opened the door on the first ring of the doorbell.

"Merry Christmas, gorgeous!" He kissed her on the cheek and stepped into the house. She was dressed as casual as he was in a pair of jeans and a sweat shirt. It was appropriate since they were going to work. The aroma coming from the kitchen reminded him of home. He smiled. Feranmi was quite the cook.

"It smells good in here."

"Merry Christmas. Yeah, I cooked. Is that for me?" she said, pointing to the gift in his hand and walking back to the kitchen to rinse the mug she had in her hand.

"Yes, my lady," he said. He followed her, but stopped at the entrance to the kitchen. She walked up to him and he handed her the bag.

"Why, thank you, kind sir." Feranmi peeked inside the bag.

"Yours is under the tree." She walked to the tree and placed the gift under it. He looked on in admiration.

"You're not going to open it now?"

"No, why don't we open our gifts together when we get back?"

"Back?" This was working out better than if he had planned it himself.

"Yeah. What kind of person would I be if I just use you and discard you? I've decided to feed you." She smiled at him. He had no words for the effect her smile had on him.

"Oh, really now? That's what I'm talking about. I knew you wouldn't let me go home to a turkey sandwich."

"I should keep a pin next to me at all times when I'm with you."

"Why?"

"To deflate your ego."

"It's not ego baby, it's confidence; confidence that's all." He winked, took her hand in his, and led her to his car.

A few hours later, for the second time that day, Alex drove into the Mello Oaks subdivision. After he took Feranmi back home, Alex had gone home for a shower and a change of clothes.

This morning had been an eye opening experience for him and he had Feranmi to thank for it. Often times he took the goodness of God for granted, especially when things didn't go his way. But at least he had the necessities. To see so many people struggling just to feed themselves. After a quick briefing by the staff on duty, they were placed in groups of five. Their assignment included stacking and loading of canned goods for families. Alex couldn't remember when something so ordinary brought him so much joy.

"Hi, I'm starving," Alex said, once he entered the house. He handed her the non-alcoholic wine and apple pie he got on his way. He was lucky that the store nearest him was open on Christmas Day.

"Thanks," she said, walking to the dining area. "So am I. Come on; everything is set."

"You couldn't have done all this today," Alex pointed to the spread on the table. She had a little bit of everything. Mac and cheese, salad, roasted potatoes, red rice, a small turkey, some dressing and Hawaiian rolls.

"I did some of it yesterday, then early this morning after talking to my folks. You call your mom yet?" Feranmi went to kitchen and returned with the corkscrew.

"Yeah, she's back home resting. I called her back a few hours ago to tell her about our experience. I did tell you she wants to meet the woman who got me to do what she has been asking me to do for some time."

Feranmi remained silent.

"Cat got your tongue?" he asked.

"Let's eat. I thought you said you were starved?" She

studied him then said, "It would be nice to meet your mom." She playfully stuck out her tongue at him.

When dinner was over, they cleaned up together and put the leftovers away. Feranmi packed some for Alex to take with him. Settled in the living room with their drinks and slices of apple pie, they turned on the TV.

"You ready to open your gift now?" Feranmi asked, excitedly.

"Let's go for it." They both got down on the carpet and she pulled the gifts from under the tree.

"Ladies first," he said.

She looked at him and began ripping the wrapping paper. When her eyes connected with the Ruby bracelet and necklace, she leaned into him and brushed her lips against his cheek.

"Thank you. Ruby for July—you remembered my birthday," she said, with undeniable admiration in her voice.

"Of course I remembered. I'm glad you like it. Here let me put it on." She extended her arm and he delicately put on the bracelet. Then she turned around, lifted her flowing mane and he put on the necklace. His fingers lightly brushed the back of her neck. He felt her stiffen.

"I love it! Thanks. Now it's your turn." Feranmi handed him his gift and he opened it eagerly. It was a British Military watch set with four additional bands. He stared at her, but was silent.

"You like?"

"I love it. Thank you."

They settled on the couch and decided to watch re-runs of *Martin*. They were on the second episode when Alex spoke calmly, "Fera, after your parents' leave, what's next?"

"I don't know..."

"So after this little idea of yours has worked out...you're telling me you don't have an idea of what comes next?" He asked again, "I've heard your story, but you're attracted to me as much as I'm attracted to you." She opened her mouth to say something but he cut her off.

"Don't even try to deny it. Your actions are telling me a different story from what your head has taught your lips to say."

"Alex, don't bully me. My sole focus right now is my parents getting here and leaving." She bit her nails nervously. She shifted her legs underneath her.

"Fera, I can't take the indecision anymore. You have to make up your mind. Four years ago, we were younger and I was moving back to Chicago. And now, for some insane reason, you still have the ability to stir my soul."

Feranmi remained silent. He got up frustrated and upset about how nonchalantly she was taking the conversation.

"Why do you insist on spoiling today? It's been wonderful and I don't want to end it fighting with you."

"I'm confused, Fera. It's been a wonderful day, but instead of building many more wonderful days, you decide to avoid them in expectation of some bad days because we're from different backgrounds? I guess I'm just a sucker for punishment." He knew his irritation was clear.

"Stop it! Please."

He began to pace. "When I decided to do this, I thought that if we spent some time together you would get to see what we really can be. I've already committed, but I will walk if by the time your parents leave, you haven't made up your mind." He heard the buzzing sound from his phone but ignored it.

She sighed. "Are you giving me an ultimatum?"

"Call it what you like, but listen to me when I tell you. We can't keep being stuck at this place—at least I can't."

His eyes roamed over her. He wanted to pull her close, but his anger overrode his attraction to her. His phone buzzed again. He located it and answered.

"Thanks, man, I'll be right over," Alex hung up the phone. He grabbed his jacket and headed for the door. "I have to leave."

"What is it?" Feranmi followed him.

"That was Phillip. The job site next to one of the smaller buildings we're renovating is on fire. I gotta go."

"Oh no... do you want me to come with you?"

He paused and studied her for a minute. This was one of the things he loved about her, the way she cared. "Thanks, but no thanks. Knowing you're at home safe will give me one less thing to worry about. Besides, it's cold out there. I don't even know if they'll let me through." He zipped up his jacket and left.

ALTHOUGH FERANMI WAS happy for the reprieve, the house felt lonely without Alex. She sincerely hoped everything was okay. She knew how hard he worked and would hate anything that would set him back. She shuddered to think how escalated their argument would have gotten had he not received that call.

Feranmi was running the risk of revealing to Alex what she wasn't ready to deal with just yet. The last thing she wanted was a repeat of the scene four years ago. She had been on an emotional roller coaster since she bumped into him a couple of months ago. Feelings she had safely tucked away were fighting beliefs she had fostered for a long time. She was tired. She was scared. Her parents breathing down her neck for a mate was only complicating matters. Close to tears, Feranmi made her way up the stairs. She needed a shower. *Take control, Lord*, she mouthed as she peeled off her clothes.

Feranmi was restless. Alex left two hours ago, but still no

word. She sent him a text before she got in the shower after getting his voicemail. He hadn't replied. She checked her phone for the umpteenth time. Deciding to call it a night, she crept into bed. Her phone buzzed.

Just getting home. Phone died. Will call you in the morning. ~ *Alex.*

ALEX CALLED her the next morning as promised. There was a little damage, but he needed to channel existing resources towards the repairs that needed to be made. This new change didn't allow them time to see each other. "I need to make sure that by the New Year, everything's back to normal." He had told her. Although she welcomed the time to herself to process what was going on, she had to admit she missed him.

It was a pleasant surprise when he called her some days later and offered to take her to see the Peach Drop to usher in the New Year. His plan worked and everything was getting back to normal. The repairs were almost done and they'd be prepared to round up in a couple of days. To her surprise, Feranmi changed clothes so many times looking for just the right outfit. She wanted to look extra special. Seemed like he had the same goal, because when he came to her door, it took all she had not to reach for him. He looked and smelled divine, giving her goose bumps. Dressed in a pair of jeans and an argyle sweater, he looked like he just stepped out of a magazine.

They enjoyed the festivities and had dinner, but she noticed Alex wasn't his usual self. No flirtatious smiles, smart quips, or playing with loose strands of her hair. He treated her like a friend. Wasn't that what she wanted? At the stroke of midnight, he kissed her on her forehead instead of the lips which she longed for. When he dropped her off a little past midnight, he also declined coming in for a cup of coffee. She did ask that they stay focused, but never counted on it feeling like this. Her heart ached. Didn't he give her 'til her parents left to make up her mind? Or had something changed when she wasn't paying attention?

CHAPTER SEVENTEEN

FERANMI WAS DRIVING WELL below the speed limit as she made her way to Hartsfield-Jackson airport. She was in her own world, but still aware of the frustrated drivers with their blaring horns speeding past her. She normally drove faster than this earning her the nickname, speed demon, but today she just needed time to absorb the range of emotions she was feeling. She was excited, guilty and nervous all at the same time. These were not the feelings she wanted to have. She was on her way to pick up her parents. For someone who hasn't seen them in a while, she should have just one emotion—joy.

In her head, it had been different. She had it all figured out, but now the reality of the deceit she was about to engage in was tugging on her conscience. However, it was something she had to do. There was no other choice; she had spent all night convincing herself of that. She really hoped she was wrong about everything and wouldn't have to go through with the scheme. That is, if she still had one. Alex had been acting strange lately. Yesterday, he did assure her that he would keep his own end of the deal, but she was still worried.

Finally, she arrived at the airport and secured a good spot at the South terminal parking lot. Good thing, since her parents wouldn't have to make a long trek to the upper level parking area. This lot was normally full, so she took it as a sign that things were going to be ok. She prayed for the Holy Spirit to take control as she stepped out of the car. Then a voice nudged at her. *You can't possibly be asking the Spirit to take control of a lie.* As soon as it came, she pushed it aside. With her head held high, she made her way into the airport.

Her parents must have made their way through customs at rocket speed because she had been there just about ten minutes when she saw them coming up the escalator.

"Mummy!!!" Feranmi screamed, running across the airport to hug her mom. Her dad, not to be left out, gave both ladies a bear hug.

"Ha, you guys were fast, oh. You made your way through Customs already? Mummy, don't tell me you didn't bring my Gala or Indomie, because with all those items to declare you won't have made it out so soon," Feranmi said, with a quizzed look on her face. Gala was her favorite snack. She had a nostalgic feeling any time she got to eat it. Without fail, when the driver came to get her and her siblings from school, they always got stuck in Lagos gridlock. To abate their hunger while they navigated through traffic, they would patronize the hawkers who were always ready to sell assorted snacks and drinks. Her favorite snack was Gala. Up 'til this day, she couldn't really say what type of meat was encased in the rubbery crust but it was good back then and still was.

"Baby girl, leave your mother alone. Don't we get a proper welcome?" her dad joked.

"Ah, daddy you know I've been waiting for this Gala and Indomie since the day you told me you would be coming to visit." Feranmi curved one arm her dad's waist and draped the other around her mom's neck while they made their way to baggage claim.

"Feranmi, don't listen to your father. He's just teasing. I have all your stuff. We met a very kind and considerate customs lady, so she didn't seize anything unlike the one your sister's husband met when he visited the last time." Feranmi remembered that story. The officer seized and trashed everything, no explanations.

"I wonder why they do that. It's just food." Her mother hissed.

"As long as they didn't touch mine, it's all good." They headed to the carousel that was assigned to the LOS-ATL flight. They didn't have to wait long; her parents' bags were out when they got there. With her dad's help, Feranmi pushed their luggage out of the airport to her car. Safely buckled up, Feranmi put the car in reverse and they made their way to her home.

HER PARENTS SPENT the weekend recovering from jetlag and by Monday they were ready to explore the town. In just two days, Feranmi had taken her parents to about every tourist attraction Atlanta had to offer. Her dad loved the CNN tour. After which he said "I will never watch CNN the same way again." Feranmi loved the look of excitement on her parent's faces when she took them to their Alma Maters. They had come to the United States in the sixties to study and were pleasantly surprised that most of the places they remembered were still there. Their only day off from sight-seeing was the day of her dad's conference.

Feranmi was happy they were having a nice time and everything was going great. She was kind of surprised that her mother hadn't mentioned marriage, Alex, or Bayo. She entered into the kitchen and headed to the sink, so she could help her mom clean up. Her mother was cooking some jollof rice while Feranmi and her dad talked in the living room.

"Feranmi, where's that your young man? Doesn't he know that when your parents are in town, he should come and greet them? Or he's not serious?" Her mom asked, while mixing the pre-boiled white rice in the tomato mixture that was simmering on the stove.

Here we go Feranmi thought.

She kept her back to her mom and concentrated on washing the dishes. Until this moment, things had been going pretty smoothly. Somewhere in her subconscious, Feranmi knew everything was too good to be true and was waiting for the other shoe to drop. Lo and behold, it just did.

"Mummy, he's serious. He's just busy, but he'll come." Feranmi had hoped she wouldn't have to use Alex after all. Now she was going to have to pull out her ace.

"I've never seen this kind of thing before. You mean he's too busy to come and see your parents that came all the way from Nigeria?" Her mother covered the pot and went into the living room. She sat next to Feranmi's dad. They were still so much in love after thirty- five years of marriage. That's what Feranmi wanted. Images of Alex invaded her mind. She couldn't afford to let her mind wander. Her mother's claws where out and she needed to be attentive.

"Dele, I was telling your daughter that I'm surprised that her young man hasn't come to see us yet," her mother said.

"Mummy, *shebi*, I just told you he's busy. He'll come." Feranmi said. She watched her dad for a reaction, but got none. Then he spoke.

"Baby girl, you never really told us about him, other than

telling your mother his name. So tell us about him." He gestured her to sit on the couch opposite them.

Twiddling her thumbs, she said, "His name is Alex. He's from *Naija*—Ibadan to be exact— but was raised here in the States." Feranmi couldn't believe how smoothly the lies were flying out of her mouth.

"Ah, ah, he hasn't been to Nigeria?" her mother asked. "So he and that your friend—Ini, are the same thing? He knows his culture, *abi*?"

"Yes, he knows." Feranmi hoped that Alex remembered all she taught him. *Please God, let him remember.*

"What's his surname?"

"Montgomery—"

"Mont *kini*? What kind of Nigerian name is that?" her mother asked, scooting forward in her seat.

"Mummy, he changed his name because they couldn't pronounce his real name in school." Feranmi avoided eye contact. She felt disgusted. She was making this stuff up as she went along. "You'll meet him during the small dinner party we'll be having on Friday." Feranmi could tell her mother wasn't completely sold on that explanation. Her mother was suspicious. But since she didn't say anything, Feranmi would let it be.

"Friday? But that will be two days before we leave. We won't have time to get to know him." Her father shook his head. "I want to see this young man tomorrow," her father said. Then he turned to her mom. "Yewande, please prepare us a meal. Let's have dinner and get to know this young man."

Feranmi was glad. No further questions. Now it was time to put on a show.

ALEX WAS BEGINNING to wonder whether his strategy was actually backfiring. He was all ready to crank up the charm, but Feranmi's continued resistance and uncertainty about them concerned him. The emergency he had on Christmas day was the perfect opportunity he needed to give Feranmi some space. He needed her to work on her feelings without him by her side. If she came to him, it was because she wanted to and not because he pressured her.

Keeping his hands and lips to himself New Year's Eve nearly drove him crazy. He had caught the look of disappointment on her face when he gave her a kiss on her forehead. And lately, he noticed the way she lingered on the phone after they said goodbye. So maybe it was working after all. He knew that she was as stubborn as they came, but he was becoming impatient. He hadn't had a decent conversation with Feranmi since her parents got into town, and truthfully it was beginning to irritate him. He thought that by now he would have met her parents disguised as her man.

Alex unlocked the door to his condo when his phone rang. Dropping his keys, he reached into his pocket to grab it. He smiled.

"Hey, stranger. I was beginning to think you've forgotten about me," he said. He waited for her usual retort but got deafening silence instead. "You ok? What's wrong?" He asked. She was unusually quiet.

"I'm okay. A little rattled that's all. I just got grilled by my parents," Feranmi said quietly.

"About what?"

"You."

"Do you want to get away and come over? Just give yourself a break."

"No, I'll be fine. Will you be available for dinner tomorrow?" she asked.

Her calmness bothered him. He was used to the feisty, stubborn Feranmi. He knew that this whole thing must be getting to her. He wanted to reach through the phone and hold her in his arms.

"Sure, what time?" Alex kicked off his shoes on the way to the kitchen.

"By 7:00 p.m." She paused for a moment. "Nothing to worry about, I'll be right by your side."

"Woman, I appreciate you offering to be my bodyguard, but I can take care of myself. Besides I'm not the one pretending—you are. Chill, everything will be okay." She was silent. He decided to try again to get her to come over.

"Are you sure you don't want to come over? I'll have Chinese waiting when you get here—"

"I'm sorry, Alex, but I won't be good company today," she said.

Not wanting to push it, he agreed. He felt the need to protect her. The thought of anybody making her unhappy pulled at his heart. At that point, he came to the realization that it didn't matter what happened tomorrow with her parents, he was prepared to fight for what he considered his. Giving her up was not an option. Even if the person he had to fight turned out to be Feranmi herself.

CHAPTER EIGHTEEN

FERANMI WALKED from the window to the bedroom door for the umpteenth time. *This is important. He better not be late.* When she got back from running a few errands, she found her parents in a fantastic mood. She assumed it was because they were well rested, but when her brother came from the kitchen with a piece of chicken dangling from his mouth, she knew the real reason. Their baby was here.

Feranmi intended to feed off the light atmosphere, but needed Alex to be on time. Feranmi was thankful to God that Deji decided to come in a day early. He would be the perfect neutralizer in case there was any tension. Deji was shocked when she let him in on the plan. He didn't like it, but supported her. That was important to her because Feranmi really needed her parents' approval.

The doorbell rang—right on time. She raced downstairs. "I'll get it," she yelled on her way down. She slowed down in time to catch her breath. Standing on tip-toe, she looked through the peep-hole just to make sure it was Alex. It was. Feranmi opened the door and gave him a worried look.

"I know. I'll tell you about it later." He gave her a kiss on the cheek. "You look good and smell good, too." Her purple and grey cashmere knee length dress fitted her curves perfectly.

"Thanks. Come on, let me introduce you to everyone," she said, nervously. Deji suddenly appeared from round the corner.

"Alex, meet Deji my brother. He came in today. Deji, this is Alex." Both men shook hands and exchanged polite pleasantries. When they were done, Feranmi said, "My parents are this way."

"Does he know about this bright idea of yours?" Alex whispered in her ear as they made their way to the living room.

"Yes and hush!" she whispered, nudging his side.

He let out a chuckle, but it was quickly muffled when he looked up and saw a man who had to be Feranmi's father staring at him above the rim of his black frames. The greys were sparingly sprinkled across his predominantly black hair. The man couldn't be more than sixty-five years old. He had on a blue, linen Dashiki.

"Daddy, this is Alex Montgomery. Alex, this is my dad." She prayed Alex remembered he had to bend and not shake her dad's hand. She didn't realize she was holding her breath 'til Alex bent at the waist with one hand behind his back, and one hand touching the floor—just as she had taught him. Feranmi smiled.

"Good day, sir," Alex said and rose to his full height.

Uh oh. It was too soon for Alex to rise, her dad hadn't acknowledged the greeting yet. But she couldn't blame Alex. She hadn't told him that part. To her relief, her dad cracked a smile and patted Alex on his back in acknowledgement of his greeting.

"Hello, young man. How are you doing?" Feranmi's dad asked.

"Good, thank you," Alex said, confidently.

"Wonderful, wonderful. Come, sit down. Let's talk so we can get to know you," Feranmi's dad said, as he walked back to the couch. Alex followed him into the living room.

Feranmi scanned the room for her mom who had conveniently disappeared. They had prepared dinner together earlier. She barely said more than two words, but that was typical. Her mother loved to give her the silent treatment when she didn't have her way. Right now, her way was Bayo.

Yewande Adewunmi appeared from the office with a frown on her face. Feranmi made eye contact and silently pleaded for her mother to be on her best behavior.

"Alex, meet my mom." Feranmi said.

"Good evening, Ma'am," Alex said extending his hand. Her mother looked at Alex's extended hand, then her dad, and then her before she shook Alex's hand. Feranmi covered her eyes. *Oh no!* She had talked about the proper way to greet her dad but she forgot to tell Alex that the same went with her mom. Feranmi knew her mom would milk this slip-up to death.

"Ehen, how are you?" Feranmi's mother muttered and sat on the other half of the love seat near her dad. Feranmi and Alex sat on the couch on the opposite side of the room. Since Feranmi could read her mom's body language loud and clear, she knew Alex could, too. It screamed she couldn't be bothered with them.

Feranmi was relieved when her dad sliced the tension with conversation. He and Alex had light talk about his job, politics, and religion. The entire time, her mother sat there showing little or no interest in the discussion. Feranmi could count on one hand how many times she nonchalantly threw in a question or remark. Feranmi knew her mother's attitude towards Alex wasn't personal. She just wanted Feranmi to marry a Nigerian. And since Alex hadn't been to Nigeria, he was more or less an American. That was really the truth, but Feranmi wasn't about to tell her that, because faster than she could say her name, her mom would be preaching Bayo again.

After a few more minutes, Feranmi went into the kitchen to bring the food out to the already set table. They were having a light meal of jollof rice with baked fish and a salad. When everyone was seated, her father blessed the food. They ate in silence for a while before her father spoke.

"So Alex, Feranmi tells you changed your name because people couldn't pronounce it in school."

Alex gave her a questioning look, then turned to her dad and said, "Yes, I did."

"So, what's your original name? Your father's name?" her mother asked.

"Mafolukwu." Feranmi blurted out. Both her parents turned and stared at her.

"Baby girl, are you Alex? Let the man speak." He father admonished her.

"*Abi o*," her mother said, then put her glass to her mouth and drank some water. "Where exactly are you from in Nigeria? Feranmi says you haven't gone home yet. Don't you want to know your people?"

Feranmi felt sweat run down her armpit. They weren't supposed to be this deep with the questions.

"I'm from Ba-dan, Inyo State," Alex said.

Feranmi nearly fainted. He had totally messed that up. Bless his heart, he was so confident when the words came out of his mouth. He probably thought he nailed it. She couldn't help but smile.

"Where?" Her father and mother asked in unison.

"He's from Ibadan in Oyo State," Deji said. It was the first time he'd spoken. He was so into his food that he hadn't looked up. But the tension was thick and her baby brother as usual came to the rescue. Her parents looked at each other and looked at her. They remained silent. Deji and Alex talked about sports and soon her father joined the conversation. Her mother remained silent.

After dinner, the party moved to the living room while Feranmi cleaned up. Alex offered to help, but she declined his offer. He needed to get to know her folks and she needed time to get rid of the anxiety that had built up all evening. At some point, her mother entered the kitchen to get some water. She was on the phone speaking to the person on the other end in Yoruba. From what Feranmi gathered, she was talking to her god mom. Her mother filled the glass filled with water and left the kitchen. Seconds later Feranmi heard the office close. Preoccupied with her own thoughts, Feranmi didn't notice it was strange her mother was talking to her god mom in the wee hours of the morning, Nigerian time.

Feranmi knew that a barrage of questions awaited her when Alex left. And she was fine with it. She hated putting Alex through this and she knew he was against it as well. But he did it for her—for her. Alex hadn't really told her he loved her, but showed time and time again that he cared. She couldn't think of anyone who'd go through what he went through tonight, for any woman. Alex told her that he wasn't pretending, and after tonight neither was she.

CHAPTER NINETEEN

FERANMI HAD WALKED Alex to his car. He was such a sweetheart, asking whether she'd be okay. She reassured him she'd be fine. She hugged and thanked him and then headed back indoors. The door was barely closed behind her when she saw her mother pacing. She was dusting her hands off, in the customary way Nigerians did to show disbelief.

"Olorunferanmi, I hope you are not about to tell me that you have fallen for one of these American men?" her mother asked.

"But, mummy—"

"Don't even lie to me young lady. I carried you in my womb for nine months and I know you very well. Who are you trying to deceive? Me?" her mother asked. Feranmi always wondered why her mother had to reiterate that fact that she carried them for nine months. Like the fact was ever in dispute. Feranmi remained silent and went to sit. There was no need pretending anymore. She was tired.

"I said it, I said it, you want to disgrace me, *abi*? Are you the only one that came to America?" her mother asked. Feranmi wanted to answer, but decided to let her mother have the stage since the curtains had been drawn for her performance.

"Your mates come home with nice, responsible, Nigerian men. They get married then come back over here if they want to. Why is your own different?"

"Olorunferanmi, are you going to tell us the truth?" her dad asked.

Everyone seems to be stuck on my full name tonight. Deciding to take the bull by the horns Feranmi said, "Daddy, he is an African-American and very hardworking. He is an only child whose mother lives in Chicago and his dad is deceased." She was already in deep, so might as well bring it home.

"How long have you known him?" he asked after a beat of silence. Feranmi was shocked. No argument, nothing. Good enough for her.

"Dele, are you encouraging her?" her mother asked. "Don't you remember what we went through when we came here to study in the sixties? Or even how the family had to come here to take Sade back home after what Roland did to her?" Feranmi saw the shocked look on her mother's face.

"I've known him for four years," Feranmi said. She wasn't sure which way this thing was going. Her father was calm, not that she was complaining.

"Mummy, daddy, I've grown up listening to the Aunty Sade stories. I've even seen a little bit of it, but Alex isn't like Roland." Feranmi stood. She walked back and forth then stopped. "For four years, I've denied myself the chance of being happy with him, because I didn't want to disappoint you."

"Feranmi, I have nothing against African-Americans. I just don't want there to be a chance of you being turned into Sade," her mother said.

"Mummy, I won't be. Alex was totally unexpected, but

mummy he's a blessing," Feranmi said. It felt good to get that out after all these years.

"Is he as serious about you, as you are about him?" her father asked.

"Yes, daddy." Feranmi wasn't really sure about that—she knew he was attracted to her—but she was going with it.

"Okay," her father said. Feranmi kissed her dad on the cheek and escaped upstairs, allowing him to deal with her mom's tantrums.

Some minutes later, her mom was still on her tirade. Feranmi cracked open her bedroom door to listen.

"Dele, I'm shocked that you would forget all the mistreatment and degradation we suffered in the hands of these same black Americans when we came here to go to school. If it were only the white ones, it would have been better. African immigrants had a hard time," her mother said.

"But we survived, *abi*? We were able to get a good education and have our kids here, thereby offering them the opportunity to be American citizens and have a wide range of opportunities when they became adults. Besides that was then. You have to see that things have changed."

"Changed, *ke*? Okay maybe they have, but marry an African-American? Feranmi should know better. She is aware of how Roland mistreated, conned, and made Sade an addict when they were married."

"But where did you hear marriage?"

"If she isn't going to marry him or have that intention, then why is she wasting her time? She isn't getting any younger. She could be getting to know Bayo. He is a nice young man—very respectful. Marriage is hard work when both people are from the same place. Why would Feranmi want to complicate her life by starting off on the wrong foot?" her mother asked.

"Marriage is hard, period. You're just upset that he is

African-American. And I can understand because of your sister. But let's give this young man a chance. He'll be here again tomorrow. We'll talk after then," her father said calmly.

Feranmi peeked and saw her mother move to the couch her dad was on. She looked at him for a while, then laid her head on his shoulder.

Ok peace for now. Feranmi shook her head and closed her bedroom door. Her eyes had tears in them. Too bad her mom felt this strongly, because Alex wasn't even a game to her anymore. She had crossed that line.

INI LISTENED with her mouth open as Feranmi recounted the events from the previous evening. The dinner party Feranmi planned was tonight. Her parents would be leaving in a couple of days so Feranmi had invited just a few people to come over. Feranmi couldn't remember the last time she was so happy to see Ini. Her presence put a dent in the tension that had been brewing between Feranmi and her mom since Alex left last night.

Ini had arrived at about noon that afternoon. Her parents were thrilled to see her. That was the side of them Feranmi loved. They had done the same thing when they spoke to Kayla on the phone some days ago. They always welcomed her friends with open arms, especially her mom. So why did she have to be so strong headed yesterday?

After a long conversation about almost everything, Feranmi and Ini left to go pick up the food for tonight's dinner party. Although not before her dad asked when Ini would visit Nigeria. She gave her standard response—someday.

It had been one whirlwind of a week. Even though her mother was having a little attitude problem right now,

Feranmi would miss her terribly when they left on Sunday. She tried convincing them to stay, but she knew Uncle Tunji's wedding was coming up and they wouldn't miss it for anything. She was contemplating surprising them during the Christmas holidays by showing up in Lagos. But that would all depend on Alex.

Alex—she had called him earlier that morning to check up on him. He was fine, but sounded a little pensive. Before Feranmi could find out what was going on, Phillip had entered his office and he had to go.

"But you can't say you weren't expecting it? I'm shocked it was Mrs. A. though. She's always so sweet," Ini said, as she maneuvered the car onto Buford Drive.

"I expected some reaction but girl, it was off the chain. Alex messing up with the greeting, then not remembering the name of the town he was supposed to be from...it was a disaster." Feranmi said.

Ini couldn't stop laughing earlier when Feranmi told her the story. And she busted into the second round of laughter now.

"If I wasn't the star in this show, I'd be laughing too." Feranmi looked around to get an idea of their location. "Don't forget to turn at the light."

"Okay, you know I always pass the place." Ini paused for a moment and glanced at her friend. "I'd hate to be you—"

"I hated to be me, too, but thank God for my dad and Deji. My mom had her attitude, but at least she was polite. Alex stood his ground, though," Feranmi said with a smile. She loved his confidence.

Ini turned into the subdivision. "Good for him. If you want something, you gotta be able to stand for it."

"That, he did. I just wish the whole thing didn't have to be this way."

Ini parked her car in front of the caterer's house. She made no attempt to get out and neither did Feranmi.

"I can't believe that after all this, you're still trying to deny that you and Alex can have something real." Ini said.

Feranmi nearly laughed at the puzzled look on her face. "That's not what I'm saying. I wish my mom didn't feel so strongly about it. I really need her approval." Feranmi paused. "I remember growing up, when they brought my aunt back from the States, she stayed with us for a while. My mom was a shadow of herself nursing her sister back to health, but my aunt was never the same. I really didn't want to cause my mom any pain, but I can't deny what I feel for Alex any longer."

"We don't often get to choose who we love. You've tried to avoid this man—Lord knows you've tried. But fate had a way of bringing you back together again. Your mom will come around," Ini said.

Feranmi paused for a moment then told Ini about Alex's ultimatum.

"You can't blame the man. You're burning hot and cold. What is he supposed to do? A man has to know where he stands."

"Look at you, giving man advice."

"Whatever. I might not have it all together, but I can tell you a thing or two." After a short pause Ini continued, "Here's a man who is obviously smitten and he loves God which happens to be on that crazy list of yours. So I guess he's tired of going two steps forward and one step back? Fera, make up your mind."

Feranmi knew she was right. "I'm scared. What if everything my mom is afraid of turns out to be true?" Ini's eyebrow rose in disbelief. "Yeah I know, my heart tells me that couldn't be, but my brain is over thinking it."

"You're acting as if we're already planning a wedding. Take a chance. We're talking dating for goodness sake," Ini said.

"I don't date aimlessly. It's a complete waste of my time. As a Christian, neither should you, but we're not going to go there," Feranmi said, with one hand on Ini's shoulder. "I might not marry the man I date if God doesn't think he's right for me, but before I even consider dating, I must to some degree believe I can end up spending the rest of my life with the person."

Ini began to laugh.

"What's so funny?" Feranmi said, slightly annoyed.

"I'm laughing at this situation. Who would've believed that one day I'd be preaching to you? You can only talk the talk, but I see when it comes to walking the walk, you get jittery."

"You see why I don't like opening up to you? You always try to get a laugh out of it. I prefer telling Kayla this kind of stuff."

Ini opened the car door. With one leg out the door, she turned to Feranmi, "That's 'cause I don't babysit you like she does. Besides, as long as you and I remain friends, I'll always tell you the truth, whether you like it or not. Now get out the car. Let's pay this lady and keep it moving. You know Friday traffic is not something to play with." Ini got out of the car and made her way to the front door.

Feranmi just sat there looking at her friend. "Lord, help me," she said, looking towards the heavens. She stepped out of the car to catch up with her friend.

CHAPTER TWENTY

ALEX CLOSED his laptop and headed upstairs. After a quick run to the office earlier, he decided to work from home the remainder of the day. Everything was going well. The two projects he was working on were on schedule and without issues. Life was great. And most of all, his personal life looked like it, too was headed down the right road.

Yesterday was the gauge he used to figure out how vested Feranmi was in him or in what her parents thought. Alex thought her parents were a nice couple. Her mother was a little standoffish, but considering what Feranmi told him, he could understand her. Despite Feranmi's determination to keep him in the friend zone, yesterday could not be faked. He fully expected her to get frazzled when he forgot some of the things she thought him–but she didn't. For the rest of the evening, she cared more about his comfort than the embarrassment he might have caused her. He believed that God was giving him a second chance at happiness and he wasn't about to blow it. Once her parents left, he and Feranmi needed to talk. He needed to tell her about Tracie and be done with it.

A few hours later, Alex arrived at Feranmi's house. There were about ten people there. Feranmi did say that there would just be a few people, mainly those from her hometown club here in Atlanta which she joined after school. She told him some of the older members remembered her dad, while some of them knew of him from his contributions to his field of study, so they had readily accepted her invitation to this get together. Deji had let him in. They exchanged pleasantries and talked briefly before Feranmi came over to take him to her parents. The smile on Feranmi's face was an indication that he got the greeting right. She quickly disappeared soon after.

He scanned the room looking for Feranmi. Other than the quick hello when he first got here—about forty minutes ago—they hadn't had a real conversation since. Alex saw her slip through the patio door. She had on an Ankara outfit. He saw something similar on her once and asked about it. It was a— blouse that stopped at her waist with a pair of hip hugging jeans. He had always thought she had the perfect figure. Her hair was styled away from her face—a style which showed off her mocha skin and slender neck. With his wine glass in his hand, he headed towards his target when he felt some fingers attempt to circle his arm. He stopped.

"Hey, you! See something you like?" Ini teased.

"You could say that," he replied.

"Have you told her how you feel?"

"I've tried to. She is bent on avoiding the obvious and it's driving me crazy."

"Hmm—that's my girl. Stubborn as can be."

"Yeah, she is. But so am I." Alex was sure his frustration could be heard in his voice.

"Good for you. Now you go tell my friend how you feel while I go get a refill." She nudged him and raised her wine glass.

The door was slightly ajar. Alex pushed a little further and then he saw her. Feranmi was deep in thought and barely noticed him. She was sitting on one of the patio chairs, gazing at the stars. There was no breeze, just a cool day. The smell of the early evening showers lingered. Feranmi was the most beautiful woman he had ever seen, on the inside and out. He watched her for a minute and his heart swelled with love.

"Hey, beautiful. What are you doing out here all by yourself? It's cold." Alex asked, moving towards her. He sat beside her and put her hands in his and rubbed them together, in an effort to warm her hands.

"Nothing, I just wanted to take a little break from the crowd. It's noisy. You know I don't deal with such on the regular. I cherish my peace and quiet." She looked at him. He could see worry in her eyes.

"I'm sorry for leaving you alone in there. Everything was a bit overwhelming. I hope Ini behaved herself?" Feranmi asked.

"She did okay. So spill, what's really bothering you. You're too quiet. Is everything ok?" He paused. "Hope it has nothing to do with yesterday?"

"No, far from it. You did great—well not great—but your best." Feranmi shrugged and smiled at him. He couldn't help but laugh.

"So what is it then?"

"I was just feeling a little homesick, that's all. My parents being here really brought back nostalgic memories from home. They made the place lively when they weren't stressing me out about marriage," she confessed.

"Hey, don't worry about it. They'd have to go back sometime. I can't say I understand because my mom is a skip, hop, and a trace away, but it'll be ok. Trust me," he said, reassuringly. "At least the trip went ok, didn't it?" She nodded and he continued, "You see all that worry for nothing. They found out the truth in the end. So…" His smiled and she did the same.

"So, have you had anything to eat?" Feranmi asked.

"Yeah, I ate some of that rice, although I liked the one you cooked for me the other day better."

"Flattery will get you nowhere, mister."

"Why would I flatter you when the truth is equally appealing? I also loved those snails. They were as spicy as you know what! But they were good." He paused when he saw her shiver.

"I don't want you catching a cold. We need to go in, but before we go I need to know something."

"Really, what?" She asked, getting up. He was about to speak when they heard the doorbell ring, then a loud shout from her brother and another male.

"Can it wait? I gotta see who's at the door."

"Can't your brother handle it?" Alex insisted.

"Yeah, he can, but it's my house. I'd love to see what all the commotion is about."

Alex put his hands in his pocket, shook his head and sighed heavily. She paused, then continued. "I promise we'll talk later. There's something I need to tell you, too."

"Okay," he said. Feranmi scurried inside. Alex followed.

After securing the door, he turned around and bumped into Feranmi who was just standing there with her mouth wide open. He followed her eyes to see what or whom she was staring at so intently. She was looking at a man, almost as tall as he was, although Alex had a full inch on him. He was dressed in a black Ralph Lauren sweater, some dark blue jeans and on his feet were black Italian loafers. The man was prostrated on the floor in front of Feranmi's father who had his hand on the man's back, patting it. Alex's eyes travelled to Feranmi's mother. Her smile was the biggest he had seen since he met her. Suddenly the man turned around and gave Feranmi a huge smile.

"There she is, my princess," he said, loudly, heading towards them. He scooped Feranmi off her feet and twirled her around. Once he put her down, Feranmi found her voice.

"Bayo Ajibade, what are you doing here?" she asked.

Alex observed as Feranmi eyes darted towards her mother. The smile on Mrs. Adewunmi's face told him told him everything he needed to know. She'd gotten her way.

CHAPTER TWENTY-ONE

FERANMI KICKED herself for underestimating her mother. She should have known better. How could she miss the signs? Her mother was a little too happy yesterday morning and that late night phone call to her god mom should have given her a clue. It was just her luck that Bayo was in DC attending a conference when her mother sent out an SOS. She knew he would be able to just hop on a plane. How could she?

Yesterday was going great and everyone was having a good time, until Bayo made his entrance. He was his usual territorial self. He took over the party like he was the host. Feranmi got over her shock in time to introduce him to Alex. Without speaking, both men nodded their heads in acknowledgement of the other.

Feranmi was puzzled at how a battle line was already drawn when both men didn't even know each other. Feranmi could sense that Alex was trying hard to control himself—his jaws clenched, searching her eyes for some kind of explanation. However, she never had a chance to be alone with him as everything happened so fast. Before she knew it, he had left.

It was just a mess. She had been in her room all morning. She needed space. The only time she left was to get a cup of coffee and see Ini off. After all the commotion yesterday, Ini decided to spend the night. She would have stayed longer, but Feranmi assured her that she would be alright. She was going to deal with this once and for all. Feranmi was still in bed thinking of her next move when she heard a knock at the door.

"Come in," she yelled.

She really couldn't deal with anyone now. Under normal circumstances, she should be snuggled up with her parents today since they'd leave for Nigeria tomorrow. But here she was hiding out. Her dad had been totally helpless, caught in the middle of the hostile stares between mother and daughter. It had always been that way. Her sister had always done their mother's every bidding so they never seemed to clash. Although she never blatantly disobeyed her mother, Feranmi wouldn't let her force a husband on her, all in a bid for her to have the title "Mrs." in front of her name. She should have listened to her friends and stood up to her parents. Now this scheme was blowing up in her face piece by piece. That all ended now.

When the door opened, her mom and dad walked in. Feranmi adjusted herself on the bed to make room for them to sit.

"Daddy, *e ku aaro*, Mummy, *e ku aaro* ," Feranmi said, slightly bending her head as a sign of respect. Her mother looked remorseful, but Feranmi didn't buy it. She waited to hear what she had to say.

"Good morning, Baby girl. I hope you managed to sleep well?" her father asked. Feranmi nodded. Her father continued, "I know you are upset, but your mother thought her action was in your best interest." He waited for a response, but she wasn't offering one. "We'll be leaving tomorrow and I know you don't want to end this vacation on this sour note."

Then her mother said, "Feranmi, I am your mother and I love you. I would never do anything that will harm you. I want what is best for you. You are getting too close to that American man—"

"Mummy, please, please stop trying to help. You raised me well. Trust that I can make my own decisions. I'm not married yet and that is not a crime. Or is it? I don't feel anything for Bayo, but Alex I really love. Believe me, Mummy. I fought it hard. Partly because I was scared after all that happened with Aunty Sade, and partly because I didn't want to disappoint you and daddy. I expected this reaction, but not to this magnitude. But in the end, it is with him that I'm happiest. He's a good man and most importantly, he's a God fearing one."

"But Feranmi... how long have you known him? You can't love him. He is not right for you."

"Mummy, how do you know that?" She was tired of arguing. "I thought you came here to call a truce. What you did wasn't really nice, oh."

Her father silenced the words that were about to come out of her mother's mouth. "Okay, okay, we are not going to start that again. It's our last day here, and we are not going to allow strangers to spoil it."

Feranmi knew her mother well enough to know she had no intention of apologizing so her dad, as always, shut the exchange down. There was complete silence.

Her father continued, "This is what we are going to do. Yewande, since you are convinced that Bayo has changed, Feranmi will go on one date with him."

Her mother smiled. Feranmi's mouth hung open.

"Baby girl, don't be close-minded. He might truly have changed, but if it doesn't work then you have both our blessings on that your young man. Sade's incident, although unfortunate, happened a long time ago and we have to move on." He turned to look at his wife and squeezed her hand. Feranmi knew he was silently telling her it was going to be okay. Now it was Feranmi's turn to smile, because the Bayo she saw yesterday hadn't changed at all.

"Yewande, you have to promise that if she still doesn't like him, you have to back down. You will leave her alone, *abi?*" Her mother did not look happy but had no choice but to agree.

"Okay," mother and daughter said at the same time.

"*Ehen,* that is better. Now you girls should kiss and make up. Let's go out for brunch."

Feranmi and her mother hugged and apologized to each other. Since that was over, Feranmi had one more person to make up with—Alex.

Right after her parents left her room, Feranmi's phone rang. She glanced at it. It was Ini and Kayla. As would be expected, Ini called Kayla to fill her in and both of them were making sure everything was okay. She loved her friends. They were always there when she needed them.

After chatting with them, she gathered the courage she needed to call Alex again. This would be the second time. She got his voicemail when she had called him earlier, right after Ini left. He was mad—of that she was sure. If she had known Bayo would show up, she would have prepared him. That didn't excuse him, though. Alex should have called her back by now.

What was wrong with him? She was becoming very irritated. He ran out yesterday without even giving her a chance to explain, and he had the nerve not to return her call this morning. She was not going to call him again. She put the phone back into her purse after checking it for the last time.

Her phone buzzed. It was a text. Her heart quickly rose in expectation, but sunk soon after. It was Kayla.

Hi girl, just checking on you. Have you heard from him? Call me back. ~ *Kay.*

Feranmi replied with a simple *"no"* then put the phone away along with all other worries. She was going to enjoy her family and let Alex be for now. Probably, he needed space. First things first—her date with Bayo. She figured it was best to get this over with. When she learned he would be leaving tomorrow, she gave him a call. They agreed to see a movie and get dinner later. She was going to fulfill the promise her parents had conned her into making. Then she would face Alex and demand to know why he was being infuriatingly stubborn. With her strategy in place, she relaxed and enjoyed the rest of the day.

BAYO WAS LATE—TYPICAL. Feranmi pulled up the blinds and peeked outside for the fifth time that evening. They had dropped Deji at the airport about an hour ago. She missed her knucklehead brother already. At the airport, her mother cried like she did all those years ago when they had dropped him off at Murtala Mohammed Airport in Lagos for the first time. If she did this now, there was no telling what would go on tomorrow when she took them to the airport.

Her mother had cheered up immediately when she found out that Bayo would be coming over to take her to the movies. Feranmi sat through another thirty minute lecture about keeping an open mind and giving him a real chance. And now, he didn't even have the decency to be on time or let her know he was running late. If she didn't know better, she would think it was a Nigerian thing—but she did. Her brother in-law, Tunde, was a pure gentleman. She also had many friends here and home whose husbands were Nigerians and were godsent.

About fifteen minutes later, she heard a honk outside her door. *Really? Did he just honk outside my house?* Feranmi made up her mind she was not going to make a big deal out of it. Dinner and a movie and she'd be home free. Her family's approval meant a lot to her. If this was the price she had to pay, then bring it on. She was just going to have to keep her mouth in check and get it over with. She braced herself, said a quick goodbye to her parents, picked up her keys and left the house.

CHAPTER TWENTY-TWO

BAYO AND FERANMI had missed the first twenty minutes of the movie. The next showing would have been at midnight, but she didn't want to be out that late. They watched the movie in silence and went to a nearby restaurant to grab a bite to eat afterwards.

The restaurant was in downtown Norcross. It was a nice chic place that had newly opened in the area. It had a black and silver theme. Bayo apologized for being late. He wouldn't let it go 'til she forgave him so she did. They used to be such good friends growing up because their parents had spent so much time together. They were content being just that—friends—'til their mother came up with the bright idea of them getting married.

He had graduated from an Italian University. No one could deny that he was well educated and smart. It didn't hurt that he was fine either—sort of reminded her of the basketballer,– Dwayne Wade. His one flaw was that he thought he was the best thing to happen to a woman. He came from money and didn't have a problem flaunting it or thinking it could get him anything he wanted.

The first and only date they went on was a disaster—at least from her perspective His pride and arrogance were just too much for her. He knew nothing about the words, "please" and "thank you." The man she saw tonight was different. He had changed. He was attentive, caring, and acted like her friend again.

"Are you sure you don't want anything else, Feranmi?"

Feranmi glanced up at Bayo and smiled. *How much does the man think I can eat?*

"Ah, ah, Bayo, *shebi*, I just told you I'm fine. Thanks." She sliced into her red velvet cake.

"Okay, I like your curves the way they are, so I'm trying to feed you." Bayo raised his hand in surrender.

She laughed. "Do I look hungry? *Fi mi sile*...leave me alone, oh." Feranmi put a piece of cake in her mouth. Her eyes rolled as the flavor played with her taste buds. It was her favorite type of cake.

"So what kind of conference are you attending in D.C?" Feranmi asked.

"Supply Chain. I want to implement it when I get back to *Naija*," Bayo replied. "Speaking of Naija, I wonder why you don't relocate. You're done with college and there are good jobs with major multi-nationals back home. Your dad is connected, so with your experience, education and connections getting one of them won't be difficult."

"Umm.. Thanks, but no my dear. I prefer here for the time being. It's good to me," she said, scooping up the last morsel of cake.

"Yeah, sure. Who are you deceiving? You want to remain here because of that Alex guy. He has got you tied to his every word. So that's why you just shunned my side?" he teased.

"We've been over this. First of all, you and I never had a shot. Our moms were in denial. You're too much for me. What you need is a 'yes sir' woman. I'm not the one," Feranmi said, then laughed. "Second, Alex has nothing to do with it. He has no bearing on my decision to remain here. Naija is just not for me right now. Maybe later." Feranmi wasn't about to tell him that the man they spoke of wasn't even talking to her.

"Come on, Feranmi, I'm not the same guy—"

"In all honesty, the person I've seen tonight is totally different from the one that took me out some years ago. I like the new you. But, my heart belongs to another," Feranmi said.

"I get it. But as for Alex, I hope you know what you're doing. Tell him he better behave because we are watching. Deji, Tunde and I won't hesitate in arranging him if he makes you shed one tear. And that, my dear, is a promise we will keep," he said sternly. Feranmi remained silent. That statement made her think of her mother and Aunty Sade. Fear began to creep up, but she quickly dismissed it.

During the car ride home, they talked about a variety of topics. He would be in DC for another week or so before flying back to Lagos. He asked her about her job and how it was, living full time in America. They reminisced over their childhood and were both thankful for how far they had come. They had changed a lot as individuals. By the end of the evening, they came to the agreement that they'd remain friends and break the news to their moms tonight. They really didn't have anything in common or want the same things.

FERANMI ALMOST LAUGHED out loud at her mother when she entered into the house. It was almost midnight. Her mother was seated on the couch with her legs crossed at her ankles. Her eyelids were drooping and looked heavy, but she wouldn't give in to nature. Feranmi knew she'd stay awake 'til she found out what went on tonight.

"Mummy, hmm...so you didn't sleep because of this gist?" Feranmi took off her shoes and sat next to her mom.

"Tell me now. What happened? How did it go?"

"Where is daddy?" Feranmi asked, ignoring the questions.

"He is sleeping, *oya* now—"

"Mummy, I kept an open mind, but my heart was already closed." Feranmi paused for a response. "He'll tell his mom and I'm telling you. We don't have those kinds of feelings for each other."

"But hasn't he changed? At least a bit?"

"Yes, he has—"

"You see, if you had given him a chance since I have been asking you. It would have worked," her mother said.

Feranmi giggled. "No it wouldn't have Mummy. I had already met Alex, but I kept pushing him away." Feranmi put her arm around her mother's shoulders, when she saw her tear up.

"Mummy, please I need you to support me here. I'm sorry about Aunty Sade. I know she was your only sister, but Alex is different. Nothing like Roland. I need you to trust me and know I can hold my own. You taught me about confidence and self-esteem," Feranmi said.

Her mother remained silent for a while, then said, "I just want you to be happy. I'm not totally convinced about this Alex, but I will give you my blessing. But mark my words, any day I hear sadness in your voice because of him, I would be on the next Delta flight." Her mother's tone was stern and serious. She stood and secured her silk scarf on her head. "Come and help me weigh these bags."

The past two hours were just like old times. Feranmi spent

it relaxing and talking with her parents in the guest room. It reminded her of her childhood—priceless. Feranmi's dad had woken up and they filled him in on the recent development. He was pleased. Feranmi helped her mother pack, making sure she didn't forget anything, especially the gifts she bought for her sister and her family. Any time her mother visited, she always bought a whole lot of things to take back home and proceeded to 'abuse' Feranmi's scale by weighing and re- weighing the bag to see if she had exceeded the weight limit. Feranmi tried with no success to tell her she wouldn't actually know that for sure until they got to the airport tomorrow.

Back in her room, Feranmi was happy this episode was finally over. As she slipped underneath the five hundred count Egyptian cotton bed sheets she had splurged on, she thought about Alex. He called her stubborn but he was just as dogged. She needed to find out what in the world was his problem. There was no way she had just gone through what she had, for him to now turn his back on her. That was not going to happen.

CHAPTER TWENTY-THREE

THE SILENCE in his house was deafening. It wasn't that Alex wasn't used to being at home alone, but memories of Feranmi filled him up—their talks and the time they'd spent together these past weeks. The hurt he felt the second time around was worse. Had her mom succeeded in convincing Feranmi that being with that guy, Bayo, would be best? His teeth clenched in anger as the memory of the past weekend replayed itself in his mind.

He had been at the site all day, in an effort to keep himself busy. He forgot that he hadn't had a bite to eat since breakfast. Alex heard about a new restaurant in Norcross that had received rave reviews, so he decided to go check them out. He pulled out his phone and placed his order. Alex had walked into the restaurant and headed towards the hostesses stand. He gave his name and was directed to the bar to wait. The atmosphere was inviting and he liked the black and silver theme. A couple of minutes later, the bartender returned with his order. Then he heard it—her laughter. The restaurant was noisy but there was no way he could mistake that sound. There was only one person he knew with that laughter—Feranmi.

Alex heard it again. He stood, his eyes following the sound. Then he saw her; he saw them. Alex's jaw tightened, his fist automatically clenched–crumbling the crisp fifty-dollar bill, he had brought out from his wallet. What was she doing with him? He watched them for a while. She seemed to be having a nice time. She had finally gotten her Nigerian man. So what they had between them was all a joke. His appetite began to dissipate. He paid and left.

It had been four days since that day at the restaurant. Alex had been tempted to call her and demand an explanation. But then again, he gave her an ultimatum and was determined to stand by it. He enjoyed a challenge just like the next man, but he had given up on games a long time ago. He still couldn't figure out where it went so wrong. He was so sure he was reading her vibe well. Alex took off his jacket and headed to the kitchen to get himself a bottle of water, although he really could use a real drink right about now. Too bad he had given that up.

One minute they were making headway, and the next she was all cozy with another guy. Why she kept calling him was beyond him. What could she possibly have to say to him? *Sorry, it didn't work out. I've found my Nigerian man.* The sound of his ringing phone startled him. He looked at the caller ID and saw that it was Kofi.

"Hey, man. Didn't you see my missed call? I called you on Saturday."

Alex had seen the call, but wasn't in the mood to talk to anyone.

"Yeah, I did—"

"So, what's up? Kay told me what happened."

"Depends..."

"Depends on what? Don't tell me that you haven't talked to Fera yet?"

"What's the point? I can't have another Tracie on my hands."

"Come on, man, that's low. You can't compare both of them. You're mad, I get it. Put yourself out of this misery and answer her calls. It's been what now— four days?"

"Kofi, I really don't want to talk about it. What she can possibly have to say to me? She wants to let me down easy? Well, I'm good. Can we change the subject?"

"I'm just saying, it's a mistake to keep ignoring her. Even if that's what she wants to tell you, at least you'll know."

"Like I said...I'm good. How is Kay?"

"She's fine. Mad at you, though—"

"Why? 'Cause of her girl? Well, we can't all be like you guys now, can we?"

He was mad at himself. How could he have been so stupid? She rejected him the first time so why did he think this time would be any different? His doorbell rang and right after there was a loud thump and then another ring of the bell. Before he could get up, the doorbell rang again and a second thump followed. He was about to go off on whoever was on the other side of that door.

"Look, man, I got to go. My love to Kay. We'll talk later."

"Alright man. Later, and one more thing...."

"Make it quick. Someone is about to break down my door." Alex's eyes darted to the door again.

"Call her. Listen to what she has to say," Kofi said.

Alex clicked off the phone and headed to the door. The doorbell rang again. He opened the door forcefully. He came face to face with Feranmi. The fiery glow in her eyes told him one thing—she was ready for war.

His heart betrayed him and skipped a beat when she

brushed past him. Her strides were forceful. She placed her bag and coat on the side table and faced him squarely. Her hair bounced around as she walked, exposing the oval shape of her face. Her hazel brown eyes and full lips took his breath away, but he had to keep it together. Tracie was also beautiful and look where that left him.

"For goodness sake, what's wrong with you?" she seethed.

"What are you doing here, Fera?" He calmly walked past her and sat on the couch. He then picked up the remote and turned on the TV. He felt her stare. He knew his calmness infuriated her more. She picked up the remote and turned off the TV and tossed it on the couch. With her hand on her hip, she turned to him.

"You haven't answered my question. What's your problem?"

"I don't have a problem," He crossed his legs and looked in the other direction.

"Really? Then why in the world have you been ignoring my calls? I even tried your office and left messages with Stacy, which I know you got. So I'm going to ask the question again. What's your problem?" Her eyes were teary with anger.

Alex stood. He couldn't hold it any longer. How dare she put this on him? He towered over her, but she didn't back down or move away. She faced him head on.

"There's nothing for us to talk about. I kept my end of the bargain, or is there anything else?" he said, angrily.

"Wait a minute. Are you actually angry? Because you lost that right considering the way you ran off on Friday and haven't returned any of my calls. You completely ignored me." Feranmi's body was visibly shaking in anger and frustration.

"I'm surprised you even noticed since you were having such a nice time at The Big Red. Where is your boyfriend, by the way?" Alex sat back down.

"What are you talking about?"

Alex saw the light bulb go off in her head.

"So you were there? You know what...I shouldn't have come." She picked up her things and began walking to the door. He grabbed her arm.

"Where do you think you're going?" he asked. She snatched her arm away and stepped back.

"Home. It was a mistake coming here. So all this is because you're jealous over something you have no idea about?"

"Oh, really? Enlighten me because I know what I saw," Alex said.

"There's no need to now. You seem to have drawn your own conclusions." Feranmi looked him straight in the eye.

"Feranmi, don't push me. I'm really not in a good mood. Now talk!" he ordered. She stared at him for a few moments then sat down.

"I had to humor my mom by going out with Bayo. She needed to be satisfied that at least I tried. It didn't work as I knew it wouldn't, but in exchange we got their blessing," she said calmly.

After a brief pause, she stood, put her coat on and walked to the door in silence. He felt like cold water had been thrown on him. He knew how much she detested being set up by her folks, but she actually went through with it just to give them a chance. She chose him.

"Fera.... wait!" He stopped her at the door.

"It's late. I have no fight left. I came here from work and I'm tired. You let your imagination run wild instead of asking me what you wanted to know."

He cupped her face in his hands. She didn't make eye contact. "Look at me." His voice was barely audible. After a few seconds she raised her face to him.

"I went crazy when I thought that you were about to be

taken away from me again. Contrary to what people may think, men have hearts. And after the story you told me about the whole Nigerian man thing, and the gaff at dinner, seeing you with him, I decided to protect mine."

"Alex, you're supposed to know me better. Whatever happened to asking before you assume? This is way outside my comfort zone, but I'm willing to try. But you are going to have to trust me as you want me to trust you." She wagged her finger between both of them. She parted her lips to continue, but before she could utter another word he leaned in and kissed her. The kiss was tender and gentle. When he released her, it took a minute for both of them to regain their bearings.

"I do trust you..."

"If you did, we wouldn't be having this argument now. I got to go," she said, placing her hand on the door knob.

She is not going to let this go he thought.

"Okay. Granted, I over reacted, but I tend to do that when it comes to you. And this may not be the last time either. Forgive me. I didn't know."

"How could you when you didn't pick up the phone?"

"Let's not go there again." His tone was final. She studied him for a moment wrapping her arms around her body.

"I love you, Feranmi Adewunmi," he said.

She looked intently in his eyes for a while. "I love you, too, Alex Montgomery," she said. There was a sparkle in her eye.

He smiled at her. "So, this is a thing? No more running?"

She smiled back." Yes, this is a thing. I'm tired of running."

CHAPTER TWENTY-FOUR

"YOU'VE BEEN GRINNING from ear to ear these days, boss," Phillip said, as they walked out of the office on Thursday evening. "

Whoever she is, I just want to thank her."

"Why does it have to be a 'she'? Can't I just be happy that work is going great?" Alex unlocked his car and placed his laptop on the backseat. Before getting in, he turned to Phillip who was parked right next to him.

"Yeah right, business can't do that to a man. I haven't seen you this way since we were in Chicago together. Just tell her I say thanks," Phillip reiterated.

"Ok, will do." Alex laughed and got into his car. "See you tomorrow and say 'hi' to the family for me." He put the car in reverse, activated his Bluetooth and dialed the number he had on speed dial.

He and Feranmi had a pretty good routine going, speaking to each other in the mornings and right before bed. They always ended their talks at night with prayer. He needed to see her. He had been in Florida for the earlier part of the week and she had been tied up with work and managing another Ada crisis. Feranmi picked up the phone on the second ring.

"Hi," she answered, with a tired sigh.

"Hey, you sound terrible. Just leaving work?" He teased.

"Such a nice thing to say. Yes, I'm just leaving," she replied.

"Do you need me to give you a foot rub?" he asked, right before he broke out into the Jackson 5 song, *"Just call my name and I'll be there."*

"You sound terrible. Don't quit your day job, okay," she said, laughing.

"I missed you. Wanna hang out with me this weekend?"

"Missed you, too. Where?"

"I got tickets to the Lion King."

"You don't have to ask me twice. I've always wanted to see that at the Fox."

He could tell she was happy and loved it. "Then it's a date. We'll be celebrating."

"Yes, we haven't had time to celebrate you getting the job with Franklin LLC. Did I tell you I'm proud of you?"

"Not today..." He opened the garage door.

"Well, I am. Is that your garage door? Say it ain't so. I'm jealous. You're home already?"

"I tell you what, I'll stay in the car 'til you get home," he joked as he got out of the car.

"Ha, ha, ha, very funny. Now get off the phone so I can focus."

"Call me when you get in."

"Sure thing."

WHY IS *she calling me this early on a Saturday?* Feranmi wanted to let the call go to voicemail, but she knew Ini would call right back 'til she got an answer. This had better be good.

"Hello?" Feranmi's voice was coarse since she hadn't used it in a while.

"Good morning. Don't tell me you're still sleeping?" Ini sounded so vibrant so early. It annoyed Feranmi, especially since she still felt dog tired.

"Ini, what do you want? It's too early for me." She pulled the comforter up to her neck and turned over.

"What plans do you have for today?"

"I don't have any plans. It's going to be a lazy day for me," Feranmi said, with a faint smile on her face. She cherished her weekends.

"Then I'm coming to get you. I have some coupons that we could use at the Dawsonville outlet. You know it's around your way. Get ready. I'm on my way."

"My bad. What I meant to say was my plan is to do nothing." Feranmi paused. "At least not 'til evening."

For Ini to call her so early wanting to go out, Feranmi figured that she and Tristan had another fight. Whenever that happened, Ini took her mind off him by going out. To her, Mr. Right was out there somewhere, and she had to be out there for him to find her. And she always insisted on dragging Feranmi along. It was okay sometimes but today, Feranmi was going to disappoint her.

"What are you trying to say? I bet if I was Alex, you would be out of the bed before he could even finish asking."

"Envy doesn't become you. Why bring Alex into this?"

"Whatever. I know you're not trying to go there with me. But seriously, you've been so engrossed in him that we don't have time to hang out anymore."

"Stop being dramatic. For your information, if it were him, I'd tell him the same thing. And guess what? He'd understand."

"What happened to Tristan anyway? You guys are normally joined at the hip." Feranmi got out of the bed and made her way downstairs to the kitchen. She needed her caffeine fix.

"Well, today we're not. So are you going or not?"

"Not. Don't be mad. I just want to chill. We'll see later in the week, though. Remember you're supposed to meet me at David's Bridal for us to pick up our dresses," Feranmi said.

"Okay, spoil sport. I guess I'll just stay home and do something else. By the way, as for Alex, glad you finally decided to live a little."

Feranmi laughed. "I'm going to hang up now. Enjoy your day and you'll see it's not that bad staying at home instead of always roaming the streets." She hung up before Ini could make her quick comeback.

Hours later, Feranmi had tidied up her house and prepared lunch. The heater was on, but she still shivered a little, probably from the cold glass of water she drank a while ago. She made a cup of tea and settled in the couch—feet under her—and savored the warm beverage. She had about three hours before her date with Alex. She smiled—she had been doing a lot of that lately. She loved that man.

Feranmi powered on her laptop. She needed to start making plans for the spring road trip with her girls from the center. She was taking them to Savannah. There were so many things she had to do before then. She opened up a Microsoft Word document and began to type her to-do list. She needed to get the donation forms, parental consent letters and some volunteers to be co-chaperones.

Her phone rang again. Ini just couldn't take no for an

answer. Feranmi put down her tea to pick up the phone. She looked at the caller ID. Bayo? She thought he had gone back.

"Hey, Smallie. I'm just checking on you. How far?" he asked. He had called her that since they were kids. It was his way of making sure she remembered he was older than her. Even though it was just by a month, he wanted to make sure she didn't forget it.

"*I dey*. What's going on? How is D.C? Missing home already?"

"Nothing much. D.C is alright, but it's not home. In fact, I called to tell you I'll be leaving at the end of next week."

"The conference is over already? I hope you enjoyed your stay."

"Yes, I did, but it's time to go. My business won't run itself. Besides that's where the money is." After a short pause, he continued, "So what are you up to today?"

"I'm at home now, but going out with Alex later. He won a new building contract so we are going to celebrate."

That's good, so at least you won't go hungry. He's hard working." Bayo laughed and so did Feranmi.

"Not that I want a lazy man, but nothing is wrong with my brain and my hands. I went to school and I have a job."

"All you independent women—"

"Don't get it twisted now, I need a strong man. I'm just not dependent on one."

"I understand. When will you be in Lagos again?"

"I'm not sure, but I'll call you. You and Alex should get to know each other. He's nice."

"Okay, but we'll still kick his ass if he causes you pain," Bayo said. A few minutes later, they hung up the phone.

ALEX SKIPPED the verbal greeting altogether when he showed up at Feranmi's house later that evening. Once the door was opened, he stepped in and pulled her closer to him. He had craved this for a week. He needed her smile, her warmth, and her lips like something crazy. He planted a light kiss on her lips, but then he needed more and kissed her deeply 'til she gasped for air. When he released her, she stepped back, shook her head and opened her eyes. Then she smiled and lifted her fingers to his lips to wipe off traces of transferred lipstick. He studied her. She was dressed in a purple dress that stopped right above her knees and leather, knee- high, black boots. Her hair was away from her face, just the way he liked it.

"Hello to you, too," she said, as she straightened her dress. "You're mighty happy."

"Just grateful, that's all. I'm so grateful to God for a new lease on life. And to top it off, He gave me you," he said.

"New lease, huh? I remember you saying that before. What's that about?"

"Nothing really." He wasn't ready to spoil the mood. He had a perfect evening planned. He needed to be more careful and hoped she would just drop it.

"Ready to go?" He extended his hand. She smiled and put hers in his and they left. Once their seat belts where safely buckled, he started the car and headed down 400S.

CHAPTER TWENTY-FIVE

THREE HOURS LATER, Alex and Feranmi stepped out of the Fox Theater, hand in hand, after seeing the stage production of the Lion King.

"Not bad at all," Alex said, as they strolled to a nearby restaurant.

"Not bad! Are you kidding me? It was awesome," she said, her voice charged with excitement.

He laughed. "Your excitement is infectious." He squeezed her closer to him. "I'm glad you liked it. I've always looked at the Lion King as kiddie stuff."

"Let me let you in on a secret. The Disney Channel is my guilty pleasure. I love watching animated features," Feranmi confessed. "When I do get a chance to spend time with my niece and nephew, I have no problems at all because I watch their shows right along with them."

Alex noticed her mood change immediately. It was pensive.

"What's wrong? You miss home?" He figured she probably became homesick in that instant. Then it hit him. He was so busy planning to keep her in his life that he didn't bother to find out if she would move back to Nigeria someday. He knew she loved her family very much, but he loved her, too, and didn't want to lose her if she decided to move back home.

"Yeah, I do, but I'll be fine. My happiest memories often leave me sad, but those are memories I cherish." They continued to walk.

"Do you think you'll ever move back to Nigeria permanently?" he asked, a little apprehensive. He couldn't believe he didn't take that into consideration before.

"I've learned never to say never, but I'm good here. I love my country dearly, but moving back to live is not for everyone, especially after living in the Western part of the world for an extended period of time. The adjustment can kill you, literally." She giggled.

He unconsciously breathed a sigh of relief.

"Because of my family, I make it a point to visit every other year."

That was just fine with him as long as she didn't make it a permanent thing. They walked in silence the rest of the way. He led her into the restaurant. As they waited to be seated, he put his hand possessively around her waist.

"Hmm...I feel safe with you," She whispered, looking up at him. He smiled down at her. She returned the favor and put her arm around him. He pulled her closer. After a five-minute wait, the hostess led them to a secluded booth in the back. She told them about the specials of the day and handed them their menus. A waiter appeared soon after to take their drink orders. Feranmi looked around taking a moment to take in the environment.

"So what do you think of the place?"

"It's quite cozy. I love that we got us a booth away from the craziness," she replied. The waiter approached with their drinks and set them down on the table. When he left, Feranmi took a sip of her sweet tea then snuggled close to Alex, resting her head on his shoulder.

"I'm glad you like it. I must be scoring some serious points. With any luck, I'll have a perfect score one day soon," he said with a grin.

"One day? I was under the impression that you'd already made your perfect score," she said, with a shrug.

"So tell me, how have you been allowed to roam the streets free for the past four years?"

She must have felt his muscles tense because she sat up. Alex paused for a minute. He didn't want to lie, so he settled for half of the truth. "The person I thought was meant for me, God showed me she wasn't."

"Oh, I'm sorry about that. Do you want to talk about it?" she asked, rubbing his arm.

"No! I will one day soon. I promise. Tonight is about you and me. Let's just enjoy it," he said in a much sharper tone than he intended. He saw her eyebrow rise, but he was not prepared for her next question.

"Are you still in love with her?"

"No, I'm not!" he snapped.

"Are you sure there's nothing you want to tell me? You're touchy."

From the way she was looking at him, he could have sworn she could see into his soul.

"What is it about her that has you so worked up, if you don't have any feelings for her?"

"I don't. Can we just drop it?" His tone much calmer. He knew that was the only way to get her to back down. "I'll tell you about it sometime, I promise. Besides, I love only you," he said, cupping her face with his hands. Her expression became more relaxed. She had accepted his explanation, at least for tonight. Alex breathed a sigh of relief when she changed the topic.

"So tell me, how is this Florida thing going to work? Do you have a license to do business there?" she asked.

"Yeah, when I moved back to Georgia, I checked and found out that Florida was one of those states that accepted reciprocity of my Georgia license. That's why I bid for the project." Alex took a sip of his water.

"It's not as big a project as the one I'm finishing up here, but it'll get my name out there and the quality of my work will make me a force to be reckoned with. I'm just grateful."

"There's nothing as sexy as a hardworking man who loves the Lord. I'm glad He gave me you," she said.

"I knew all that fight in you was just a front," he teased. But she didn't have her usual quip.

"Talk to me."

"How would this thing work? Will you have to move out there for a little bit?" she asked shyly with her head down, playing with the straw in her drink.

"She misses me," he said, lifting her head with his finger.

"Stop playing with me and answer my question." Feranmi slapped his hand playfully.

"Ouch woman, that hurt," he said, rubbing the back of his hand, faking pain.

"For the first couple of months, I'll be in Florida at least three days out of the week. You should know by now that I can't stay away from you too long."

"Ok, I guess that'll have to do. Will this project last as long as the current one?"

"No, it won't. I should be done in about eight months. I guess they're trying to be careful, too, since I'm an out of town builder. This project is just a small one," he said.

She wasn't smiling, so he said, "Come on, baby. Let's not spoil this mood. We're here to enjoy ourselves and celebrate.

The work won't start 'til we're back from Chicago, so let's enjoy right now," he said. She smiled. Alex looked up and saw the waiter approaching with their orders.

Their dinner was eaten in semi-silence as each one of them seemed to retreat into their own separate worlds. His reaction to her questions scared him. He was still angry at Tracie and he had to deal with that so that his demons didn't spoil his future. He could just hear his mother, *for everything that is hidden will eventually be brought into the open, and every secret will be brought to light.*

AFTER DINNER, they made the short trek back to the parking lot. Alex helped Feranmi into the car and kissed her again before closing the door. He got into the car and turned on the radio to the jazz station. He then put the car in reverse and backed out of the parking lot. Feranmi leaned back and closed her eyes.

"You okay?" he asked.

"Yeah, just thinking about what a perfect evening it's been."

"I aim to please, my darling...I aim to please," he said.

"You're doing a fine job so far," she teased.

"You tired? Want me to drop you off?"

"Honestly, no. I just want to be here with you," she said with a smile.

"It's chilly. You want to get some coffee?"

"Sounds great."

It didn't take too long to get to the small coffee shop Feranmi often frequented near her home.

Alex ordered a latte and she ordered a dry cappuccino. Feranmi had never been to the shop this late so the dimly lit, romantic setting was new, but she liked it. It resembled one of those hang-outs for poets and writers. They located a comfortable table by the corner and pulled their chairs together. With both hands wrapped around her drink, Feranmi took a sip and let out a moan. It was just what she needed for the chilly night.

"Now that's the stuff," she said with her eyes closed. She opened her eyes to see him staring at her with an intense gaze. "What?"

"I love it when you're not giving me a hard time."

"I didn't give you that much of a hard time," she said, winking at him.

"If that's your story, then stick to it. I know what you really put me through," he said, kissing her forehead. His intense stare caused Feranmi to play with her drink stirrer.

They chatted and flirted until it was time to leave. They were the last of the two couples there when they left. The ride back to her house was too short in her estimation. She didn't want the night to end and she could sense that neither did he. Getting out of the car, he went around to the passenger's side to help her out. With one hand on the roof of the car and the other on the door, he caged her in.

"Thank you for giving us a chance," he said.

"No. Thank you for not giving up on me. I had a great time this evening."

Feranmi's heart was racing. He was so close. Her cheeks felt flushed and heated, and her lips trembled. Alex didn't stop staring at her, but took one hand and put it in her hair. He released it from its clip. Her hair tumbled down. He drew her head to him and lowered his lips to stops hers from trembling. His lips were sweeter and softer than she had ever tasted them. Whether it was the moment or that was actually true, she didn't know. The kiss lingered a little longer than usual as he placed his other hand on the small of her back, pulling her closer.

After what seemed like eternity, he abruptly stepped back in anger or frustration, she couldn't tell which.

"What's wrong?" she asked, still flustered.

"Are you really asking me that?" Then he looked straight into her eyes and said "Babe, I adore and love you so much but it sometimes feel like I'm losing control. We can't let that happen, so I gotta go."

She remained silent. They had been so careful not to cross the line and she was thankful that he had enough control for both of them.

"You wanna go to church with me tomorrow?" he asked, diffusing the tension.

"Sure, you'll come get me? Or never mind, I'll drive to you," she offered as he walked back to his side of the car.

"I will be here early. Be ready." He got in his car and left.

CHAPTER TWENTY-SIX

AS SOON AS the praise team finished their rendition of Smokie Norful's, "I Understand" there was a prayer and a couple of announcements. Then everyone was seated. Not long after the congregation had settled down, a man dressed in a double-breasted suit stepped to the podium. He kind of reminded her of Don Cheadle. Feranmi assumed he was the pastor. Alex put his arm across her shoulders drawing her closer to whisper in her ear, "That's Pastor Edwards. He's our Senior Pastor. Get ready, he's about to drop a serious word." She smiled at him and nodded.

"Good morning, church," Pastor Edwards began. Not getting an overwhelming response, he repeated the greeting. The response was thunderous. He nodded his head, pleased.

"Let us pray..." After a short prayer, the pastor opened his bible. Then he looked into the crowd.

"Today we're going to talk about trust. Trust in God the Almighty." After a brief pause and a sip of water, he continued, "Turn your Bibles to Matthew chapter 6-let's read verse 24. *No one can serve two masters. Either you will hate the one and love the other, or you will be devoted to the one and despise the other. You cannot serve both God and mammon.*

"The whole essence of this passage is Jesus teaching us about trust. You either trust in God or you don't. There is no middle ground. If you read further down to verse thirty-four, Jesus goes on to illustrate the goodness of God. If we understood His abounding, limitless love for us, worry will be a thing of the past. We'll not look to those things that can't satisfy and put our trust in them. Or try to do things our way.

"As children, we trust that our parents will give us what we ask for because they love us. Our trust is unwavering because we can see. But today, we're going to talk about trusting God, a God you can't see. We all have preconceived plans for our lives, needs that we want met. We pray to God and expect it to go exactly as we have planned out. Or for Him to give us exactly what we want, how we want it. Then life happens and things don't work out that way, but we get so engrossed in the plan we have for our life that we fail to see when the Lord has changed the course of the journey."

Feranmi heard shouts of, "preach" and, "yes pastor" coming from the congregation as the man of God continued. "God knew you even before you were formed. He knows the plans He has for you. Our job is to trust in His plan and believe that it will be for our good. Romans chapter 8:28... *And we know that in all things God works for the good of those who love Him, who have been called according to His purpose.*

"He knows the plans that will make your future hopeful and bright, but you have to trust His ways and not yours. You have to let go and let God and watch Him do miracles in your life."

At the conclusion of the message, there was thunderous applause as some people stood up shouting, "Amen" and, "Hallelujah." The rest of the service was pretty much like what she was used to. There was an altar call, tithes and offering were collected, and the closing benediction wrapped things up.

After the service, Feranmi and Alex walked out of the sanctuary hand in hand. They greeted a couple of members Alex had gotten to know since he had joined the church. When they got to the car, he opened her door and waited for her to buckle her seat belt. When he saw she was secure he asked,

"Hungry?"

"I'm famished," Feranmi replied, rubbing her stomach.

"Okay, hang on." He closed the door and walked around the car to get in.

On the drive back to Alex's place, the mood was meditative. Feranmi laid her head on Alex's shoulder and was deep in thought. The message today spoke to her and her situation. She had long ago decided to give Alex a chance and open her heart to him, even though he wasn't the plan she had for her own life. But somehow, today's sermon seemed to be the confirmation she was looking for.

"Wake up, babe," Alex said. She had drifted off a little.

"Oh, we're here already? You've got some food in this house? If not, we're at the wrong place because I'm hungry," she teased, as she got out of the car and headed towards the house.

"Babe, today is Sunday...I rest!" He tried to keep a straight face, but not for long and laughed. Feranmi just glared at him.

"You do not joke about your stomach." he teased, unlocking the door and pushing it open.

"Make yourself comfortable and I'll go and get the Chinese. I placed the order on our way back."

"Are you serious? So you still gotta go get it?"

He kissed her forehead, "It's just around the corner so I'll be back before you blink. It wasn't ready when we passed by and I wanted you be comfortable in the house rather than waiting in the car."

"How sweet. Okay, hurry back. I'm starving," Feranmi kicked off her shoes and made her way to the half bath. She heard the front door close just as she closed the door to the restroom.

A FEW MINUTES LATER, a refreshed Feranmi came out of the restroom. She wanted lunch to be an informal affair and thought it would be a good idea for them to sit on the floor. She pulled the ottoman that was in the center of the room, closer to the couch. She went into the kitchen and found two serving trays and a bottle of grape, nonalcoholic wine in the refrigerator.

On her way back to the kitchen to get the wine glasses, she saw a piece of paper on the floor. It had been underneath the ottoman. *Men, never put things where they belong.* Feranmi picked up the folded paper. It was from the Illinois State Department of Public Records. Feranmi looked at the date— two years ago. The letter was informing Alex that his driver's license information had been updated with the State of Georgia. Feranmi wondered what that was about. She placed the letter on the mantle and continued to the kitchen.

True to his word, Alex was back in a jiffy. He had shrimp lo mien while she had chicken fried rice. They both ate with light discussion between them occasionally eating off of each other's plate. Then she remembered the letter.

"Baby, I saw a letter from the department of public records. It's something about your driver's license," Feranmi said.

"Where?" Alex asked.

Feranmi could have sworn she saw him tense up, but decided to ignore it.

"It was underneath the ottoman. I left it on the mantle." Feranmi took a piece of shrimp from Alex's plate. He stood and walked to the mantle.

"What's that about?"

Alex crumpled the letter, "There was a mix up about my license when I first moved back to Atlanta. I had to get a letter which cleared it up." He sat down and continued to eat.

"Honey, that much I can read. What happened? Why was there a mix up?" she asked.

"I got a speeding ticket, but didn't appear in court and so my license was suspended. But I didn't know that when I moved. When I went to get my Georgia license, I was told of the mix up, so fixed it." Alex said.

"Hmmm. Okay, those driver's license people can be picky sometimes." Feranmi said. She wanted to ask him why he didn't appear in court, but his tone had some finality in it. She had a feeling there was more but she once again decided to ignore it.

Alex and Feranmi finished the remainder of the meal in silence. When they were done, they both cleared the area and selected a movie to enjoy. Within ten minutes of the movie, Feranmi, who was perfectly snuggled in next to Alex, began to snore lightly. Alex placed a pillow on his lap and laid her head on it. He turned off the television, laid his head back, and drifted off.

ALEX WALKED into Home Depot and headed straight to the lumber section. His supply came in, but they were short a few pieces. He made a call to his contractor, but wasn't going to delay the project because of it. He was looking for just the right pieces of wood when his phone rang.

Alex had been waiting for this call. He had told Kofi about the weekend with Feranmi—especially the part about her finding the letter. The reason he didn't appear in court was because he had been sitting in jail in another part of the state. But that wasn't something he was about to tell her at that moment. So he had to lie again. Kofi couldn't talk at the time so he was calling back now. Alex activated his Bluetooth.

"Hey, man. Everything sorted out?"

"Yeah, I'm good." Kofi paused. "Man, you're making a mistake. You're the happiest you've been in a while and I'd hate to see you blow it because you're too scared to tell Fera the truth."

"Don't you think I know that? What scares me the most is that if I tell her, she'll look for the nearest exit and take my happiness with her," Alex said.

"But that's not your call. You have to tell her before somehow or the other she finds out. You're putting Kayla and me in a very awkward situation because we know."

"Fera is my business! I know what I'm doing," Alex replied, a bit irritated. He knew that Kofi was right. "I'm not trying to be deceitful deliberately, but I love her so much and given the opportunity, I would make her my wife today. I'm just scared."

"I understand, but then you can't keep it from her either. It's by God's grace that you two are even together considering the hurdles you've been through. But you have to trust that the same God will keep her if she's meant to be yours. We all have a past. We've all done things that we wished we didn't or situations we wish we weren't in. If she's really for you, she'll understand, but you won't know unless you tell her," Kofi said.

"I hear you, man. I'll tell her before I ask her to marry me."

"Marry her, huh? She must really be something."

"That she is. When I'm with her, the world stands still. She fills me up in ways I can't explain. When I don't see her, it's as if a part of me is missing. When I do see her, I have to have her close, always having some form of contact. Since I'm still a man with blood running though my veins, only my walk with Christ keeps me from going too far. I've got to make her mine before I go completely insane," Alex confessed.

"Wow! I feel you and I'm so happy for you. You deserve more than the best and judging by her friend, my baby, you couldn't have found anyone better. Now do us all a favor and clear the air so we can really celebrate."

They talked a little bit more before hanging up. Alex thought about what the pastor said about trust. The sermon made him see the hypocrisy in his stand. He wanted Feranmi to trust him and give him a chance despite the plans she and her family initially had for her. But he wasn't willing to trust her or God that if he told her about his past that she would still be there. He was so unsure of what would happen if he told her that he had been in jail for six months.

"Help me, Lord. Show me the way." Alex whispered a little prayer. He would tell her soon. With his mind made up, he continued his search for the lumber. He and Feranmi had a date later on, so he would swing by the site and drop it off, then head straight home. Lately, he left the site earlier than usual. Phillip was coping just fine and everything was still in order.

He found what he needed and made his way to the cashier when his phone rang again. Thinking it was Kofi with another sermon he let it ring. Alex paid the cashier and left the store. After loading the pieces of wood in the trunk, he got in the car and pulled out his phone.

Hi, honey. I won't be able to make it tonight. I'm meeting with Ada's mom. Miss me, okay~ Fera.

Disappointment swept over him. Alex loved that Feranmi

had this program she was passionate about, but sometimes when things happened that were beyond her control, it consumed her. She was so attached to those girls, especially Ada, and her inability to keep her on the straight and narrow path had been frustrating her lately. They didn't always agree on her level of involvement, but he was still supportive. But when it started to interfere with them, he drew the line. He put on his Bluetooth back on and called her number.

"Hi, got my text? I tried to call you, but it went to voice-mail," Feranmi said.

Alex could tell she was upset when she answered the call.

"I did. You wanna tell me what this is about?" His tone was somber.

"It's Ada. She got into some trouble and her mom has just about had it so she's threatening to send her home to live with her grandmother. Ada called me so I'm going over there to see if I can help," Feranmi explained.

Alex remained silent.

"You there?"

"Yeah, I'm here," he replied, contemplating what to say next.

"You're not saying anything. I know we were looking forward to tonight, but I'm sorry. I'll make it up to you."

"That's not the issue here. Helping out is one thing, but when it begins to interfere with us, that's another issue entirely."

"Come on. Don't you think you're blowing this out of proportion?"

"Not when it's the third time. There are some things you can't fix. At a certain point, you just have to step back. Things can't always go the way you expect them to."

"Where is this coming from? Because I'm going to help Ada?"

"This is about the fact that the last time you couldn't help one of the girls, it put you in such a mood that it took days for you to let it go. We suffered as a result. Now this." Alex spoke calmly.

One of her girls had a pregnancy scare, but it turned out she was fine. It didn't end well, though, because her parents still withdrew her from the program.

"Why are you bringing that up? Besides you said you understood and I apologized."

"Because I see a pattern. What's wrong with Ada now?" he asked.

Feranmi was silent for a brief moment.

"She was held for shoplifting. But she was just in the wrong place at the wrong time and with the wrong gang. The shoplifting charges have been dropped but her mom is still bent on sending her back to Nigeria to live with her grandmother."

Neither of them said anything for a while. Images of Tracie flashed before Alex's eyes. He had been too busy to notice the way things slowly started began coming between them until she slipped away from him completely. Alex knew Feranmi wasn't Tracie, so decided on a calmer approach.

"Listen to me. I love that you care so much about those girls, but your job is to mentor and guide. Not to solve every problem."

"Alex, I'm sorry. I got to do this. Please, can I call you later?" she asked.

"Do what you gotta do," Alex said and clicked off the phone.

CHAPTER TWENTY-SEVEN

"OKAY, we're tired of waiting on you to give us the skinny on what's going on. We've given you ample time without badgering you, but if you think you'll just keep this from us, you got another thing coming," Ini said.

Feranmi was really not in the mood to talk about this. Especially since the topic of discussion was mad at her at the moment. She remembered just staring at the phone when he hung up. He had never hung up on her before. Feranmi called Alex later that evening, but could still tell he was disappointed. She had taken half a day off work to get her dish repaired. But now she was so ready for the cable man to leave so she could go see Alex. She was half watching the man fix the dish when she heard Kayla's voice.

"I agree. Fera, are you keeping secrets now?" Kayla asked.

"Slow down, y'all. I would've gotten around to it. But don't be expecting a report every time. I love you girls to pieces, but my relationship is between me, Alex, and my God." Feranmi tried as much as possible not to laugh. She knew Ini would react first.

"Wait, wait, wait. Nobody's trying to be all in your business so I don't know what the speech is for," Ini retorted.

"Okay, now since you don't want to know, hang up so I'll give Kay the 411."

"Whatever! Just tell the story," Ini said.

"I thought you didn't want to hear." Feranmi was enjoying taunting them.

"Okay, settle down you two. Fera spill it. I've got things to do. Your antics are creeping into my time," Kayla said.

"There's nothing to report really. Alex and I have been seeing each other."

"We know that," Ini said. "How serious is it? That's what we want to know."

"We love each other," Feranmi announced, smiling from ear to ear. The screams of her friends could burst her eardrums. Feranmi moved the phone from her ear.

When the screams died down Kayla asked, "Are you happy?"

"Yeah, are you happy because I know this scared you to death," Ini said. Feranmi loved her friends. It was always about her first.

"Yeah. Thanks for pushing me and being there to listen when all I wanted to do was whine. I never thought I'd say this, but Ini's little sermon some weeks ago really opened my eyes. And what Alex went through with my parents for me— that sealed it."

"Aww, that's so sweet. But we just gave the push. It was all up to your ability to let go," Kayla said. "Have you experienced those challenges you were so afraid of?"

"No. Just adjustments. Like my cooking and the pidgin or random Yoruba phrases I often say. I have a bigger family and we're all close. He, on the other hand, just has his mom so sometimes doesn't understand all the phone calls I get from home or the numerous people I call auntie and uncle. The little things."

"So do we hear wedding bells?" Ini asked.

Feranmi thought a moment, then said, "That's an Alex question, but I don't want to focus on that now. We're having a good time. I love him, he loves me, and we love God. It's just great." She was getting misty eyed. It amazed her how much she could feel for him once she let herself out of the emotional bondage she had created. "But he's mad at me right now."

"Oh. Lawd. What have you done?" Kayla asked.

"Why it gotta be me?"

"Because Alex is sweet, that's why. Confess—what did you do?"

Feranmi narrated the events of yesterday to her friends. There was silence, and then Kayla spoke, "Diva, come on now. You know that you're wrong on this one, right?"

"Why?" Feranmi asked. She knew why, but just wasn't ready to admit it yet.

"Like seriously, you need us to tell you?" Kayla asked.

"But those are my girls, I have to be there when they need me," Feranmi explained.

"Not to the detriment of your relationship. You know better," Kayla said.

Finally Ini spoke, "You gonna be mad at me, but your need to prove that women can have it all consumes you. News flash; those girls have to walk their own path. You can only mentor and coach, but you have to leave room for them to make their own mistakes. You can't put them above Alex because you wouldn't like it if he put something above you."

The silence on the phone was deafening. Feranmi looked at her wristwatch; Alex would still be at the site.

"I know you get the picture, so we're going to let you go do what you need to do," Ini continued.

"Girls, I got to go. I've gotten the gossip I needed and Kofi is waiting for me," Kayla said, jokingly.

"Oh, so you only call me for the gossip?" Feranmi asked, mentally rehearsing what she was going to say to Alex.

"All right, see you tomorrow, Kay. Fera, are you guys coming to pick me up so we can ride to the airport together?"

"No, we ain't. You live closer to the airport than Alex and I. You're just too lazy to drive that's all."

"Whatever...better keep your man on time. The flight is at 11:00 a.m."

"We'll be there. Can't wait to see you, Kay...muah."

They hung up. Feranmi raced up the stairs. She was just about to open her closet door when she got a text.

Call me later- Kay.

Feranmi wondered what that was about. Why didn't Kayla say whatever it was when Ini was on the line? She pushed the thought to the side. She'd call her in the car. Now, she needed a killer outfit since she had some begging to do.

Some minutes later in the car, Feranmi dialed Kayla's number. She answered on the first ring.

"Hey, that was pretty quick," Kayla said.

"Got your text, what's up?"

"Didn't want Ini giving you a hard time. You know how she gets." There was silence. Feranmi suspected Kayla wanted to say something, but was hesitant.

"Kay, what's going on? You're not saying anything. I'll soon get to the site and will have to hang up."

"So this thing between y'all is pretty serious?"

"Yeah, it is and I couldn't be happier. He is my everything, for real."

"That's nice. What has he been up to the last four years?" Kayla asked.

Feranmi was silent for a moment because she wasn't sure

she was speaking with Kayla. Kayla was sounding weird and out of character, as though she was fishing for information.

"Working, I guess. Oh, there was this girl he dated for a period of time. Apart from that, nothing out of the ordinary. But I should be asking you that. Didn't both of you stay in touch?"

"Yeah, we did kinda."

"All I can tell you is that silliness I used to assume about all African-American men is a thing of the past. Alex changed all that," Feranmi said in contentment. She was lost in her own world and forgot for a moment that Kayla was on the line. That was kind of easy to do since Kayla hadn't said anything.

"Kay, you there?"

"Yeah, girl, I'm here. I'm happy for you."

"You don't sound like it. What's wrong?" Feranmi could hear her tone totally change.

"Oh, nothing. I just got a headache."

"Okay, feel better, I'm about to turn into the parking lot. Love you. I'll call you later." That was the strangest phone call. She would have to talk to her later or when they got to Chicago. Right now, she was on a mission.

"BOSS, you can go home now. I got it from here. Besides you're scaring the men," Phillip said.

Alex knew he wasn't in a good mood, but was asking for quality too much? He wasn't getting that right now.

"Are you trying to handle me?"

"No, I'm not. But they'll be more productive if they weren't so nervous. You've been yelling since you got here. Don't worry about it. Go prepare for your trip. I got this."

Alex looked at Phillip with skepticism in his eyes.

"Have I let you down before?"

Alex thought for a moment. He really did need to run a few errands before tomorrow. He hadn't spoken to Feranmi to solidify the plans yet. Alex knew he had over-reacted yesterday, but that didn't take away the disappointment he had felt.

"Ok, I'll be in touch every day while I'm gone. Be back on Sunday. Call me if you need anything."

"Got it! Just go and have a good time," Phillip shouted, making his way to the other end of the building where the workers were.

For it to be February, the weather was nice. A very comfortable 65 degrees with lots of sunshine accompanied by a cool breeze. He loved it. Alex made his way to the parking lot. He saw Feranmi and stopped dead in his tracks. She sat on the hood of his car. Her hair was being tossed around by the gentle breeze. It made her look so care-free. She held up an arrangement of exotic flowers. But his expression remained unreadable as he walked towards her. When he got to her, she slid down right in front of him. They were just inches apart.

"I'm sorry," she said, making a sad face. She handed him the flowers. Alex admired them and placed them down on the hood of the car.

"You've been a bad girl."

"I know and I'm sorry." Feranmi stood on her toes cupped his face and kissed him. Alex wrapped his arms around her, lifting her off the ground. Her kiss was soft and tender. After a few seconds, he put her down.

"You little fox. Are you trying to seduce forgiveness out of me?"

"Is it working?"

"I don't know. You might wanna try again," he said, with a grin on his face

"Come on, babe. I'm sorry. Say you forgive me."

"Before I say anything, I want to make sure you know where I stand."

"Yeah, I do, and you're right. I need to set boundaries. Be patient with me. I've been doing it on my own for a long time."

"Understandable, but we're a team now. We can't let anything take precedence over us."

"I'll try. I promise." She said.

He looked at her in admiration. How did he get so lucky? "So what happened? Everything okay?" Alex asked, tucking a stray lock of hair behind her ear.

"Her mom was really adamant. But in the end, she was willing to give her one more chance to prove herself or it's a one-way ticket back home."

"Home might not be so bad for her." Alex leaned against the car beside Feranmi and put his arm across her shoulders.

"Yeah, it might not be. I grew up there and it's not bad. It's just that she has so much potential. Why she's acting up, I have no idea." Feranmi snaked her arm around his waist.

"Hmmm, keep doing what you are doing and we'll pray for her as well."

"So you ready for tomorrow?"

"Yep. Was gonna run to the store and pick up a few things." He turned his head and pursed his lips aiming for her forehead, but Feranmi reached up to meet his lips with hers.

"Hmmmm, you taste sweet. I think you should get in trouble more often. I love this attention," he said, with a smile.

"Do you now?" She asked. Her alluring eyes gleamed up at him. They were his favorite part of her face.

Alex walked Feranmi to her car and gave her directions to where they would be going. As she pulled out of the parking lot —with him closely behind—Alex smiled in satisfaction. Feranmi was more than his woman. She was his life and he couldn't wait to officially make her his. But first there was one very important thing he had to do. It was time to come clean. He would lay everything out in the open and let the chips fall where they may. He prayed they fell in his favor.

CHAPTER TWENTY-EIGHT

"HEY, SLEEPY HEAD, WE'RE HERE." Alex planted a kiss on her forehead. He, Feranmi and Ini had just arrived at the gate of Chicago O'Hare International Airport. The flight was a smooth one. Alex hoped the next three days would be just as smooth. He watched Feranmi stretch, brush her hair, and apply lip gloss. He touched the ring box in his pocket. God help him, he intended to take Feranmi back to Atlanta as his fiancée.

"So, what's the plan?" she asked.

"We'll get a car and I'll take you girls to the hotel. Then I'll head over to Mom's." Alex turned on his phone and dialed his mother's number.

"It's freezing," Feranmi said once they were seated in the shuttle bus that was taking them to the car rental kiosk. She tightened her scarf around her neck and moved closer to Alex. He could feel her body shiver so wrapped her in his arms, trying to provide warmth. Winter in Atlanta was nothing compared to Chicago.

"Good thing we took Kay's advice and pulled out the heavy sweaters. I'm gonna need some cocoa when we get to the kiosk," Ini said, rubbing her hands together. Alex, who was used to the Chicago cold, looked at both ladies and chuckled.

"Welcome to my hometown, ladies. Relax, once we get inside the car, I'll crank the heat up."

"Perfect!" Ini said.

An hour later, Ini and Feranmi were checked in at the hotel. Once they got in the elevator to go to their third floor rooms, Alex rested against the wall and pulled Feranmi to him. She gave him a playful pat on his chest, signaling him to behave since they weren't alone. He smiled and turned her around so that she was leaning into him. He glanced up and saw Ini looking at them shaking her head.

"What?"

"Y'all need a room.... But umm you can't have one now... can you?' she asked, with a hint of sarcasm.

Alex grumbled. Feranmi was still laughing when the elevator came to a stop. They found their rooms almost immediately. After making sure that Ini was properly settled, Alex walked Feranmi to hers. He leaned against the doorway of her room. She rolled her luggage to the corner and went back to the doorway and stood directly in front of Alex.

"You just had to show off, didn't you," Feranmi said, jokingly referring to his little performance in the elevator.

"I have no idea what you're talking about, baby", he said, stroking her cheek. "If you're talking about me pulling you close in front of your girl, get used to it." Inching closer to her, he bent his head as if he was about to kiss her but stopped short. "You're mine and that qualifies me to display my affection anywhere I deem fit; within reason of course." Alex paused. "I thank God every day for bringing you to me. I love you deeply."

Without kissing her, he straightened. Feranmi felt robbed. She wrapped her arms around his neck she drew his face down closer.

"I love you, too. Oh by the way, hope you sent out a public service announcement telling your old girls that there is a new sheriff in town. I may be saved, but I do not play like that," Feranmi teased.

"It's not even like that. Trust me. Now get some rest. I'll swing by in about two hours to take you to my mom's, and then drop you off later at Kayla's. We'll meet back up for the rehearsal dinner. How does that sound?"

"Sounds like a plan," she said. She stood on her tip-toes and brushed her lips across his. She'd finally gotten that kiss that he had robbed her of a few moments ago.

FERANMI HAD SPOKEN to Amanda Montgomery on the telephone a couple of times and she seemed like a warm and friendly person, but Feranmi was still nervous about meeting her. It showed, as her hands trembled a bit as she reinserted the earrings she removed before her nap. She smiled as she remembered her friends teasing her earlier about her initial hang-up of getting involved with Alex.

Right after Alex left, Kayla had come by to pick up Ini. Feranmi would be meeting up with them later. Kayla and Ini were genuinely happy for her, although when she thought about it, Kayla did seem a little bit uneasy when they talked about Alex and Feranmi meeting his mom. Kind of how she was when they talked over the phone yesterday. She still couldn't believe that Feranmi had fallen in love so deeply and quickly.

What was wrong with her? She had been the one pushing me and Alex together in the first place. Feranmi pushed the thought aside, deciding that she was reading too much into her mood. Perhaps Kayla was just having last minute jitters.

Feranmi applied another coat of lip gloss, and then checked herself out in the mirror one last time. She'd decided on stretch, knit, orange dress with three-quarter sleeves. It was fitted at the waist and had a flair skirt. Since she was going to meet Alex's mother, she wanted to look extra special. When a guy took you to meet his family, it was a huge deal. Mothers and their sons had special relationships and Alex being an only child made the stakes higher.

Feranmi zipped up her brown, knee-high, leather boots and tied her scarf around her neck. Just as she was about to zip up her jacket there was a knock on the door. *Alex*, she thought. By the time he knocked the second time, she opened the door. He stepped into the room and just stared at her. Her anxiety instantly disappeared. He hadn't said anything but his eyes spoke for him.

"I take it you like what you see." Feranmi twirled around to give him the entire picture and then giggled at her vanity.

"I do." He nodded and took a few steps to close the space between them.

Alex looked snazzy in his casual, baby blue, turtle-neck sweater and dark blue, denim jeans and he smelled so good. Feranmi felt a strong magnetic pull between them.

"You don't look too bad yourself," she said. Their eyes locked and she knew they needed to get out of the hotel room. "We need to get going. I don't want to keep your mom waiting. How is she?"

"She's good. She can't wait to meet you." Alex placed his hand on the small of her back. He led her out of the room and they made their way to the elevator.

Forty-five minutes later, Alex pulled up in the driveway of a red, brick bungalow. The lawn was well groomed, although the weather had turned the grass brown. Except for the couple of kids playing in the residual snow in the cul-de-sac, the neighborhood was really quiet. They got out of the car and walked hand in hand to the front door. Before ringing the doorbell, Alex put his hands squarely on her shoulders and turned her to face him.

"No need to be nervous. You look lovely and my mom is cool." He planted a kiss on her forehead. Then he tilted her head up with two fingers. She lifted her eyes to meet his. "And most importantly, remember I love you with everything that is me." She nodded and then he turned around and pushed the doorbell.

Amanda Montgomery opened the door and the warm smile Feranmi had sensed over the telephone welcomed her. She was a beautiful woman. Feranmi immediately recognized where Alex had gotten his good looks. She was petite, no more than 5ft. 1 in. Her hair was a mixture of gray and black curls. She was dressed smartly. Alex had informed her that his mother would be fifty in three months. She didn't look a day older than forty-five. Although nothing was set in stone, Alex was thinking of having a surprise 50th birthday party for her.

"Come in, come in. Welcome to my home," Amanda said.

Alex led her into a magnificent house that was inviting and cozy. Just like Alex, his mother seemed to like contemporary and traditional art paintings and sculptures.

"Ma, this is Fera. Fera, this is my mom," Alex said.

"Hello, Mrs. Montgomery." Feranmi extended a hand.

"Come on, child. Give me a hug," she said, with a smile. She pulled Feranmi into an embrace. Amanda was about an inch taller than Feranmi's own mother and had less weight on her. The hug helped to calm Feranmi's nerves a bit.

This might not be bad after all. Standing to her full height, Feranmi caught the gleam in Alex's eye. He quickly looked away, and headed towards the living room, leaving them alone.

"So, how are you my dear? How was the flight?" she said, as

they made their way to the living room.

"It was fine, ma'am." Feranmi followed Mrs. Montgomery through the foyer, admiring all the fixtures and fittings. "You have a lovely home."

"Thank you, dear. Please call me Amanda."

Calling Alex's mother by her first name was going to be a challenge for Feranmi. Where she came from, it was improper to address someone older by their first name. That was why she prefixed the name of anyone older than her with 'aunty' or 'uncle'. She had been in the U.S for about eight years now, but was still having a hard time with the first name thing. It didn't have anything to do with formality, which her boss and most of her colleagues thought. It just had to do with respect. At work, she had learned to adjust, after all when in Rome....

"About the house, thank you, dear. It's been my home for the better part of thirty years. Alex insists on adding new touches and redecorating once every couple of years, but the basic structure has remained the same, thankfully." Mrs. Montgomery tapped Alex on his shoulder, signaling him to move his outstretched legs so they could get through to the sofa.

"How do you like the city so far? I know you haven't been here long, but make sure you both find time to see some of the sights."

"I hope to do a little before the rehearsal dinner tonight. We won't have time tomorrow because of the wedding and we leave on Sunday." They chatted for a couple more minutes before Mrs. Montgomery excused herself to the kitchen. It was time for lunch. Feranmi stood and followed, giving Alex a kiss on the forehead on the way.

"Can I help with anything?" Feranmi asked, looking around the kitchen. It had all stainless steel appliances with a beige color scheme and granite counter tops. The cabinets were elongated and had a rich, mahogany stain that made the kitchen warm and inviting. In the middle was an island that was covered with the same brown granite that covered the countertops.

"No, dear. Just sit down. Everything will be set in no time," Amanda said, walking from the china cabinet to the oven to place the barbequed chicken on the platter.

My mother would have my head if she got whiff that I sat down and let an older person serve me. It's not done. There were some things that she couldn't do whether she was in America or not. Feranmi thought.

"Please, there must be something I can do."

Mrs. Montgomery looked at her with a smile. "Okay, dear, you can set the table while I dish out the food."

Both women worked in silence. Alex left the living room to help Feranmi set the table, stealing little touches and kisses here and there. Feranmi turned to see Mrs. Montgomery watching them. Mrs. Montgomery quickly turned away, but not before Feranmi saw her look up to the heavens and mouthed the words "Thank You." Feranmi saw happiness all over her face.

AFTER LUNCH, Alex and Feranmi shooed Amanda out of the kitchen. Before she agreed to leave, she looked at them and smiled.

"What, Ma?" Alex asked.

"Nothing, I'm just happy seeing both of you together," she said and walked out of the kitchen.

After the kitchen was tidied, Feranmi walked into the living room and saw her favorite channel on. "Mrs. Montgomery, you like Lifetime too?" Feranmi had seen this movie before. In fact, she was sure she had seen all their movies.

She sat down next to Alex's mother and said, "I think I've watched this one before. Alex gives me such a hard time when he sees me watching Lifetime." She giggled as he shook his head. They sat and talked for some minutes before he stood abruptly. He headed to the staircase, then paused just as he was about to climb.

"I'm going to get ready. We'll see the town, then go for the rehearsal dinner." He took the stairs two at a time, then he paused and shouted, "Ma, don't embarrass me. No pictures."

"You see. I had forgotten about that. Now that you reminded me, I might as well," Amanda said jokingly.

"Well, my baby loves me anyway so go ahead," he replied.

Feranmi blushed. It was a very true statement.

Feranmi expected Amanda to bring out the albums which she could see in the middle compartment of the table, but instead she turned to her and pulled both of her hands into hers.

"Thank you," Amanda said.

Feranmi smiled and lowered her eyes before asking, "For what?"

"For making him happy," Amanda said. "My son has been sad for almost two years and I'm just happy that after all he went through, he's able to find someone that would make him smile again."

"Alex and I make each other happy, but honestly God had to intervene, because I was hesitant about getting involved." Feranmi was puzzled. "Can I ask you a question?"

"Sure, my dear. Anything."

"You just said considering all he went through. What did he go through?" Feranmi asked. Alex hadn't told her anything out of the ordinary. Feranmi caught the puzzled look Amanda gave her.

She shifted in the chair and cleared her throat, then said,

"I'll let Alex tell you since it's obvious he hasn't. But just know that he loves you dearly."

Feranmi was about to respond when Alex came running down the stairs. She looked at him and smiled.

He smiled back. "Ready to go?" He picked up his keys from the mantle. Feranmi stood. Amanda walked them to the foyer.

At the door, Alex kissed his mom on her cheeks. "Don't wait up, Ma. I got my key." He turned to Feranmi, "I'll go warm the car up." He opened the door and walked to the car, leaving her with his mom.

Amanda spread her hands and Feranmi walked into her embrace. After a few seconds, Amanda released her.

"I had a lovely time, ma'am. It was a pleasure."

"Child, haven't I told you to call me Amanda?" Mrs. Montgomery smiled. "It was nice meeting you. It was good seeing my son laughing again. All thanks to you."

Feranmi felt embarrassed. Alex's mother was giving her way too much credit.

"I'll be back on Sunday before we head to Atlanta."

"That'll be great. Run along now and you kids have fun." Feranmi hurried out to meet Alex in the car.

When they were settled in the car Alex said, "Hope you enjoyed yourself." He inserted the key into the ignition.

"Yes, I did and your mom is very nice. She really welcomed me with open arms."

"You see, I told you there was nothing to be nervous about." He leaned across the seat and kissed her cheek. Then he fired the engine and put the car in gear and pulled out of the driveway.

Alex was right. His mother was a sweetheart, but she wasn't quite sure there wasn't something to be nervous about. Alex hadn't told her everything about his past. She was determined to find out what he was keeping from her.

CHAPTER TWENTY-NINE

ALEX AND FERANMI had been at the Sears Tower for about an hour when her phone rang. Alex watched as Feranmi searched frantically for her phone. He made a mental note to buy her on of those phone pouches he had seen on an infomercial once. She found it and answered.

"Hey, girl...out with Alex, wassup?" Feranmi said, as she playfully swatted Alex's hand from her neck. He continued to tickle her so she placed her palm across the mouthpiece of the phone. "Behave."

"I'm sorry, boo. No I didn't." Feranmi said. Alex saw her expression change to remorse. From the one-sided conversation he heard, he figured her friends were giving her a hard time. This was the second time she had taken a call from one of them since they left his mom's house.

"My bad. Totally lost track of time. Don't be mad, I know this is your weekend. I'm on my way." She disconnected the call and faced Alex.

"You're going to get me in trouble. You know where this spa is, right?"

"They'll be all right. Yes, I do. Come on, let's go," he said, taking her hand and heading towards the exit.

With that phone call, Alex knew that the hour they had just spent together was about all the time he would have alone with Feranmi until after the wedding since he had to be at the golf course. Kofi and Kayla weren't going to have the traditional bachelor and bachelorette parties. They instead opted to treat their wedding party to a spa day for the ladies and a game of putt-putt for the guys. This was the way they chose to celebrate their last day as singles while also relieving some pre-wedding day stress.

ALEX HAD BARELY PULLED into the parking lot of the golf course when his phone rang. It was his mom.

"Ma," he said, as he got out of the car." You ok?" He leaned his body against the locked door.

"Is Fera there with you?"

"No, I dropped her off at the spa. I'm about to catch up with the guys to play golf."

"Son, I think I made a mistake with Fera this afternoon."

"What are you talking about?" he asked nervously.

"You said she was the one, so I assumed you would've told her about the ordeal of two years ago—"

"Ma, what did you do? Did you tell her anything?" he asked, rubbing his hand over his head anxiously.

"No, I didn't. I just told her I thank God for giving you a new lease and she questioned me on what I meant. But I told her that's a discussion for you and her to have," his mother said, with a sigh. "I guess with all the festivities, she forgot to ask you about it."

Alex wiped the bead of sweat that had formed on his forehead. Feranmi did seem a little distracted earlier. Maybe she had thought about it, but got distracted by Kayla's phone call. And with everything going on, he doubted she remembered.

"Okay." He sighed. He needed to talk to Feranmi. He'd been so caught up in the euphoria of their relationship that the days seemed to just pass by without him telling her. At least that's what he told himself.

"Son, if she hasn't asked you anything, you need to tell her quickly. She trusts and loves you. I like her; she's a far cry from Tracie. It'd be a shame for her to hear it from anyone but you," Amanda advised.

"I will. I plan to propose to her when we come to the house on Sunday. I'll talk to her before then. Hope she's able to still accept me."

"Your fear is unfounded. You're innocent and she'll see that. It's the deception she won't understand. Trust me. I'm a woman—I know."

"I wasn't intentionally trying to keep things from her. In the beginning, she had her hang-ups, then when she finally let her guard down, things have just been moving so fast," he explained.

"Nonsense! She wouldn't see it that way. Besides, whatever you're afraid of, it's still best coming from you. If she is meant to be yours, it will work out. Trust God." After a few moments of silence, she continued, "I gotta go, baby. Some of the ladies from my bingo club are coming over. Love you."

"Love you, too."

THE REHEARSAL DINNER was fantastic and everyone had lots of fun, but Feranmi couldn't help but feel that Alex was preoccupied. She asked him what was wrong, but he just smiled and kissed her forehead. There was something about that smile that bothered her. It didn't seem to reach his eyes. She was about to make an excuse for her and Alex, so they could go outside. She wanted to find out what was really wrong. But just then the attention seemed to shift from Kayla and Kofi to Alex and her. Everyone teased them about how long it took them to get together.

After dinner, the crowd dispersed, and Alex led her to the car. Leaning on his car, he held her close.

"Not too cold, are you?" Alex adjusted the scarf around her neck.

"Not when I have you to keep me warm," Feranmi said, snuggling close. "And I lied before; I like Chicago, but I still prefer Atlanta," she said, with a smile.

"Surprisingly, me too. It's still home, but I prefer Atlanta. Have I told you I love you lately?"

"Not in the last hour," Feranmi said.

"Well I do and don't ever forget it. Babe, I need to talk to you about something."

"Okay. That reminds me I need to ask you a question, too. But you go first..." she said, dusting off some nonexistent lint from his shirt.

As Alex was about to open his mouth, an SUV full of women pulled up. They had the Mary Mary song, "It's the God in Me" on blast.

Ini stuck her head out of the window, "Haven't you told him yet? We got to go. Y'all are just too much for me." The other women in the car laughed.

Alex gave Feranmi a puzzled look when the door opened.

Kayla came out of the car and grabbed Feranmi's wrist, "Alex, dear you'll see her tomorrow—duty calls. We love you, though."

Stealing one last kiss before Kayla dragged her away, Feranmi whispered, "I'll call you from the car."

THE LADIES HAD MADE a quick stop at the hotel to pick up Feranmi and Ini's dresses. It was just past midnight before they got back to Kayla's house. Feranmi made her way to the bathroom. She knocked on the door and immediately heard the faucet being turned on. She waited a few seconds and knocked again. Then she heard whimpering. She turned the knob and saw Kayla drying her hands. The tell-tale sign of dried tears still marked her face.

Feranmi entered and closed the door. "Why are you up, missy? You should be in bed. Tomorrow is your big day."

Then out of the blue Kayla hugged her tight. Feranmi gave her some time before loosening the embrace to see her face.

"What's wrong?" Feranmi asked, motioning for Kayla to sit on the closed commode. She didn't want to go back into the room since there were girls littered everywhere. There was another knock. Not waiting for an answer, Ini entered. Feranmi saw the puzzled look questioning the solemn mood in the room. Ini looked at Kayla then at Feranmi.

"What's going on?" Ini asked.

Feranmi shrugged waiting for Kayla to speak.

Finally Kayla stood and spoke with a shaky voice. "Am I doing the right thing? Will I be a good wife? I don't want to be a failure."

The three friends hugged each other tightly for a few seconds before Feranmi spoke, "Kay, those are just last minute jitters. Kofi is a fine man and you are the most caring, God fearing woman we know. You too will make a perfect couple and have cute little children together," Feranmi said with a smile as she rubbed Kayla's shoulders. "That's just the spirit of fear and self-doubt. Remember you can do all things through...."

"Christ who strengthens me," Kayla finished the verse and smiled.

Feranmi knew that would brighten her mood. They used that saying in school a lot and 'til this day when either one of them was facing a difficult situation.

Ini, who had been silent all this while, started to rub Kayla's back, too and said, "Boo boo, if you wouldn't be a good wife, then there's no hope for me." Their laughter sliced the tension in the room.

"I can't quote or preach, but I know somewhere in the bible it says let your light shine so that others will see God through you. Believe me, I've seen Him through you...not so much through Fera, but you for sure," Ini said.

Feranmi gave Ini a light shove. They laughed again.

"Come on, y'all. Let's go to bed. It's gonna be a busy day tomorrow. Hopefully not so busy that I won't be able to hitch one of Kofi's boys," Ini said.

"Oh, Lawd, here she goes," Feranmi and Kayla said in unison.

CHAPTER THIRTY

"OH, my baby girl is getting married. You look beautiful."
Kayla's mom stood in front of the full-length mirror admiring
her daughter. Ini and Feranmi were both standing at the side
with Tasha, Kayla's maid of honor. They worked together in
Chicago and had developed a relationship over time. The other
three bridesmaids were scattered around the house getting
ready. Kayla looked stunning, and eyes would surely turn when
they saw her, especially Kofi's.

Kayla had her hair in a loose chignon up-do with a white
rose in it. She was dressed in a white, lace, gown that had an
empire waist. At the waist was a satin purple and orange
formed bow tied at the back. And on her head was a traditional
chapel length train. Feranmi and Ini had gasped when they saw
the detail of the dress.

"Thank you, Mum. Where is dad? Hope he's ready? I don't
want to be late to my own wedding," Kayla said. Feranmi
caught her glance at the clock hanging on the wall.

"Let me go make sure he's ready. You girls don't be too long.

The car will be here soon," Kayla's mom said, leaving the room with Tasha in tow. Tasha also looked fabulous in her purple, one strap, flowing gown that had an orange tie around the waist.

"You girls look beautiful," Kayla said, looking at her two best friends. They were holding hands in a circle. Feranmi and Ini had on one strap flowing orange gowns, a replica of the purple gowns the bridesmaids wore. They both had their hair in half up-dos.

"Okay, we're not going to cry and mess up our makeup," Ini said.

KAYLA'S bridal party arrived at the church in two cars. One for the bridesmaids, Tasha and Kayla's mom. The other was a white limousine for Kayla, her dad, Ini and Feranmi. Feranmi listened attentively as Dr. Bell became emotional when he gave Kayla some last minute advice on sustaining a healthy and happy marriage. He said that the secret behind his long lasting marriage with Kayla's mom was they made God the third cord in their union and never went to bed angry.

They pulled up at the back of the church and headed straight for the waiting room. Kofi and his groomsmen were ready and in position. Just as they were settling in, there was a knock on the door and Reverend Father Winston entered. He was the presiding priest. He walked over to Kayla and clasped her hands in his.

"Today is the beginning of a new chapter in your life. Are you ready?" he asked. Kayla nodded without speaking. Feranmi observed as Kayla struggled to hold back tears.

"Okay, let's not keep that groom of yours waiting any

longer," he said. With that, he blessed her with the sign of the cross and headed for the door.

"Let's go get you married," Feranmi and Ini said in unison as they ushered her out of the room.

The wedding was solemn and beautiful. Kayla and Kofi had written their own vows and there was total silence as they recited them. It was so poignant. The whole ceremony lasted about one hour. The newlyweds were outside the church, surrounded by family and friends.

Feranmi was about to exit the church lobby to join then, when she felt tingling goose bumps appear on her arm and she knew that Alex was nearby. She turned around and he was leaning against the wall. Their eyes connected and spoke volumes. She went over to him. She brushed her lips against his and smiled. He gave her a puzzled look with a raised eyebrow.

"What? You look too fine. I've got to let them know you're mine," Feranmi said.

"Is it just weddings or does me being back home bring out the green-eyed monster in you?" Alex asked jokingly. "By the way, you look really amazing."

Feranmi blushed.

"We're headed to the hotel for cocktails, right?" Alex took her hand and they strolled out of the church lobby.

"Yes. I'm riding with the girls. See you there," she said. She noticed his pursed lips and smiled. "You are so cute when you purse your lips like that."

"Woman, I'm not cute! I guess I'm not going to have time with you today at all." He sulked.

"Duty calls. We'll have time when the partying actually starts. Then my work will be done. Now, I've got to attend to the new Mrs. Addo," Feranmi said, then turned and left.

THE RECEPTION BALLROOM was simply elegant. The pillars that were at strategic places in the ballroom had the same flowers that made up Kayla's bouquet hanging around them. At the corner of the room was a four-tier wedding cake with different layers of filling; velvet, buttercream, coconut and chocolate. The cake sat on a satin covered table. Delicate piping adorned the cake making it almost a sin to cut into it. Nestled cozily at the top of the cake were a miniature bride and groom. Right next to it was a smaller, but equally attractive groom cake. Kofi was a huge baseball fan. He was a die-hard fan of the White Sox, so his cake was made with a White Sox theme. All of the guests were going to receive a miniature remake of the wedding cake as souvenirs.

Feranmi was blown away by how all the talks they had—the planning and re-planning— had come together so beautifully. She was sure Kayla's wedding planner, Cora, was tired of all the changes they had made. She was so gracious though, because if indeed she was, she never showed it. Not to Kayla's face anyway.

Each guest table had a small, framed picture of Kayla and Kofi. As is tradition in most African countries, the guests always left with a handful of souvenirs given by everybody from the couple's immediate family to their second cousins removed. Everyone wanted their name on something that was given to the guests. Feranmi had seen enough Nigerian weddings where people went crazy and rowdy over these gifts. Therefore when Kayla mentioned it, she suggested they all be tied together with a satin purple and orange ribbon and be placed on the chairs for each person to pick up.

"Hey, girl let's go. It's time to dance in," Ini said, as she dragged her away. The reception was about the start. Everyone was seated and they were about to dance in with the couple.

The bridal party danced in first and lined the way for the couple to make their grand entrance. This was the best part of any wedding for Feranmi. She loved to dance.

IT WAS LATE. The newlyweds left the reception about thirty minutes ago and the celebration was winding down. Feranmi and Ini were gathering Kayla's money. Feranmi smiled when she remembered Kayla whispering to them, "Make sure you get all of it." It was customary for guests at African weddings to 'throw' money on the bride when she danced. The bridesmaids were usually the ones who would scamper around to make sure all the money was recovered.

Feranmi looked across the room and saw Alex making his way over. Reaching her, he put his hands around her waist from the back and said, "You ladies must be worn out. I didn't know African wedding receptions could be so tedious."

"Tell me about it. Fera is used to them because she's been to countless, but this was just too much. Fun, but too much." Ini took the knotted bag from Feranmi.

"What's that?" he inquired.

"The money we picked up from the floor when people sprayed them. Americans call it the money rain, *abi*? We call it 'spraying'." Feranmi laughed. Alex and Ini laughed right along with her.

"You ready? I'll walk you to your room, then head on home. It's a good thing our flight isn't 'til noon, so we'll have time to rest a little before we leave.

I'll come get you by eight so we can spend some time with my mom before we leave." After a brief pause Alex looked over at Ini.

"Ini, hope that's alright with you?"

"Oh, I'm surprised y'all even remember I'm riding with you. The way you're just planning and leaving me out.

Feranmi nudged Ini, "Stop it. Alex won't know you're teasing and will take you seriously."

"But, I'm not," Ini said, walking ahead of them.

"Don't pay her any attention. We'll be ready." Raising her voice so Ini would hear her, Feranmi said, "She'll get with it or be left behind," she giggled.

They continued to walk to the elevator hand in hand, when Feranmi paused abruptly.

"Okay, hold on. I really gotta go to the ladies room." She looked around to locate the nearest restroom. "And before you ask, no, I can't wait to get to the room. I'll be right back." She gave Alex her heels, which she had long replaced with slippers, and her purse. Then she made a dash for the ladies room in the lobby.

Locating an empty stall, she began performing the routine that was like second nature whenever she had to use any public facility. She hurriedly cleaned the commode, flushed then placed a toilet cover on the seat. She heard shuffling of feet. Some other ladies had entered the restroom. They were so loud, Feranmi quickly figured out that they apparently didn't think anyone else was in the restroom or they didn't care. They both located free stalls on either side of her and started talking.

"Hey, Tamara! That was some wedding. These Africans can party," the first lady hollered to the nearby stall.

"Yeah, girl. They sure can party and I'm glad we came. As soon as Nadia extended the invitation, I was right on it, picking out my dress. I've heard about these African parties."

"That was really nice of her. When she told me her cousin was getting married, I was kind of skeptical, but it turned out alright. There were some things they did I didn't get, but when I see her at work, I'll ask her."

"Oohhh, girl. Did you see who I saw dancing on the floor wrapped around this fine African girl as if he had no worry in the world?" At the mention of "African girl" Feranmi stiffened. She knew she shouldn't be eavesdropping, but couldn't help it. Finishing, but not wanting to flush, she listened.

"Alex, that's who." Now Feranmi really needed to know what they were talking about.

"Alex Montgomery! Yeah, I thought that was him, but he's changed. He's filled out a little bit, with some serious toning. He looks really fit, unlike the last time I saw him."

"I'd look toned and filled out, too, if I had the liberty of being cleared of a murder and then moved, to Atlanta to start over."

"Yeah, I heard he's in Atlanta now. Hmm, hmm, poor Tracie. She's dead now and he's just living the life." There was a short pause and then the ladies started again.

"Did you see that lady he had on his arm? She's pretty. Wonder if she knows he's a murderer."

"Come on, now. He's not a murderer. At least the court says he's not. It took a while, but he was released and the charges dropped."

Feranmi's mouth gaped open as her lips began to quiver. She placed her hand over her heart as though she could stop its accelerated pace. She couldn't remember how long she sat on the toilet. It was the sound of a flushing toilet and the water running from the faucet that brought her back from her trance. What had she just heard? The tears had started rolling the minute she heard Tracie, murder, and jail all associated with Alex's name. Her heart hurt like it had just been ripped out of her. Like a robot, she got up, flushed, and exited the stall. She still couldn't get the tears to stop, but she had to get her self together.

She just couldn't believe it. She had to get away from him. She needed a plan. This just couldn't be. She washed her hands, dried her face, and left the rest room. She was fuming, but didn't want to lose it in front of Ini. She didn't need the pity or a lecture. She just needed to get away from him.

CHAPTER THIRTY-ONE

IT'S ABOUT TIME! Alex thought when he saw Feranmi walking towards him. He had been waiting for quite a while. As she approached, he noticed she wasn't smiling. Instinctively, he was worried. She came to a halt next to him and folded her arms across her chest looking straight at the closed elevator doors. Her stance seemed to shut him out. He studied her.

"Ini was tired and couldn't wait any longer, so she went on ahead to her room. She said she'll see you in the morning."

Feranmi didn't respond. Instead, she continuously pressed the UP button on the elevator as though her action would force the doors to open. It was as if she was trying desperately to get away from him.

"What's wrong?" Alex asked.

"I'm fine," she said harshly without looking at him. He tried to touch her and she stepped back. The elevator doors opened and she got in. He followed.

"Fera! Talk to me. What happened?" He made another attempt to touch her again. She moved further away from him.

She pressed hard on the number three button. The doors closed, taking them up.

"Leave me alone, Alex," she said, tapping her feet.

It wasn't looking good. She only did that when she was angry.

"That's not gonna happen. Now tell me what's wrong. You go to the restroom as one person and come out as another," he said, his patience waning. The doors opened and Feranmi began walking quickly to her room. She got to the door and slid the key through. Once in the room she turned around to get her things from him.

"Goodnight, Alex." She tried to close the door. He used his foot to stop the closing door, then entered into the room.

"Not on your life." He leaned against the now closed door and put his hands in his pocket.

She began to pace back and forth. With a single swift motion, she turned around. Alex noticed a tear slide down her cheek and the fiery look in her eyes. He felt anxiety, ready to hurt the person who had done this to her. No, he would not be turning the other cheek. He wasn't there yet.

"You want to know?" she asked, her eyes challenging him. When he didn't respond, she continued, "Okay, here it is...I overheard the most intriguing conversation in the ladies room." She gave him a questioning look. She probably expected him to say something but he had made up his mind not to speak 'til she got it all out.

"Turns out the man I thought I knew was once jailed for killing his girlfriend...what's her name again? Oh yeah, Tracie." Her tone was sarcastic.

He could see and feel the fire in her eyes as she glared at him. In them, he could also see a trace of disgust and pain. Alex felt like he had been punched in the gut. He stood straight and walked over to her. She backed away.

"Don't you dare touch me. Ever. "

"It's not what you think," he said quietly, as he moved to close the gap. In an instant, his mind went back to the conversations he had with Kofi and his mom. This was his worst nightmare come true.

"You don't want to know what I think right now."

"It's not like that, Fera—"

"Oh really? So you didn't spend time in jail for her death?" Her laughter mocked him.

"I did, but—"

"That's all I needed to know." She walked to the door and opened it. "You need to leave." He went over to her and shut the opened door.

"Fera, stop it and listen to me before we both say something we'll regret."

"Regret? I've already begun to regret." She began to pace again and stopped. With one hand on her hip she asked, "Did this have anything to do with the mix up with your drivers' license?"

Alex remained silent.

Feranmi threw her hands in the air and said, "You know what, never mind." Then she muttered something he immediately recognized as Yoruba—he had heard her talk to her brother and parents in the language. *"Mi o ba ti duro ara mi jeje."*

"What does that mean?"

"It means, I should've stayed on my own."

"What are you talking about? I'm not going to let you throw away what we have over a misunderstanding. Let me explain," he pleaded.

"No, Alex, save it. You should've 'explained' a long time ago. You had ample time to tell me whatever it is you now want to 'explain'!" she screamed.

231

"How could I? I mean you already had all these hang ups about us. It was almost exhausting just to get you to give us a chance," Alex said, raising his voice to meet hers.

"So it's my fault you lied to me? Wow!" Feranmi shook her head from side to side.

"I did not lie to you," he said, with emphasis on the word *lie*.

"Oh, yeah, that's right. You just omitted the truth. Let's be politically correct here."

He hadn't seen this side of her before. This was different. He wished she would calm down so he could explain, but somehow he knew he wasn't going to get that wish tonight. She was hurt, tired, and wasn't listening.

"This is going downhill fast. When you cool down I'll be able to explain everything. And for the record, I did not kill anybody." He opened the door and left.

THE SECOND he walked into the lobby the next morning, he was met with Ini's angry eyes. She was seated there packed and ready to pounce on him when he came close. His first thought was that Feranmi had told her what happened between them and she had moved into protective mode. Without warning, she started to walk briskly towards him.

"What did you do to her?" she asked angrily.

"Good morning to you, too. What are you talking about?" He looked around for Feranmi while trying to determine how much Ini knew about the situation.

"I'm talking about this." Ini shoved a note into his hand.

Not taking his eyes off her, Alex straightened the crumpled piece of paper and read it. She was gone. He couldn't believe it. "Let's go," he said, as he started heading towards the door.

Alex was fuming. *How childish could she get?* He had barely slept. The look of disgust Feranmi gave him was etched deeply in his mind. He hadn't shared what was going on with anyone. Kofi was too busy and his mom would just worry unnecessarily. He wanted this to be between him and Feranmi. Now with this little stunt, everyone would know because he had one of her angry, best friends sitting next to him.

NINETY MINUTES LATER, they were checked in when the hostess announced that their flight would be delayed for an hour.

"This is just great," Ini said. "I'm going to the restroom. Can I get you anything on my way back?" she asked.

"Yes, please. Some coffee." Alex rubbed his hand across his forehead.

"How do you want it? Cream and sugar."

"No, black. Thanks."

Ini turned and left. Alex stood and walked over to the window. It was a rainy morning. The grey skies reflected his mood. He had messed up big time. He just had to find a way to get Feranmi to listen to him. Minutes later, he saw Ini walking towards him with two small coffees. Alex sat back down and Ini handed him a cup.

"Here you go. You look like you haven't slept a wink. I think you need a pick me up 'cause you're going to need enough energy to grovel." She sat in the empty seat beside him.

"Thank you. And what makes you think I need to grovel?" Alex took a small sip of his hot beverage. He looked at her with a half-smile that was met with her raised eyebrow. "We'll be alright." At least he hoped so.

"I'm going to snap her head for running off like that." Ini

contemplated for a few minutes, and then continued, "I just don't get it, Alex. You must have really messed up. Out of all of us, Fera is the slowest to anger. Kay may be like the mother hen, but she can get really feisty quickly. Fera is normally well planned out and weighs all the possibilities. She never makes rash decisions. What did you do?"

Alex sighed, then said, "Ini, I know all that. If only I can get her to calm down and let me speak, this would all be cleared up." With that, he took another sip of his coffee.

They both sat in silence for a while, then started chatting about other things, both of them still trying to call Feranmi, but getting no answer. The PA system came on announcing the plane had arrived and they would be ready to board shortly.

FROM THE TIMER on her nightstand, Feranmi could tell that she had slept for five hours. She sat up and dangled her feet over the side of the bed. The events of the last twelve hours came flooding back.

Thirty minutes after Alex left, she was still very upset. She willed her tears to stay in their ducts, but they had minds of their own. Determined not to wallow in, "had I known", she got up immediately and took out her phone from her purse. With one phone call, she had changed her flight to 6:50 a.m. She wouldn't have been able to pretend on the flight in the morning.

Her head spun in pain. A couple of minutes and two painkillers later, she was packed and ready for bed. Feranmi tossed and turned all night. It took her a few minutes to get dressed and make it to Ini's room. She knocked on the door a couple of times and got no answer. Perfect, since she really didn't feel like talking. She scribbled a note and slid it under her door.

She had gotten home before noon and had gone straight to bed, so had been disconnected from the outside world for five hours. That was bad. Her family would have tried to contact her and when they couldn't, they would have tried Deji. He wouldn't have known her whereabouts since her phone was off. She needed to call her mom. It was an unspoken tradition that either they called her or she called them every Sunday. She mentally calculated the time difference and figured she still had a few minutes before they went to bed.

She picked up her phone from the nightstand and powered it on. The voicemail icon popped up and she had ten messages. She dialed in her passcode and found out that some of the messages were from Alex, Ini, and one from Deji. She would deal with Alex and Ini later. She had to call her mom quickly. After that she would give her brother a call, to calm his nerves as well.

A couple of hours later, dressed in an old CAU t-shirt from her alma mater, lounge slacks and a pair of socks to keep her feet warm, Feranmi was stretched out on the couch. She had spoken to her folks for about thirty minute then decided to take a bath. She felt better after a long soak in the tub. Her growling stomach reminded her that she hadn't had anything to eat in a while. Not feeling like cooking, she had ordered a pizza which she expected any minute.

Her mother had berated her as usual for having her phone off for so long with a family so far away. She asked of Alex—his relationship with her mother had gotten better, largely due to Alex's efforts. The mention of his name made her come to the reality that her life was more messed up now than when she was looking for a pretend man.

What had Alex done? How could he be accused of killing

someone? Six months in jail? These were all questions she longed to have answers to. Admittedly, she was too mad to listen yesterday when he was trying to explain, but he shouldn't have let her find out from others. What else was he hiding from her?

The ringing doorbell brought her out of her trance. Her pizza must have arrived. The medium, meat lovers' pizza smelled divine. She paid the delivery-man, and then headed to the refrigerator to get herself a can of Coca-Cola. Legs folded underneath her, she changed the channel to TBN; Trinity Broadcasting Network. She didn't go to church today so she might as well look for a televangelist to worship with.

Just in time. One of her favorite pastors was just starting his telecast. She reached for the pizza box on the center table when the doorbell rang again. The delivery guy must have forgotten something. Had she mistakenly kept the wrong part of the signature slip? On her way to the door, she checked the slip in her hand. It said, "Customer copy" so that couldn't be it. Feranmi stood on her toes and looked through the peep-hole. On the other side of the door was Alex Montgomery and he didn't look too happy.

CHAPTER THIRTY-TWO

ALEX WAS furious and had no qualms showing it. His flight back was horrible. The minute the plane took off, he couldn't wait for it to land. Granted, he owed Feranmi an apology and an explanation, but she shouldn't have run off like that. Making matters worse, she had turned off her phone so he hadn't been able to talk to her for about six plus hours. He was so mad he could shake her. Ringing the doorbell a second time with no answer, Alex knocked on the door.

"Fera, open the door, I know you can see me and I'm not leaving 'til we talk. I'm tired and starving, so don't test me," Alex shouted. He was sure she was standing on her tip-toes, looking at him through the peep-hole while plotting her next move. He was about to raise his hand to knock again when he heard her pushing the code into the alarm that she always set whether she was at home or out. Then the locks started turning and the door opened. She turned around immediately heading to the couch leaving him to tend to the door.

"What's wrong with you?" Alex stepped into the house. He

caught up with her and grabbed her arm, staring down at her. "How could you just disappear like that?"

Feranmi remained silent. Her eyes went to where his hand circled around her arm and back up at him. He let go immediately. She continued to walk to the living room and sat on the couch.

"Fera, I'm asking you a question." He sat adjacent to her. The aroma of the pizza upset his stomach and it growled. He hadn't eaten anything since that coffee in the morning. All he had time for when he landed was a quick shower and he was back out again.

"Alex, I'm not in the mood now. I'm starving and I can hear you are, too. So you can grab something to drink from the fridge and we can talk later if we must," she said, calmly. They ate their meal in silence, each contemplating what to say next.

Minutes later, all done, Feranmi emptied the remaining contents of her soda can down her throat. He watched her with a million thoughts running through his mind. He was trying to feel her out so he could know how to start.

Turning around to face him, she asked with a raised brow, "Why are you looking at me like that?"

"Nothing, I just wonder how my Fera can turn into someone who wouldn't even give me the benefit of a doubt and then run away from me." His voice was steady and low.

Sitting up straight she cocked her head to the side "Is that the best you've got? Are you trying to make light of this situation? I can't believe this. Men! Funny, if the shoe were on the other foot, would you be this blasé?" She stood up, hastily packed up the empty pizza box and soda cans then made her way to the kitchen

Bowing his head, Alex knew she was right. He beckoned on the Spirit to take control. He didn't mean to be offhanded about it considering she was still upset and hurt. Alex followed her and saw her throwing the items into the trash with more force than necessary. He watched her.

Feranmi turned around and saw him standing there looking at her. She walked the short distance to the sink and leaned against it. She wrapped her arms around her body and lifted her eyes to meet his.

"You've got five minutes. Start talking and tell me why your name is even in a sentence that has jail and murder in it and most of all, why you kept it from me?" She raised her voice. Before he could say a word she continued "I told you my story. I shared my fears about our relationship because of what were misguided stereotypes. I guess they weren't misguided after all."

Alex sighed and wiped his forehead with his hand. Lifting his head, he looked directly at her and said, "You're right. I knew about your inhibitions, but when you let go and let me in, everything happened so fast that I couldn't bring myself to upset anything. I was scared that if I told you my story, that would be the last time I'd see you."

Not waiting for her to say anything, he walked over to her. She walked off to the living room and sat down. He followed closely behind and sat down next to her. After a brief pause, he began to tell his story.

Alex recounted his time with Tracie. He kept his eyes on Feranmi the whole time, trying to read her reaction. She was uneasy when he talked about the good times he had with Tracie. She was jealous. That was a good sign.

"So how did she die? And you end up in jail? Did you have anything to do with it?"

Alex stiffened. "I told you I didn't kill anyone. If you don't believe that, then there's no point in all this."

Feranmi was silent.

"So do you?"

"Do I what?"

"Do you believe me?" He was asking for her trust when he hadn't given her his, but he needed to know before they continued. He squeezed her hand.

"Look at me, Fera, and tell me you believe me when I tell you that I didn't kill anyone, even without hearing the rest of the story," Alex pleaded.

Feranmi looked deep into his eyes, "I believe you. What happened?" she whispered.

He continued to describe the last night at the restaurant when he and Tracie had gotten into a fight and he stormed off. "That was the last time I saw her and I got in my car and just drove aimlessly. I needed to clear my head."

"By the time I got back to my house, it had been turned upside down and I found Tracie on the kitchen floor in a pool of her own blood with my hand gun next to her," Alex said.

Feranmi gasped.

"I panicked and didn't know what to do. I was in shock. It was not looking good for a brother, so I called, Kofi."

"Which Kofi? Don't tell me Kayla's husband, Kofi, because if he knows, that means she does, too. So everyone knew and you all deliberately kept me in the dark." Feranmi punched Alex in the chest. She stood up.

"I can't believe you and even worse, Kayla. Now her weird phone calls and questions are all making sense."

Alex rubbed the spot where her fist made contact with his chest.

"Babe, calm down. Don't blame anybody but me. Please, I'd hate for anything to happen to your friendship with Kay because of me. I swore them to secrecy. I wanted you to hear it from me."

"We see how that turned out," she said, sarcastically. "Just finish the story."

Alex took a deep breath. "I called Kofi who came right away, then we called the police. After a couple of days I was taken into custody, but only as a person of interest. With the lack of any new leads and the fact that Tracie's dad was the Lieutenant Governor and needed someone to answer for his daughter's death, I quickly became the suspect." His anger began to rise.

"The gun only had one set of prints on them—hers. But the autopsy concluded it was a murder and not a suicide. Coupled with the fact that I didn't have a reasonable alibi that could vouch for my whereabouts, my fate was pretty much sealed. What made matters worse was that there were a number of people at the restaurant that witnessed our argument and were willing to testify to that fact."

Feranmi sat in awe. "This sounds like an episode of *Law & Order SVU*."

He was silent for a bit. It did actually sound like something out of the movies.

"So I was charged and detained without bond. I didn't want to become a statistic, so I liquidated my business to hire an experienced and quite expensive attorney. Then I also hired a private investigator. His sole job was to comb the streets and find out what exactly happened to Tracie," Alex continued.

"Some months later, my detective discovered that her new boyfriend was into drugs. Nobody was talking because of his strong connections. But he also owed a lot of people money. One of his creditors had followed her to my home and I'm assuming that Tracie got scared and went for my handgun. The rest is history." Alex stood up and began to move back and forth. Feranmi still hadn't said a word. She watched him pace. When he glanced at her, her expression was empathetic.

"Then they let me go, but not before six months of my life was taken away from me. My business crumbled and the rumor mill was churned. After months of self-pity, I picked myself up and took the next flight out of town, back to Atlanta. I put all my heart and soul into re-building my business," he explained.

He kneeled in front of her and he placed his head in her lap. Feranmi was still.

"I've kicked myself so many times for not doing what I needed to do and letting you find out the way you did." His eyes pleaded with her.

Feranmi thought for a moment then cupped his chin with both her hands. He knew he looked tired and drained. He felt it.

"Alex, I'm so sorry for what you had to go through. I cannot even imagine how you must have felt. Being betrayed by your girlfriend was not enough, you had to be charged with her murder as well," Feranmi said softly.

Alex lifted himself off his knees and sat down beside her. Taking both her hands in his, he said, "Babe, I'm not looking for your pity. It happened. I survived and God gave me a fresh start. It drew me closer to Him and allowed our paths to meet again. I am no longer bitter about my journey because it led me to this destination. All I need is your forgiveness."

"You have to give me time. You laid a lot on me tonight. My head was spinning just listening to you. You betrayed my trust. I opened up and showed you everything about me, even when I came up with the ridiculous fake man plan. In all those times I was sharing my ugliness with you, you hid yours from me. How can I trust you won't do that again out of some fear that it will tear us apart?"

He said nothing.

"I can't do this. Remember, I told you before, without trust we can't make it."

"What does that mean? Are you breaking up with me?" Alex's tone was defiant.

"I think you should go." Feranmi got up and calmly walked to the door. Alex stared at her. He got up and walked to the door, standing there for a minute.

"Fera..." he whispered.

"Please leave, Alex," she said, firmly with her eyes downcast. Without another word, he turned and walked out the door.

Feranmi slid down the door and cried.

CHAPTER THIRTY-THREE

"SHE'S UPSET. I get it, but it's been weeks and she hasn't returned any of my calls or answered my texts," Alex said, with annoyance.

"Calm down, man. She needs time that's all," Kofi said.

"How much time? I'm not going to wait forever."

"Alex, you have a right to be angry, but I hate to break it to you—this is entirely your fault."

"Don't you think I know that?"

"Then you have to chill and wait for her to make her way back to you."

"It's been four weeks. How much more time does she need?"

"As much time as it takes. Kay said she's pretty upset."

"You mean, she needs more time to come up with a number of excuses for why we can't be together," Alex said, frustrated.

"Trust is a fragile thing. She has to be sure she can rely on you."

"I know that, but..."

"But nothing. Check it, suppose she did the same thing to you?"

"Whose side are you on anyway?" Alex asked.

"I'm on the side that needs you to calm down so you can get your woman back. Pushing it any further would further drive her away," Kofi explained.

Alex contemplated for a minute. The more he thought about the situation, the angrier he became. The past four weeks had been nothing but hell for him. Their parting four years ago was nothing compared to this. He hadn't been able to sleep. It was a good thing that the Anderson Group building was wrapping up and Phillip was the best foreman there was, because he hadn't been able to concentrate on work either.

He had given Feranmi a couple of days before calling her, but she refused to answer. The text he got from her telling him to let her be and that she needed time was the last one he got. He knew it was pointless going to her house and he couldn't take their problems to her office.

He hated being in limbo when it came to his heart, but that was what this was turning out to be. He was tired of begging Feranmi to give them a chance. True love forgives; it doesn't keep scores of wrongs. It's patient and kind. He deserved a woman who would be all that to him.

He had been a fool to let himself get caught up with her a second time and give her another opportunity to hurt him. Her rejection the first time drove him into the arms of the next available woman; Tracie. As if the hell he went through then wasn't enough, he decided he needed more. It was clear from Feranmi's actions that their love was one sided and he was done trying to salvage it. Feranmi really didn't love him, at least not the way he deserved to be loved. He was the first to admit that he messed up, but love should have softened her heart so she could see it from his point of view.

"What we need is to get you two together. You were made for—"

"Don't worry about it! I'm done."

"What?"

"It took me a while, but I have finally figured that Fera isn't the woman for me. I should have left well enough alone."

"Alex, I've seen you with Tracie and I've seen you with Fera. There's no way you can convince me she isn't the woman for you."

"Leave it alone, man. I'm tired of dealing with it. I've got to go. "

"Running won't solve this. You need to face it and come up—"

"Man, let it rest. I'm done."

"When do you leave for Florida?" Kofi asked, exhaling deeply. Alex knew at that moment he had given up on the conversation. At least for today.

"Sunday. First I've got to do this community building project thing I committed to a while back. I really don't feel like being out tomorrow, but it's just one day. Then I'm off the next day."

"How long will you be gone for?"

Alex remembered his conversation with Feranmi a while ago in the restaurant. He had promised to be gone just three days a week. Now that she wasn't around, he didn't have to worry about commuting back and forth.

"Two weeks. I'm pretty much done here so I can commit my time there."

"Got it," Kofi said.

"Be easy. I'll talk to you later. My love to Kay." Alex hung up the phone.

He swung his legs off his desk grabbed his keys and jacket and walked out of his office. He stopped by Phillip's office.

"Hey, I'm going to get something to eat. You want me to bring you back something?" Alex asked.

"No, thanks boss, my wife packed my lunch herself today, full of my favorites," Phillip said, smiling.

"Must be nice. All right, I'll be back." Alex tried to conceal his anger as his mind went to Feranmi again. He was all set to propose when this mess happened. Yes, he had been wrong to keep the truth from her but she didn't make it easy either. He had been jumping through hoops to get her to go out with him. It was a huge mistake trying to recapture the past. When she came up with her little scheme, he should have run the other way.

FERANMI LACED up her sneakers and pulled her hair up in a bun. It was a pollen-filled spring day and she really didn't feel like going outdoors, but she promised the girls that she would take them on this building project a long time ago. The community center was partnering with a local organization that helped low income families with repairs and to build new houses. She really didn't want to be around any kind of construction right now. It reminded her of the mess her life had become.

The day Alex walked out of her life the second time was even worse than the first. When he narrated the story, she could still see some pain in his eyes over what he had endured. She wanted to reach out to him, but her anger kept her from comforting him. He should have trusted her. Whether he committed the crime or not was not the issue. She knew he didn't, but he deliberately deceived her. He hid himself from her while she bared herself to him.

Feranmi cried herself to sleep every day, mourning over her lost love. She loved Alex, but couldn't bring herself to be in a relationship with someone she didn't trust. Her sad nights turned into brighter mornings and day by day she was coming to terms with the fact that hooking up with Alex again wasn't such a good idea after all.

Feranmi ran downstairs to the kitchen to get some water when her phone rang. Only two people could be calling her this early; her mom or Ini. She quickly swallowed her allergy pill and picked up the phone. *Ini.*

"Hey, lady. What's good?" Ini said, too excited for so early in the morning.

"Nothing much, about to go for the building project I told you about."

"Oh, yeah that I forgot, hold on..."

"No, I..." Feranmi tried to say but Ini had already put her on hold. That meant only one thing—Kayla was on the other end.

Feranmi and Kayla's relationship had been strained but cordial since the breakup with Alex. Ini had tried to get both ladies to understand the other's point of view. In the end, they apologized for harsh words towards each other, but there was still some strain there.

"Hey, Fera, you there?" Feranmi didn't answer immediately so Ini said again, "Fera...."

"I'm here. Girl, you know I got to go. I need to go pick up some of the girls from the center and then head out to the place. I got to be there by 9:ooa.m," Feranmi said, a bit irritated.

"Ugh...since the breakup, you've just been cranky," Ini said. "Chill, I got Kay on the line...Kay, you there?"

"Hello, Kay."

"Hello, Fera."

"Y'all got to be kidding me. Are we doing this again? It's been weeks and we said back in school that no man will ever come between us," Ini said.

There was an extended silence, then Kayla spoke, "Fera, how long are you going to be mad at me? I'm apologizing again. I really didn't think he would go so long without telling you. We have been through too much for you to think I deliberately tried to hurt you."

After a while, Feranmi spoke, "Yeah, I guess so, but I was really disappointed and felt betrayed. I'm trying to put the whole episode behind me."

"Great, I'm glad we got that out of the way," Ini said. "This is the last time I'm going to do this...the next time I'm going to have to whoop y'all behinds. We have come too far for all this drama."

"Yes, ma'am," Feranmi and Kayla said, at the same time. The friends laughed. Feranmi looked at her watch. It was a quarter to eight. She had to go.

"So why did y'all call me this early?"

"We wanted to know how you're doing," Ini said.

Feranmi knew what her friends really wanted, but decided to stall.

"What do you mean?" She opened the garage door and got into her car. She put the car in reverse and eased out of the garage.

"Stop playing. You know what we mean," Ini said.

"We're worried about you," Kayla echoed.

"If you're asking about Alex. I haven't seen him."

"Don't you think you are carrying this thing too far? That man really loves you," Kayla said.

"Did you hear me say I don't love him? I do, but I refuse to be with someone I don't trust. What else is he keeping from me?" Feranmi said, cruising down the highway. "It might take a minute, but I'll get over him."

"But everybody deserves a second chance. Are just going to

suffer because you can't bring yourself to forgive him?" Ini asked.

"We've seen you two together...twice now. You have to admit that out of all the guys you dated no one brought out the very essence of you other than Alex," Kayla said, calmly.

That much was true. He awakened something in her that she didn't even know she had. He filled any room he entered with his large shoulders and killer smile. It made everything around him seem so small. Feranmi shook her head in an effort to clear it. Her friends were breaking down the resistance that took weeks to build.

"Girls, I got to concentrate on the road. Call you later?"

"Fera, darling, I won't bring this up again, but let me say this and I'll let you go. The very thing Christ stands for is love and forgiveness. If you really love Alex, you should be able to forgive him. We can't expect to be forgiven if we can't afford the same courtesy to our fellow man. I believe once you forgive him, you'll be able to find your way back to him. Alex is a good man. You can't be so blinded by anger that you can't see that," Kayla said.

Nobody said anything for a while, then Ini spoke "Ok, dearie. We'll talk later."

FERANMI HAD BEEN in a somber mood since she got off the phone with her friends in the morning. She had a good mind to turn back and curl up in bed, but needed to keep herself busy to stop herself from breaking down and crying. She had avoided her friends for weeks because she was so angry. Today was the first time they'd discussed the breakup and more than anything, Kayla's last words to her struck a nerve.

There was no doubt about it—Kayla was right. How could she be so blinded with emotion that she forgot the very thing that she had prided herself at being—Christ-like. She was far from perfect, but liked to believe that she walked in His footsteps. Feranmi felt ashamed and unworthy. Before she picked up the girls, she made up her mind to go by Alex's house afterwards and talk to him. She owed him an apology. Whether they could salvage their relationship was left to be seen, but at least she needed to forgive and apologize to him. Truthfully she hadn't made it easy for him.

Hours later, Feranmi and her girls were halfway into their assigned task.

"Miss Fera, can we take a break now? We need something to drink," Shay asked. She was one of the sixteen year-olds that accompanied Feranmi. Feranmi looked around and saw a small kiosk that was set up for water and popsicles.

"Sure, we'll soon be leaving anyway." Feranmi and the girls made the short stroll to the kiosk. The jovial atmosphere was interrupted by Ada's raised voice,

"Miss Fera, there goes your boyfriend." Feranmi stiffened then turned around. She saw him. Alex looked as sexy as sin in his jeans and white tank top that he covered with a short-sleeved, plaid shirt. Feranmi wanted to reach out and touch him. As though sensing her gaze, Alex turned around. Their eyes stayed locked in place for a few moments 'til he looked away, picked up his small water cooler, and started walking towards the parking lot. This was her chance. Looking at the girls, she said, "Ada, you're in charge. The three of you stay together. I'll be right back, then we can leave." She ran after him.

"Alex, wait!" she said, but he continued to walk. She met up with him and grabbed his arm. He looked at her as if he had just been stung. She quickly removed her hand.

"Yes?" he asked. She could see his muscles tighten with tension.

"I didn't know you would be here."

"You lost the right to know anything about me or my whereabouts weeks ago. Did you need something?" he asked, irritated.

She cleared her throat, looked down then up again. "We need to talk." Her eyes pleaded with him.

"Why? Why now? I've been trying for weeks to reach you. To get you to talk to me. What changed?" He looked at her with an eyebrow raised.

"Kay, Ini and I talked and I owe you an apology—"

"So, now I'm worthy of an audience because you consulted with your girls?" he asked with his teeth clenched.

"Did you think I should just listen to you and sweep it under the carpet? I had a right to be mad and I needed to think. You can't hold that against me." Feranmi's eyes darted from the kiosk back to him.

"I do!" he retorted. "All I've heard about was your plan to marry the perfect Nigerian man. When you finally gave us a chance, I couldn't bring myself to tell you for fear of losing you. But then I wasn't wrong was I? Because at the first sign of an imperfection, you run." he sneered. "What exactly does love mean to you?" His burning stare made her uncomfortable.

"Love brought me to you now. I was going to come to see you after this. I had no idea I would see you here. Maybe I handled everything wrong. I'm sorry."

"Maybe?" His laughter was laced with sarcasm. He unlocked his car and got in. "Okay, you've apologized. Do you feel better now? As for us, I'm done. I deserve someone who loves and wants me just the way I am." Alex closed the door and drove off.

CHAPTER THIRTY-FOUR

IT WAS OVER and there was no one to blame but herself. Feranmi replayed the conversation with Alex over in her head so many times during the past couple of days, looking for how it all went so wrong. She felt hopeless, having strayed so far away from God, she didn't even know where to begin asking for His guidance. The whole thing had blown up in her face just as Kayla said it would. She tried to manipulate everything and everyone to work according to her desire instead of trusting God to lead the way. The ache in her heart convinced her that Alex was what God had for her all along. She rejected him the first time, but was given another chance and she didn't even have the sense to make good use of it. She preached forgiveness all the time, but the one time she actually had to practice it, she failed and now it was too late.

Alex hated her. She couldn't fathom how she had been so blinded by anger and pride that it took her so long to forgive a man whom she knew loved her. Now she believed that subconsciously, it was her way of pushing him away since he wasn't in her plan.

It had been a week since he left her standing in the parking lot. She gave him a day to calm down and made a trip to his office Monday, but Stacy told her he had gone to Florida. She was devastated.

Her friends called her to know how she was holding up. With tears running down her cheeks, Feranmi told them about the encounter in the parking lot. It was over and done with.

It must be true what they say that hindsight is always perfect she thought. Deciding not to dwell on it any longer, Feranmi got up from bed.

Today was the last day she would have with her girls from the center, before they went off to summer camp. She would miss them terribly, but in order to keep herself busy, she had signed up to mentor another group of girls. Feranmi was taking them to Savannah to see the Savannah History Museum. The forecast predicted severe thunderstorms in some parts of Georgia later on. Savannah was just three and a half hours away. She figured that they would be back before any of it hit. Right now, it was so gorgeous outside that she hoped the weather man got it wrong.

She knelt in prayer—she had been talking to God a lot lately. She desperately needed Him to fix her heart. If only she talked to Him as often before, she might not have made a mess of things. She opened her bible and her eyes fell on Psalm 61. She read it, concentrating on verse 2;

"Hear my cry, God

"Listen to my prayer.

From the end of the earth, I will call to you, when my heart is overwhelmed.

Lead me to the rock that is higher than I".

Then she prayed,

"Please, Father, I repent of my sins, lead me and fix me right. I know I don't deserve it but please soften Alex's heart so that he

would accept my apology. I look to you, Oh Lord to help make this thing right. Also as I take the girls out today I ask that you be with us every step of the way. In Jesus' name, amen."

An hour or so later, dressed in a floral, flare dress, Feranmi slipped her well-manicured feet into her sandals, picked up the keys to the rental SUV she got yesterday and headed for the door. The sky was bright and clear. The sun had made its appearance. It was going to be a great day. Her talk with God this morning had given her a new perspective. Alex had made up his mind and she had to respect that, but with God she knew that all things were possible. Alex would come to see that he was wrong about one thing though; she did love him. Although she understood why he didn't believe her.

She wasn't going to keep beating herself up about her failed relationship. She had cried enough tears. If it was the will of God, they would be together again. If not, she would chuck it up to life experience and keep her head up. There was always joy in the morning and Feranmi decided this morning that her joy had come.

Once in the car, she activated her ear piece and dialed Ini. The other chaperon cancelled at the last minute which would have made Feranmi cancel the road trip, but Ini stepped in and saved the day. Feranmi knew that this wasn't really Ini's thing, but she did it just for her.

"Hey, girl, I'm on my way. Please be ready."

"All right. See you in a bit."

IT HAD BEEN A GREAT DAY. The girls talked about everything they saw 'til they began to fall asleep. The car was so quiet without their chatter that Feranmi could almost hear herself think. She glanced to her side and saw that her friend was also fast asleep. Ini drove in the morning so Feranmi was the designated driver on their return.

The girls were so fascinated by everything, especially the women's fashion of the early 19th and 20th century. They really liked being able to see some of the things they read about in school. Feranmi and Ini really thought they enjoyed the road trip more than the actual tour of the museum. Feranmi enjoyed seeing the look of contentment on their faces. She loved making them happy and teaching them that anything was possible no matter what anyone else thought.

It had started to drizzle a little bit when Feranmi dropped the first girl off. She looked at the clock on the dashboard, it was 8:00 p.m. She had one more stop and that was Ini's. She had safely dropped off the last girl.

"Girl, wake up. We're almost at your place," Feranmi tapped Ini on her shoulder.

Stretching, Ini let out a yawn. "I don't know how you cope with these girls. They wore a sister out."

"You get used to it. It's fun for me," Feranmi replied, with a smile. "Stop yawning, you know I still have to drive home. I don't want to start sleeping."

"You sure you don't want to stay over? The rain has gotten heavier and I'm not comfortable you driving in this weather."

"I'll be fine. Besides I want to go to church tomorrow. If I stay here, I won't be able to make it back in time," Feranmi said. She felt Ini's stare boring a hole into her.

"Ask me what you want to ask me. You've been staring at me funny all day."

Ini hesitated. "I know you don't want to talk about it, but I'm worried about you. Have you heard from Alex?"

Feranmi went still at the mention of his name. Ini had been extra nice to her all day. Feranmi knew she was dying to ask, but she forbade her or Kayla to mention his name. She needed to heal without his name constantly being thrown in her face.

"No, I haven't. I called him once, but he didn't answer. I've left that whole situation to God. I'm not going to beat myself up about it anymore. I messed up, but everyone does."

"I know you don't want us to intervene, but don't you think it will help?"

"No! If we're meant to be together, we'll find our way back to each other. If not, then so be it."

"Ok, you're stronger than me and I admire you for it."

"Don't make me start crying. Let's change the subject," Feranmi said, dismissively. They talked about work and Kayla who would be visiting soon for a two-day conference.

A few minutes later, Feranmi pulled into Ini's driveway. The rain had gotten a little heavier so Feranmi pulled up as much as she could. Ini gathered her bag and souvenirs and turned to Feranmi, "I had fun. I might even considering volunteering a day or two. Don't hold me to it, though." She looked outside, "Are you sure you don't want to stay?"

"Positive. Love you, sis and I'll call you the minute I get home."

"I won't sleep 'til I get your call," Ini said, with a worried look on her face. She hugged Feranmi and ran out of the car.

The rain was getting heavier and was now accompanied by winds. Feranmi could feel the winds as she tried to steady the SUV. If this was her Maxima, she would have no problem, but maintaining control was becoming a challenge. Making the turn off the highway, she was thankful that she would soon be home.

She came across a deserted car. Did they run out of gas? Feranmi took her foot off the accelerator to maneuver around it when she hit unexpected pool of water that splashed on the windshield blurring her vision. By the time she regained sight of the road, there was another car coming down the two-way street that sent her into a panic.

Feranmi swerved to avoid hitting the car. She screamed, "Jesus" and lost control of the steering wheel, which sent her crashing right into a tree on the other side of the road. The last thing she remembered before losing consciousness was the air bags being deployed.

CHAPTER THIRTY-FIVE

ALEX TOSSED AND TURNED. It was the same thing every night. Peace eluded him, even in sleep. The fact that he had been in a hotel for the past week didn't help his insomnia either. But he preferred to be here than in Atlanta—another city that held bad memories for him.

He was about to turn over when his phone rang. It was too early, the person calling him better have a good reason. Alex picked up the phone from the side table. He looked at the caller ID. It was Ini. His half-shut eye lids flew open. What did she want?

"Hello, Alex. This is Ini. You need to get here. Fera's been in a car crash." Her voice was shaking.

"How? When? Is she ok?" His stomach clenched in fear.

"We don't know. She's been unconscious since they brought her in. I called her brother. He's on his way."

"What hospital?" he asked, too scared to ask anything else. Ini gave him the information and he hung up the phone. Dread came over him. He had spent the last week working himself to the bone and nursing anger and bitterness over what Feranmi put them through. He replayed their conversation in the parking lot and was content with the hurt look on her face. He wanted to give her a taste of her own medicine. He even ignored her call all in an effort to cause her the same pain she caused him. But the phone call from Ini changed everything.

RUNNING through the wet parking lot, Alex entered the emergency room. He hadn't been able to shake the gut wrenching fear that had accompanied him on the one and a half hour flight. This news sent him on an emotional roller coaster. What if he never got the chance to hear her laugh or see her smile again? On the plane, he thought about how short life was. Today was all that was promised, and it was important to make the best use of it. *She has to wake up, she just has to.*

Ini came rushing to him the minute she saw him.

He acknowledged her with a nod. Then asked, "How is she? Is she awake now?"

"She's in with the doctor. No, she's still out," Ini said.

Alex could tell that she hadn't slept in some hours. "Is Deji here yet?"

"He just called from the airport. He's on his way."

Dropping down on the chair, Alex rubbed his head. He looked back up at Ini. "What happened?"

Ini sat down next to him and narrated the trip to Savannah and how she pleaded with Feranmi to stay with her that night. She was worried when she didn't hear from her by midnight, then she got a call from the police telling her what happened. They had gone through her phone and dialed the last number Feranmi called.

Nurses and doctors were walking through the halls, but not stopping to give them any new information. Deji arrived and they filled him in. Deji took out his phone and placed a call. Alex began to pace. From what he heard, Deji was talking to their parents.

A doctor dressed in scrubs entered the waiting room. "Feranmi Ade..." he was having trouble pronouncing her last name but they knew who he was referring to. Deji and Alex rushed to him.

"I'm her brother. Could you tell me what's going on?" Deji asked, anxiously.

Alex groaned. If things weren't so bad between them, he should have been her next of kin.

"Your sister came in with head trauma and minor bruising on her arm and leg. We should be thankful that the airbag deployed. If not, it could have been a lot worse." The doctor studied them for a minute, then continued "We've made her comfortable, but won't know the extent of her head injury 'til she wakes up. Hopefully it'll be soon, but all we can do is wait... and pray. I need you to come with me for paperwork."

"When can we see her?" Ini asked.

"When the nurses have settled her into a room." The doctor left with both Deji and Ini closely behind him. Alex stood there feeling hopeless and hating that there was nothing he could do.

IT WAS three hours later before Feranmi was given a room and there was still no sign of her regaining consciousness. Deji was the first person to go in to see her. When he came out twenty minutes later, Alex could see that he was noticeably shaken by what he saw and only male pride kept his tears in check. Alex consoled him while Ini went in to see her. Alex had been on the phone with Kofi giving him an update. Kofi had to literally hold Kayla down from taking the next flight to Atlanta. They tried to tell her that with Feranmi unconscious, there wouldn't be any need for her to come.

"She is going to be okay, man." Alex patted Deji on the back. He wasn't sure whether her brother knew the present state he and Fera's relationship. If he did, he didn't show it.

"I pray. It's scary seeing her like this. Let me update my folks. They're worried." Deji excused himself and placed another call.

Alex continued to pace 'til Ini came out. He braced himself and he walked into Feranmi's room with a combination of fear and eagerness. He had to see for himself that she was still alive. He sighed with relief as he saw her chest move up and down.

Her exquisite facial features still stood out, despite the swelling and bruises. She had bandages on one arm and one leg. He stared at her. He wanted to hold her, but feared he would cause her pain. No matter what happened between them, he wished she would open her eyes. He would do anything to have those hazel brown eyes stare at him.

That day passed by without him getting his wish. Feranmi still hadn't opened her eyes. Alex stayed by her side the whole time. The only time he left the hospital yesterday was to get Deji settled in his place since it was closer to the hospital than Feranmi's place. Ini and Deji went to rest at night and returned this morning.

Deji brought Alex a change of clothes and Ini brought him something to eat. Alex only left her side to go to the restroom or when the doctor or nurse asked him to step out. He was exhausted. He hadn't slept, spending the night praying and asking God to bring Feranmi back to him.

It was now noon. The doctor came in for his routine check. With Ini and Deji close by, Alex excused himself to take a walk. He was on his way back when Ini came running to him.

He was gripped with fear, not knowing what she was about to say.

"She's awake Alex.... she's awake," Ini cried, running back to Feranmi's room.

He was gripped by emotions. His eyes blurred with tears he held back. He looked up to the heavens, mouthed a, "thank you". He ran after Ini.

———

THE DOCTORS WOULDN'T LET anyone see Feranmi until all tests had been completed. For two hours, she had been poked and prodded by nurses drawing blood and conducting various other tests. The results of the MRI— to determine the extent of her head injury—showed no serious damage. She would have serious headaches for a couple of days but it should disappear with enough rest and medication.

Feranmi had to remain for observation overnight. The doctor gave strict instructions that she could have only one visitor at a time. Family first. When Deji entered her room, Feranmi could see that he had been shaken up by the whole episode. She smiled to put him at ease.

He called home and she spoke to her parents. Her parents were relieved that she was awake. Despite her pain, Feranmi smiled when her mom broke into a Yoruba praise song. It took a lot of persuasion, but she and Deji were able to talk her out of taking the next flight to the U.S. Deji didn't leave her side until he got a call that required him to go back to school. So he took the next flight out, but promised to be back in a couple of days.

When Deji left, the nurse came in to take Feranmi's vitals and give her some medication. Ini was right behind her. She rushed over to Feranmi and a stray tear fell from Ini's eye. "You better not try this stunt again."

Feranmi smiled. The single effort made her head throb. "Okay, I won't."

Ini hugged her aching body. After visiting a little while, Ini stood to leave. Feranmi could see she was hesitant.

"It's okay, you can go home. I'll still be here tomorrow," Feranmi said. Ini was silent, so Feranmi asked. "What?"

"I called Alex," Ini blurted out.

Feranmi's stare was blank. She knew how Alex felt about her. She didn't need his pity if she couldn't have his love.

"Alex was here all through this ordeal. He's outside. I should go. You guys need to talk." Ini walked over to Feranmi and kissed her on her cheek. "Behave. I'll see you tomorrow."

Feranmi touched her head and moaned. The throbbing pain caused her to be still.

"You've always been so stubborn. Shouldn't you be lying still?"

"Alex?" she whispered. He must have entered when she shut her eyes for a moment.

"Shouldn't you be lying still? I can see you grimace in pain." He walked over to her tossing his keys on the table. "How do you feel?" He whispered. His voice soothed her soul. His powerful frame filled the room.

"Better than when you saw me..."

"You knew I was here?"

"Ini told me..."

"You had me so messed up with that extended nap." His eyes roved all over her.

She shifted, and then moaned almost immediately.

He rushed over to her side. Holding her hand, he asked "Do you need me to adjust the pillow?"

His unique masculine scent played with her senses, making her want to reach out and hug him. She observed him for a while then asked, "Were you actually here the entire time I was unconscious?"

He remained silent. Then for the first time their eyes connected. She could see strain in his.

"Yes," he said, stroking her forehead.

"Why? You were pretty clear about what you thought of me the last time we were together. So why did you come?"

He chuckled. "Which do you want me to answer first?"

"Your choice," she said casually, but her beating heart betrayed her as she anxiously awaited his response.

"I came because despite what happened, we're friends first. I care about you," he said, not taking his eyes off her.

Feranmi nodded, trying to hide her disappointment. She thought love brought him to her. But it was out of obligation to her as a friend. Her head throbbed and she scowled. He touched her head. "Babe, are you ok? You need me to call the nurse?"

"I'm not your babe and no, you don't have to do anything else, Alex. There are nurses here to cater to my needs so you don't have to stay," she retorted.

"Why?"

"Why what?"

"Why are you upset?"

"I'm not upset. You can go now. I need to rest."

He stiffened, but instead of leaving he sat on the chair next to her. "I'm not going anywhere 'til you tell me what this is about."

Her eyes welled with tears. She hated that he was treating her like a friend. She loved him, but apparently he had stopped loving her. She was determined not to let him see her cry. An unruly tear escaped and Alex wiped it away with his finger. She flinched at his touch.

"Stop being nice to me. It's making me sick. I can't stand

the friend treatment." There, she said it. No need wasting any time. A near death experience made her see things differently.

He smiled. "You don't like us being friends?"

"You're not going to make this easy are you?"

"I have no idea what you're talking about," he said, with a smirk on his face.

"I can't be your friend because I'm in love with you. I know you don't love me anymore, and I prefer to nurse my pain in peace, so please leave."

"I never said I don't love you. You made me so mad I wanted to shake you 'til you came to your senses but I have always loved you. Never stopped."

"But you were so mean to me..."

"I wasn't on my best behavior that day because I was angry. Besides, you almost died. That trumps anything that's wrong with us." He paused. "I'm sorry for keeping my past from you, making you doubt my sincerity. I never want to go through what I went through these past weeks again."

She used one hand to stroke his face. She loved him so much it hurt. "Baby, I'm the one who should be sorry. I was scared of us. You were my unexpected blessing and I had no idea how to handle it. So I saw that as the perfect excuse to push you away."

He kissed her so hard on the lips that she winced in pain.

"Oh, I'm sorry, my love," he said with a smile. He cupped her face with his hands. His stare was so intense. "Four years ago you captured my heart, but I let you walk away that time. I almost made the mistake of letting you go again. Whatever hurdles we come across, we fix together."

"Deal. I no longer have the strength to run. I knew what I wanted, but God knew what I needed—you. And I accept wholeheartedly."

Alex reached inside his pocket and pulled out the half-carat princess cut, diamond solitaire on white gold. Feranmi gasped, blinking several times to hold her tears back. Her head was spinning with discomfort, but this moment was all worth it.

He took her left hand in his and got down on one knee. He glared at her.

"I have been carrying this around since we got on a plane to Chicago. I know this isn't the right place or time but I need to get this out now. I felt so hopeless when the doctor asked for family and I didn't have any rights." He watched for a reaction but she just stared at him. He continued, "Feranmi Adewunmi, when God was creating my Eve, He created you. You're truly are my missing rib. Will you marry me, share my life, and give me a houseful of babies?"

"Yes, yes, I will marry you. I don't know about a houseful, but we will definitely have babies," she replied, with a smile.

He slipped the ring on and kissed her. He got into the bed with her and wrapped her in his protective arms. "Now go to sleep...we need to get you healed so we can get out of here."

She closed her eyes and fell into a deep sleep.

EPILOGUE

DECEMBER, 2012
Lagos, Nigeria

"STOP IT, girls. You're going to make me cry," Feranmi said. She was sitting in the middle of the room and Kayla and Ini were going over Alex stories. A couple of her cousins fanned her while the makeup artist worked on her face. Even though the air conditioner was on full blast and the big fan blowing in the room, it was still HOT!

Feranmi grew up in this same house, but after staying away for so long, the heat wasn't something she could come back and get used to so easily. It irked her when people said, "But you grew up here..." That was then, this was now.

Her heart went out to Alex. She wondered how he was fairing. It was cooler in the mornings, because this was the Harmattan season. But it was not even close to the kind of chill they would have been experiencing if they were in Atlanta. It was the day after Christmas and everyone was still in a festive mood. The excitement was double because the day had finally come. In about five hours, she and Alex would officially become a married couple. At least in the traditional sense.

Everything had happened so fast after they became engaged. She stayed in the hospital for an additional day and Alex took her back to his house and nursed her to health. He was the perfect gentleman, giving up his bedroom for her and staying in the guest room. He catered to her every need. Within a week, she was well enough to go back to her place. The minute she was up and about, Alex insisted they start planning. He didn't want to wait a day longer than they had to. They, however, ended up having to wait eight months to give him time to finish up the project in Florida.

They had called her parents and his mom to tell them about the engagement when she got out of the hospital. Her mom was in shock, but got over it quick enough to be happy for them. The added bonus of planning a huge engagement party didn't hurt either. Her dad on the other hand, was happy for them but wanted to know why Alex hadn't called him first to ask for her hand. He was truly old fashioned, but Feranmi could understand, since that was the way Tunde, her sister's husband, had done it. Her father quickly got over that and then wanted to know when they were coming to Lagos to complete the traditional rights. He insisted it had to be done at home, although Feranmi did know of some people who performed the same rights in the States.

Feranmi loved the look on Alex's face when she explained what the traditional rights entailed. His facial expressions went from confusion to astonishment to understanding. Finally, he pulled her close to him and said, "That's cool. Just so there is no mistake, at the end of the day I'm bringing the new Mrs. Montgomery back home with me."

"Yes, baby, you will. It just has to be done. I have witnessed a lot of traditional weddings, now it's my turn," she giggled. The thought of her knight in shining armor doing what he had to do to claim her made her smile.

"You are my queen, and I'll do whatever I have to do to make you mine. I've to call Kofi to start getting his stuff together because this is one trip he's going to make with me. I won't be laying down by myself," he said, referencing the part of the ceremony where Feranmi told him that the groom and his friends laid down flat on the floor in front of the bride's parents "begging" for a wife. She also explained the bride price negotiations part, but clarified that it is usually returned because the bride's parents are not selling a wife, but giving a daughter.

Her parents prayed for them over the phone just as Amanda did. Her friends were the worst; they nearly screamed her ear off when she told them. They were deliriously happy.

"All done," her makeup artist said.

Ini and Kayla came around to look at her. She had on an *Iro* and *Buba* sewn out of a yellow *Aso-Oke* with blue little faux diamonds all over it. Her mother made sure the knot of the *Iro* was firm and she had ample space to move her legs so she could dance. Her *gele*—head wrap—which had been professionally tied earlier, sat perfectly on her head. It was not too tight or too loose. Her mother had also made sure her hand fan matched her shoes, which were also yellow and blue.

"Girl, are you ready?" Kayla asked. She, Feranmi and Ini were all holding hands just as they had a few months ago back in Chicago.

"Yes, I am and I'm so thankful you girls were able to come and celebrate this with me. We will do it again in Atlanta in two months."

"Isn't this it?" Ini teased.

"Don't even try it. You know that the church wedding is in

Atlanta in February. Just enough time for my parents, my sister and her family to tie up loose ends and fly over."

"I know, girl, just teasing. We've gone dress shopping, remember. Okay, hold still. I got to cover you up like Mrs. A said. I don't want her to have my head," Ini said, as she covered Feranmi with a white see-through veil.

Feranmi's mother entered the room with a couple of her aunties.

"You girls haven't finished? *Oya! Oya!* They are calling for you," Yewande said, clapping her hands together, hurrying them up. She stopped for a minute to admire her daughter, then left with the women she came in with.

"Let's go get you married," Kayla said, and they hurried out of the room.

THE END

FINAL NOTE

Thank you for reading Feranmi & Alex's story. Please consider leaving a review on the platform you purchased the book. I greatly appreciate honest feedback. They really go a long way. The number of reviews a book receives greatly improves how well it does.

If you liked this story, I trust you might like some of my other titles. But before we get to those, never miss a sale, new release announcements, or freebies. You can ensure that by joining my mailing list. I'd love to stay connected.

If you want more of Alex and Feranmi, they make a cameo appearance in another standalone title He Changed My Name

ALSO BY UNOMA NWANKWOR

Pretend Bae

Away To Africa

New Year's Kiss (Prequel)

Rent-A-Bae

www.ingramcontent.com/pod-product-compliance
Lightning Source LLC
Chambersburg PA
CBHW021111110726
47900CB00007B/2131